Maine Men Book Seven

Levi's LOVE

K.C. WELLS

Levi's Love
Copyright © 2022 by K.C. Wells
Cover Art by Meredith Russell
Edited by Sue Laybourn
ISBN: 978-1-913843-91-5

Warning
This book contains material that is intended for a mature, adult audience. It contains graphic language, explicit sexual content, and adult situations.

<u>Maine Men</u>
Levi, Noah, Aaron, Ben, Dylan, Finn, Seb, and Shaun.
Eight friends who met in high school in Wells, Maine.

Different backgrounds, different paths, but one thing remains solid, even eight years after they graduated – their friendship. Holidays, weddings, funerals, birthdays, parties – any chance they get to meet up, they take it. It's an opportunity to share what's going on in their lives, especially their love lives.

Back in high school, they knew four of them were gay or bi, so maybe it was more than coincidence that they gravitated to one another. Along the way, there were revelations and realizations, some more of a surprise than others. And what none of the others knew was that Levi was in love with one of them…

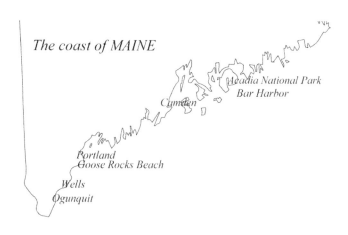

The coast of MAINE

Acadia National Park
Bar Harbor
Camden
Portland
Goose Rocks Beach
Wells
Ogunquit

Prologue

From *Finn's Fantasy*:

Joel followed him into the tiny dining room where the table had been covered by a sheet. On it sat several pieces of shaped wood in different sizes. "What's this?"

"I'm making a rocking chair for Levi's grandmother. It's her seventieth birthday soon, and he commissioned me to make it." Finn smiled. "As if I'd say no."

Joel stroked one of the pieces. "I think you're very talented. I also think it's a great idea." He frowned. "This the same person Lynne was talking about? The one who makes cookies?"

Finn smiled. "That's Grammy. She's a very special lady. Not many people would do what she did."

Joel was intrigued. "What did she do?" Finn bit his lip, and Joel regretted his curiosity. "Look, if you don't want to tell me, that's okay. It's none of my business."

Finn sighed. "It's not a secret—I mean, all Levi's closest friends know, and so does most of Wells, if it comes to that, because you *know* how things get around—but Levi doesn't talk about it much." He pulled out a chair and gestured to the one facing it. "Please, have a seat." Joel did as instructed, Bramble beside him, his nose on Joel's knee. "The thing is…

Levi's mom got into bad habits when she was younger. We're talking younger than Nate, by the way. Bad habits—and worse friends."

"What kind of habits are we talking about?" Joel asked cautiously. Not that he didn't already have an idea.

Finn's gaze met his. "You do know Maine has an enormous drug crisis going on, right? It's in the news often enough. It's been that way for years, but I think it's worse in inland areas."

Joel nodded. "I think drugs are becoming a bigger problem wherever you live in this country." He knew Nate was sensible, but Joel hoped to God his son didn't start along that particular road. *It has to be a temptation, right?* One he prayed Nate was strong enough and wise enough to resist.

"Anyway, when Levi's mom was eighteen, she left home. She made a whole lot of excuses about feeling trapped and having no freedom, and she was of age, so there wasn't a whole lot her parents could do. She got herself a job, moved away from Wells, and *sort* of stayed in touch."

"How do you know all this?"

Finn shrugged. "Levi told me. He shared it with all of us. He said Grammy was worried sick. And then the day came when his mom turned up on Grammy's doorstep, pregnant."

"Oh God."

"Yeah. She didn't know who the father was—or at least that's what she said—and she swore to Grammy she'd turn things around."

"Why do I get the idea that didn't happen?"

Finn met his gaze. "Because you've seen enough to know how these situations usually work out? And you're right, of course. It wasn't long before she slipped back into her old ways."

"But… she was *pregnant*." Joel couldn't understand how *any* woman could abuse their body with drugs when they knew there was a life growing inside them.

Finn nodded, his face somber. "Apparently, she stuck around for a while, then moved back to wherever she'd been living. Grammy was going out of her mind. So when they woke up one morning to find a baby on the doorstep, with a note saying he'd be better off with them, they weren't really surprised."

"Did they try to find her, to make sure she was okay?"

"Yeah. Grammy had social services working on it, and she even went so far as to hire a private detective. But the thing is, most social services are in the southern Maine/Portland areas. That's a very small part of a very large state. People living outside the area don't often have access to the help they need."

"Did they eventually find her?"

Finn shook his head. "No one in Wells has heard from her since she left Levi with Grammy. Levi doesn't know if his mom is alive or dead."

Joel's heart went out to Finn's friend. He'd burned his bridges with his own parents when he and Carrie had divorced, but at least Nate and Laura still had a relationship with their grandparents. "So Levi's grandmother raised him?"

Finn nodded. "She became the mom he needed. Which got tougher when his grandfather died, not long after Levi was born. Levi said it was his grandfather's heart condition that killed him. I'm not so sure."

"No wonder you hold her in such high regard.

It sounds like you saw a lot of her when you were growing up."

Finn smiled. "I spent most of my time at Levi's house. I guess we're more like brothers than friends."

Chapter One

Early June, 2008

Levi Brown tilted his head and relished the sun's warmth on his face. Only fifteen minutes remained before his next class, and it was too nice a day to stay in the noisy cafeteria once he'd eaten his lunch. Besides, Noah White was sitting alone at the top of the bleachers, his long, pale legs straddling the bench, his attention on the magazine spread out before him.

For God's sake, just go over there and talk to him.

Yeah, like it was *that* easy.

Levi could chat with his best friends Finn and Seb for *hours*, but the thought of engaging Noah in a simple conversation tied his tongue in knots, sent his heartbeat into overdrive, and made his hands clammy.

You're not going to shake hands with him, you're just going to say hi.

Even that felt beyond him. Noah had joined Levi's English class at the start of ninth grade, and they'd barely exchanged greetings. And here they were, the last day of the school year coming right at him, and summer vacation right around the corner.

So get your ass over there and talk to him before it's too late.

Levi knew why he'd kept his distance. There was no freakin' way he was going to let Noah know just how much Levi was crushing on him, and he didn't trust his mouth to function. Hell, he couldn't give a talk to his class without his cheeks burning and his words tumbling out all wrong. And that was *exactly* what would happen when Levi got too close to Noah. It didn't matter that Noah was all arms and legs, a tall, gangly student with sharp elbows and even sharper cheekbones, his blue eyes hidden behind glasses, a recent thing.

Noah was beautiful.

Noah was all the proof Levi needed that at fourteen years old, he was most definitely gay.

Noah was looking right at him.

Shit.

Levi took a deep breath and walked over to the bleachers, ignoring the cries and shouts from the boys practicing their football skills out on the field. He held his chin high, and Noah didn't break eye contact as he approached.

Then he closed his magazine, and attempted to stuff it into his backpack.

Interesting.

Levi came to a halt at the foot of the bleachers. "Hey." Noah gave a single nod, and Levi's heart thumped. "Can I join you?"

"Sure. It's a free country."

Levi climbed up to where Noah sat. "What were you reading just now?"

Noah blinked. "Excuse me?"

Shit. Shit. Shit.

"I'm sorry. It's none of my business."

Noah's eyes gleamed. "What did you think I was reading?"

Oh God. "Maybe something you didn't want anyone to see." Levi still had no clue where Seb had gotten that gay magazine from that one time, and he didn't *want* to know, but Seb hadn't tried to hide it.

That's because Seb really doesn't give a shit.

Noah bit his lip, and Levi couldn't tear his gaze away, fascinated to watch his full lower lip become redder and even more full. Then Noah reached into his backpack, removed the magazine, and handed it to Levi.

He stared at the glossy cover, and it took him a moment to realize it showed an intricate, beautifully painted layout. "*Model Railroader*?"

Noah coughed. "Anything wrong with that?"

"God, no, absolutely nothing. I mean, whatever floats your boat, right?"

Noah snatched it back. "I get these from my grandpa. He's really into his trains."

"I guess you are too," Levi surmised.

Noah's cheeks pinked. "Yeah. I go there most weekends and help him run the trains. He's got this amazing layout. Takes over a whole bedroom."

"I bet your grandmother loves that."

Noah chuckled. "She doesn't mind. She's used to him." He cocked his head to one side. "Didn't you ever play with trains when you were little?"

"Not that I remember."

"Not even *Thomas the Tank Engine*?"

Levi shrugged. "Can't say I was ever interested."

"Oh." Noah folded the magazine and replaced it in his backpack, then leaned back on his arms. "You don't talk much, do you? I think this is the most I've ever heard you say."

"I get nervous around people, I guess. Until I get to know them better."

Noah nodded toward Levi's right shoulder. "He's

one of your friends, isn't he?"

Levi twisted to look, and found Finn striding toward the bleachers. "Yeah, that's Finn Anderson." And now he'd finally gotten enough courage to break the ice with Noah, Finn's timing sucked. Then he berated himself for his mean thought.

"Hey. Been looking for you." Finn flopped onto the bench below them. He gave Noah a smile and a nod. "You're Noah, right? I sit three rows behind you in math. You're the smart one."

Noah laughed. "I like math."

Finn grimaced. "*No one* likes math." He peered at Levi. "Whatcha doin' tomorrow?"

"You mean, apart from Grammy dragging me around Hannaford's? And doing my homework, of course." He grinned. "Or have you already done yours?"

Yeah right. Finn was a last-minute kinda guy.

Finn rolled his eyes. "Oh, come *on*. The only homework we've got is the pile of summer reading for English, and I'm sure as shit not gonna start *that* yet. Anyhow, it's the weekend. Me and Seb are going to the Leavitt. Come with us."

"What's showing?"

"*Iron Man.* I was telling you about it last week."

Levi grinned. "Sounds good. I'll ask Grammy when I get home, but she won't mind." Grammy liked Finn and Seb. She said Seb reminded her of someone she knew when she was younger.

"I was going to see that myself."

Finn smiled at Noah. "Then why don't you come with us three?"

That was one of the many things Levi loved about Finn—his generous nature.

"Really? But—"

Finn folded his arms. "Look, we're going there anyway. What you gonna do, sit on your own, or sit with us?" His eyes sparkled. "That way, you get to share Grammy's cookies."

Noah frowned. "Whose cookies?"

Finn pointed at Levi. "His grandmother makes the most awesome cookies. Every time we go to watch a movie, she sends Levi with a bag of them." There was a glint in his eyes. "Unless you don't like chocolate chip cookies."

Levi sighed. "Ignore Finn. You don't have to come with us just because he says so, or because he's bribing you with cookies. You might have plans of your own." Like visiting his grandfather and running his trains.

Noah's cheeks grew pink again. "You know what? I'd love to come."

Finn beamed. "Great. We'll meet outside Harbor Candy. I think it's showing at two-thirty, so let's meet up there by two."

"I'll be there. And I'll buy popcorn for us."

"*Now* you're talking." Finn's brow furrowed as Noah got to his feet. "Where you going?"

"Just remembered. There's a book I've gotta get from the library." He nodded toward Levi. "See you in English."

"Sure." Levi waited until Noah reached the bottom of the bleachers, taking long strides, before sagging.

I did it. And I didn't screw up.

Not only that, there was also the prospect of an afternoon with Noah at the movies. Levi didn't know if the idea thrilled him—or terrified him.

"So…" Finn glanced at him. "Is he gonna be one of us?" When Levi gave him a puzzled look, Finn rolled his eyes again. "You know, the three gay musketeers. Are we gonna be four?"

"No clue about the gay part, but I wouldn't say no to him hanging around with us. Would you be okay with that?" Levi's heartbeat quickened.

"Sure, why not? He seems okay. I kinda like him."

Levi watched as Noah reached the school building and disappeared from view. "I like him too." The simple statement didn't come close to how he really felt, but that was going to be his secret. Because if *Seb* found out…

My first crush.

The thought of sitting next to Noah in a darkened movie theater sent trickles of anticipation up and down his spine, and he decided to make sure that happened.

Just being close to him would be enough.

Chapter Two

Sunday, June 13, 2021

Noah White took his bottle of beer and wandered over to the summerhouse. It was five o'clock, and the temperature had to be in the high seventies, with scattered clouds drifting in greater numbers across the blue sky. He glanced back to where the others sat around the fire pit, talking and laughing. Noah liked how Dean draped his arm across Aaron's shoulders, as natural as breathing, making it appear as if it had always belonged there.

Well, what do you know? Aaron I'm-straight turns out to be Aaron I'm-bi.

Noah was happy for him. Dean seemed like a great guy, and Noah had never seen Aaron look so content. *Who would have thought so much could change in one year?* Finn and Joel had been talking about the wedding, and the light in their eyes was beautiful to behold. The joy on Levi's face when Finn asked him to be his best man… It made sense. Those two had been friends since forever.

Our first wedding. Noah gazed at the couples, wondering who would be next. Not that everyone had to get married, but none of his friends seemed averse to the idea. *Give it time.* He was sure about one thing: Finn and Joel might be the first, but they wouldn't be the last.

The French doors opened, and Grammy stepped out onto the patio. The others greeted her, and Levi got up to get her something to drink.

Noah remembered why he'd left them. He stared through the glass windows of the summerhouse, taking in the sofas, the table, and the extra folded chairs Grammy kept in there. His heart sank.

Damn it, I was right. This is not going to work. It had been a wonderful idea in principle, but now he saw the available space, he knew he'd have to come up with an alternative.

"Lookin' kinda thoughtful, Noah." Grammy came to stand beside him. "You imaginin' your trains in there?"

There was no point putting it off.

"That's just it, Grammy. I appreciate the offer, I really do, but being practical… it won't work."

Her brow furrowed. "Why not? I can find somewhere else for the furniture. All you need is a big table, right?"

Noah sighed. "No. I mean, the layout *could* go on a table, but then there's all the wiring, the stuff you don't see *under* the layout." He surveyed the summerhouse's interior. "There's not enough space either." He patted her arm. "So thank you, but I need to come up with another solution. The most I could do in there is store everything, and the point was to have a place where I could run the trains."

Grammy gazed at the summerhouse, deep in thought. She pursed her lips. "An' what if I *have* a solution?"

He smiled. "You're a great lady to have offered me the space in the first place. Don't worry about it. I'll think of something."

She crooked her finger. "You come with me. I might just surprise you." She picked her way over the stone slabs marking the path to the patio, then headed for the house, pausing at the French doors. "Levi? Can I borrow you for a second?"

"Sure." Levi got up from his chair and joined them. "What's up?"

"Something I want to run by you." Grammy walked through the house, and Noah and Levi followed her up the carpet-covered staircase to the second floor. She paused at the door to the attic. "Now, I want you both to have an open mind for a second." Grammy opened the door, switched on the light, and climbed the narrow stairs that turned, opening out into the attic with its peaked roof, the brick chimney breast poking through its center. She frowned at the opening where they'd emerged. "Damn thing needs a rail around it."

"Why? We never come up here, except for those." Levi pointed to the boxes piled near the top of the stairs, from which spilled tinsel, strings of lights, and other Christmas paraphernalia.

Grammy snorted. "I haven't been up here in years."

"So why are we here now?" Levi asked.

Noah got where she was headed. "You think I could store my trains up here? There's enough space, sure…" Except there were a lot of boxes.

"Wasn't quite what I had in mind." Grammy flung out her arm to encompass the clutter. "I was thinkin' more 'bout goin' through all of this stuff—an' most of it will prob'ly end up in the trash or Goodwill—and then you settin' up your trains."

He blinked. "Here?" Noah glanced at the space. He imagined it would get real cold in winter.

"Why not? It'd need some work doin' first," Grammy admitted. "Startin' with insulatin' the roof. Levi's grandpa put up that fiberglass waddin' between the rafters and secured it with wire nettin', but I'm thinkin' sheetrock would be better. You boys must know someone who could tackle that, or at least advise you on how to go about it. What about Finn? He's handy." She pointed to the chimney. "I know that's kinda in the middle of everything, but... you could make it into a... what's the word? ... a feature."

Noah's mouth fell open. A whole attic? Dear Lord, the possibilities...

She grinned. "*That's* given you something to think about."

"What about power, Grammy?" Levi frowned. "And lights. We've only got two bare bulbs up here."

"I'm just puttin' it out there as a solution. Of course, there's a ton of work to be done first, but after that..." Her eyes gleamed in the light from the bulb. "Well, Noah?" She gestured to the cluttered space. "I know there's a whole lotta crap, but try to see beyond that, see what it *could* look like." She grinned. "Hell, you could put together a small town up here. What do you think?"

His throat tightened. "I love it." His mind was already turning over ideas.

"Ah, but you haven't heard the catch yet."

Noah figured there had to be one. "And what is that?"

"You two boys will need to go through all these boxes. I'll leave it up to you to decide what stays an' what goes."

"But Grammy," Levi protested. "They contain your life. *And* Grandpa's. Don't *you* want a hand in making those decisions?"

She gave him a sweet smile. "Child, it's been decades since I went through any of this. If I haven't looked for something in all these years, it's not worth my time. But sure, if you find something you think I need to consider keepin', show it to me by all means. As for the rest, I'll abide by your decision." Grammy pointed to the stairs. "But before you do anythin' else, get Finn to put a rail around that openin'. I don't want either of you boys to go sailin' ass over tea kettle down them stairs. You'll break your necks."

Levi kissed her cheek. "I'll go get him. Let's see what he has to say about it." He hurried toward the stairs.

Noah couldn't stop smiling. "Grammy, you're awesome."

She waved a hand. "It was just a thought."

"But it was a good one." He gave her a hug. "Thank you."

When he released her, Grammy was smiling too. "Then you'll do it? You'll use the attic?"

"I'd be crazy to say no."

"That's settled then." She beamed. "I suppose we're gonna be seein' a lot more of you around here. Not that I'm complainin' 'bout that. You've been part of this family since you were barely in your teens." She shook her head. "An' this family just keeps on growin'."

Noah wasn't complaining either. Any chance to spend more time around his best friend… When Walt had suggested him moving into one of the rental apartments, Noah had seized the opportunity of living within walking distance of Levi's house. Wellington Manor wasn't ideal, however. As the season got into full swing, the noise level rose in direct proportion to the number of vacationers staying there. Working from home was a pain, and more often than not, Noah drove to Inn on the Blues at Short Sands Beach. He could sit on the upper deck with his laptop, enjoying the breeze off the ocean. The manager, Stacey, was a friend, and as long as he bought the occasional beverage or snack, she was happy to let him work there.

Except he knew it would get noisier there too once the season really got going. More traffic, more people on the beach…

Noah had no plans to move out of the rental apartment until he absolutely had to, and that wouldn't be until August. Two months of being a stone's throw from Levi. But the prospect of using the attic for his trains brought him even closer to the person dearest to him in the whole world, the guy he thought of as his brother.

Only, hadn't there been a couple of times when he'd seen Levi as more than that?

Noah shut down those recollections. They didn't fit into the box. They weren't him.

"Where'd you go, boy?" Grammy's voice broke through.

"Sorry. I zoned out for a sec."

She cackled. "You're already plannin', ain't ya?"

Yeah, something like that.

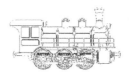

Aaron watched as Levi and Noah followed Grammy into the house. *I wonder what that's all about?*

Seb cleared his throat, leaned forward, his elbows on his knees, and spoke in a conspiratorial whisper. "Okay. We all know what's coming, right?"

Aaron frowned. "Maybe *you* do, but I have no clue what you're talking about."

Seb rolled his eyes. "Oh, come *on*." He inclined his head toward the French doors. "Those two."

"What about them?" Aaron kept a straight face but his heartbeat quickened. *Damn Seb and his intuition.*

Seb's eyebrows went skyward. "You don't think they're made for each other? Lord, even their names match. Brown and White." He gave an exaggerated shiver. "Gives me chills. Like they were meant to be."

Marcus coughed. "You missed your vocation, sweetheart. You have this innate desire to matchmake, don't you?"

"Hey, it worked last time, didn't it?" Seb gestured to Aaron and Dean. "Look at these two. Proof." He sat back, his arms folded.

Aaron couldn't suppress his smile. "So I started dating Dean because of you? Sorry, dude—I started dating Dean because he was Dean."

"I know where Seb's coming from." Finn nodded. "Levi and Noah, a couple? Makes sense. It'd be the next logical step for them."

"So we'd all be paired off, is that it? Everyone gets their Happy Ever After, everything tied up neatly in a big red bow?" Aaron forced himself to take deep breaths. He couldn't lose his shit over this. "You can't just push them together. Not if one of them doesn't want that."

In the silence that followed, Aaron's stomach clenched. *Aw fuck.*

Ben's eyes gleamed. "You know something. 'Fess

up."

Aaron leaned back, arms across his chest. "I have nothing to say." He'd already said way too much.

Dylan whistled. "One of them has the hots for the other? Is that what you're saying?"

"I told you, I'm not saying *anything*."

"But you're thinking plenty. You think they *should* be together, same as Seb does."

Before Aaron could utter a response, Finn rejoined the conversation. "Like I said, it makes sense. They've always been close."

Shaun's eyes widened. "Oh shit. Dylan nailed it, didn't he? Only, it's Levi who has the hots for Noah. Doesn't make sense to be the other way round, not after what Noah said last summer. He doesn't have the hots for anyone."

"Doesn't mean it has to stay like that," Ben mused. "All they need is a little push." His eyes sparkled.

Aaron lost it. "Hell no. You'd be as subtle as a train wreck." His heart pounded. They could be back any second. "We can't talk about this here."

"But we *are* gonna talk about it?" Shaun countered.

Aaron knew when he was licked. "Fine. Yeah. I'll text you, and we'll meet at my place. Anyone who's interested in helping these two see what's right under their noses is welcome to come along." He froze as the French door opened and Levi appeared.

"Finn, you got a minute?"

"Sure." Finn got up and went over to him. They disappeared inside.

Seb rubbed his hands together gleefully. "An intervention. I like it."

Aaron didn't. He knew they meant well, but judging by the glances from Mark, Joel, Marcus, and Nathan, not everyone was enamored by the prospect. Maybe age had given them more insight than their partners.

I've got a bad feeling about this.

And he had no one to blame but himself.

Chapter Three

"So what do you think?" Levi pointed to the roof. "Grammy said it needs sheetrock."

"And she's right," Finn remarked. He grinned. "As usual."

Grammy waved a hand. "I'll leave you boys to work out the details. I'm gonna see if my guests have eaten every scrap of food in the house." She headed for the stairs.

Levi waited until he heard the door to the attic close. "Then when can you start?"

Finn laughed. "Whoa there. You're gonna have to hold your water. I have a lot of jobs I'm working on right now. You know, like building a house for me and Joel? It isn't anywhere near finished, and we get married next month, or did you forget that part?" His grin widened. "Which reminds me, Mr. Best Man... you'd better start writing your speech."

"You want me to do that?" In his delight at being asked, Levi had clean forgotten the duties of a best man. And now he thought about it... "I'm no good at speeches. You remember what I was like in English class when I had to give a talk? I'm okay with you guys, but put me in front of an audience, and I get tongue-tied." He swallowed. "Maybe you should choose one of the other guys."

Finn snorted. "Like Seb? Hell no. Can you

imagine the kind of stuff he'd come out with?"

"Don't you worry about your speech. I'll help you," Noah assured him.

Levi blinked. "Really?"

Noah smiled, and warmth barreled through him. "You saw every performance I ever gave in high school. You think I can't coach you? Just leave it to me. I'll have you word-perfect in time for the wedding." His confident air settled the waves of anxiety rolling through Levi's stomach.

"There," Finn said triumphantly. "Noah will take care of you. And speaking of Noah…" Finn turned to him. "You're gonna have to wait a while before you can set your trains up. Sorry."

"It's okay. Work is piling up right now, so that's the last thing on my mind." Noah glanced at their surroundings. "I still can't believe she's letting me use all this space."

"Don't forget we have a job to do before that can happen." Levi pointed to all the boxes. "God knows what we're going to find in those."

Noah's eyes glittered. "Grammy's secret past. Who knows what she got up to when she was younger?"

Levi chuckled. "You mean, we discover Grammy was a spy? A secret agent? Hate to burst your bubble, but I don't think she's ever taken a step out of Maine."

Noah gaped. "Seriously?"

"Pretty sure. At least, *I* can't remember her ever traveling out of state."

"She had a life before you, you know," Finn observed. "And I know it's difficult to believe, but she was our age once." He grinned. "Why do I have this image of Grammy in the sixties, flowers in her long hair, knee-high boots, sunglasses…"

Noah's eyes widened. "Oh my God. Now I want to see photos."

"We'd better get back to the party too." Levi didn't want Grammy tiring herself out. For as long as he could remember, she'd been a ball of energy, but this past year there'd been a change. Before, Grammy would have scoffed at the idea of taking a nap, but now they were becoming more frequent. She claimed she was fit as a flea—God knew where she got that phrase from— and Levi regretted not going with her to her most recent checkup. Not that he thought she'd lie to him, but—

Who am I kidding? Of course she'd keep information from me, especially if it was bad news, but only because she wants to protect me. And that would be down to her stubborn independence more than anything.

That did it. Her next appointment, he was going with her, whether she liked it or not.

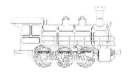

Shaun nudged Levi's arm. "Look at those two," he murmured, inclining his head to where Aaron and Dean strolled around the yard hand-in-hand. "I remember how damn good that felt, knowing I was at the start of something that promised to be amazing."

"And is it?" Not that Levi needed to ask. Shaun had never looked happier. It seemed as if the weight of the last ten years had rolled off him, revealing a man who smiled more, laughed more, and stared at Nathan as though he hung the moon. Now and then Shaun would twitch his shoulders.

He feels lighter.

Levi wasn't one for envy—he had little time for negative emotions—but Lord, it had been creeping into his mind lately.

Shaun sighed. "It's not only amazing, it's perfect." Then he gave Levi another nudge. "Look over there." He was staring at Nathan, who stood in a little group comprising Joel, Marcus, and Mark. Shaun's eyes sparkled. "Why do I think they're up to something?"

Levi understood his reaction. He wasn't close enough to hear their conversation, but their occasional glances toward their partners gave the gathering a secretive air. "Joel's getting married too, remember? Maybe he wants to arrange a bachelor party with guys his own age." The thought wasn't that far out of left field. Levi figured Finn's idea of the perfect party would be whooping it up in Ogunquit, probably at Maine Street. *And that'll be a first.* Levi had heard some of them talk about the gay bar often, but he hadn't even crossed its threshold. Not that he'd shared that piece of information.

But Joel and his present company? Levi couldn't see them getting down on the dance floor. They were all in their forties, and while not one of them acted as if they were ready for a pipe and slippers, they had more gravitas than their respective partners. Levi could picture them going out for dinner someplace quiet, a much more low-key event.

He gazed at Noah, who was telling the others about Grammy's offer. Noah's face glowed, his eyes twinkled, and the joy in his voice was unmissable.

Levi's heart sank, his limbs numb and heavy. It

was time to face the truth.

He'll never look at me *with that same light in his eyes.*

He watched Ben and Wade as they leaned into each other, noting Ben's hand on Wade's neck as they kissed.

He watched Dylan and Mark casting longing glances toward the fence that marked the boundary between Grammy's house and theirs.

He watched Seb whisper in Marcus's ear, noting the way Marcus squirmed a little in his chair, accompanied by Seb's rough, dirty chuckle.

He watched as Shaun strolled over to Nathan, only to be gathered into his arms, Nathan kissing the top of Shaun's head.

Levi didn't need to be a mind reader to guess at the thoughts that passed between them all.

They can't wait to be alone.

The man he loved—the man he'd waited for since he was fourteen years old, surely too young an age to know what he felt was love, but Levi had known, balls to bones—stood there oblivious to Levi's turmoil. If Noah had so much as glanced *once* in Levi's direction with an *ounce* of that same longing Levi saw in his friends' expressions, Levi's heart would have done a somersault.

He doesn't want me.

Okay. Enough torture. His friends were moving on, finding love.

It was time for Levi to make a break with the past and move on too.

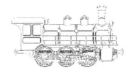

Noah closed the door and gazed at the apartment. It wasn't much—one bed, one bath, and most of the space was taken up with boxes containing his belongings—but at least it was just him. No interrogations, no dramas…

And speaking of dramas…. Yet another gathering where there had been revelations.

He smiled to himself. Despite Aaron's protestations that he wasn't looking for love, it appeared love had had other ideas. Dean seemed like a great guy, and judging by the performance they'd given in the truck outside Levi's, things were already getting hot and heavy.

His phone vibrated, and one glance at the screen was enough to make his stomach clench into a tight little ball. Ignoring it was not an option. She'd keep calling until he answered, and then there was always the ball-shrinking thought that she'd turn up on his doorstep.

Hell no to that.

"Hey Mom." He steeled himself for whatever was coming right at him.

"Are you okay?"

"Of course I'm okay. Why wouldn't I be?"

"So you're going to stay there?"

Another roil of his stomach. "Mom, we talked about this."

"I don't see why you felt you had to move out in the first place."

Because you were driving me crazy.

"Mom, I'm almost twenty-seven. Don't you think it was time I moved out? None of my friends live with their parents."

"What about Levi? He lives with his grandmother."

"And? What's your point?" He sighed heavily. "Is this why you called, to ask if I'm staying put?"

"Actually, your father had a question for you. He wants to know when you're going to collect your trains. And everything else that's above the garage."

Noah's head was spinning. "Talk about a one-eighty. First you want to know why I moved out, and then you tell me to pick up the rest of my stuff? Which is it, Mom?"

"He thinks like you do, that it's time you moved out. So he wants the space. He's talking about making it into a craft room. God knows I'd be glad to get all his toolboxes out of the way. Can't walk through the garage without tripping over something." She paused. "So... are you seeing anyone?"

"Mom, we talked about this too. I—"

"You moved out over two months ago. I thought that was because you wanted privacy."

"Mom... No, I'm not seeing anyone, okay? And right now, I don't have time to see anyone. I'm snowed under with work."

"It's not tax time. Why would people need a bookkeeper at this time of year?"

"Because not everyone is like you and dad. A lot of small businesses do their taxes as they go along, so that they don't fly into a panic at tax time. I'm not complaining."

"I see." Another pause. "Then you'll come over

and pick up your stuff?"

Noah thought quickly. He could store the boxes in Grammy's summerhouse until the attic was ready. It wasn't the best solution, but it would have to do.

"Yeah. How about next Saturday?" He'd need a day to dismantle the layouts, box up the trains, and sort out the cables.

"That works. And if you want to stay the night…"

He chuckled. "Thanks for the offer, but I'm thinking of going out Saturday night." He needed a night of dancing, of losing himself in heavy, pulsing music.

And whatever else Maine Street had to offer.

He wasn't averse to the idea of a hookup—there had been a few of those—and it had been a while. And Maine Street was the place to meet guys who would be up for getting off.

Noah's mind went back to Aaron's cookout the previous summer. Sharing his asexuality had consumed him for so long, and yet his friends had readily accepted it as part of him. But he doubted he could make them understand the complexity of his sex life. He loved a good orgasm as much as the next man. He could appreciate porn. He didn't feel attracted to the guys who blew him or those he fucked, but that didn't detract from his enjoyment of it. Not that he'd had many opportunities to enjoy it.

A memory surfaced. An earnest guy who'd engaged him in deep conversation one night, asking if Noah just hadn't found the right person yet. He'd seemed appalled that Noah hadn't experienced sexual attraction.

But that's not true, is it? What about—

There had been brief *pangs* as Noah labeled them, in the past, brief moments where yes, he'd felt something that might have been sexual attraction, but he'd logicked his way through them. Those feelings didn't fit into the box he'd created for himself, so it was easy to dismiss them. They didn't conform to his view of who he was.

What was less easy to dismiss was the fact those feelings centered around one person—Levi.

Noah wasn't stupid. He'd moved to Wellington Manor to be closer to Levi. He'd jumped at the idea of using the attic because while it would give him space, it would also mean spending more time with Levi.

He's part of my life. Of course I want to be near him. That was all it was.

Wasn't it?

Chapter Four

Saturday, June 19

Levi took a last look in the mirror, and his heart raced. *That isn't me.* Not that he was wearing anything out of the ordinary.

Except that wasn't true. His new skinny jeans clung to his legs like a second skin, and God help him if he got a hard on, because no one would be able to miss it. His equally new black tank top was a loose fit, with larger openings for his arms that showed off his torso. He'd trimmed his beard too.

Nobody there will know this is my first time at a gay bar. Nobody there will even know *me.*

Levi was about to step out of his comfort zone big time, and the prospect terrified him. That didn't mean he was going to chicken out. *A new look for a new Levi, remember?*

He glanced at his phone. It was too late to call Aaron and ask him to go, even though they'd discussed it. *If I'd wanted him with me, I would've called him at some point during the past week.*

This was a solo mission, one requiring every bit of courage he possessed, and he didn't want any of his friends around to see him, just in case it turned out to be an epic fail. *After all, I'm nothing special. Who's going to be interested in me?* He could understand why guys had flocked to Seb. The man was gorgeous, from his shaggy, sexy hair to his long legs, and as for those eyes… Seb exuded a confidence Levi could never hope to possess. *Me? I'm going to be like chum in an ocean of circling sharks.*

Waiting for one of them to take a bite….

Despite his churning stomach, he gave his reflection a wry smile. *They'd better not leave any teeth marks.* Not with Grammy around.

Levi picked his phone up and clicked on Uber. He didn't plan on sticking to soda all night, so no way was he going to drive the short distance to Ogunquit. Once he knew the car was en route, it was time to go say goodnight to Grammy.

He hadn't mentioned his night out to her either.

Levi went downstairs and into the living room where Grammy sat in her chair. She blinked as he entered, placing her book in her lap. "Goin' someplace?" She glanced at the clock on the mantelpiece. "Bit late, ain't it? Are you meetin' some of the boys?"

"No, I'm just… going out. On my own."

Grammy arched her thin eyebrows. "Mm-*hmm*." She gazed at him from head to foot. "That's a different look for you, ain't it? 'Cause I sure don't remember you wearin' jeans like *those* before now." She cocked her head toward the window. "Is that a taxi?"

"Yeah, it's for me." Levi went over to her and bent to kiss her cheek. "I'll see you in the morning." His heart hammered. "Goodnight, Grammy."

Grammy narrowed her gaze. "You okay, child?"

"I'm fine," he lied. "Don't stay up too late."

"Says the man who's goin' out on the town at nine o'clock." Her eyes twinkled. "In that getup, you're gonna be mighty popular." She curved her hand around his cheek. "Be safe, okay?"

"I will, I promise." He tried not to think about the condoms and packets of lube in the pocket of his sports jacket.

Outside, a horn blasted, and he straightened. "Okay, gotta go." He hurried out of the living room, through the front door, stopping short of opening it. *The jacket is going to be a pain if I want to dance.* He removed his wallet, phone, and the condoms and lube, shoved them into the pockets of his jeans, and hung the jacket on a hook.

Why did I choose skinny jeans?

Levi opened the door and hurried down the path to where the car waited to whisk him to a gay bar, and hopefully something he'd been fantasizing about for most of his adult life. Maybe his heart was thumping because during all that time, he hadn't pictured losing his virginity to a stranger, but to the one person who'd captured his heart.

It should be with you, Noah.

Then he shoved such thoughts aside. This *wasn't* the big deal he'd made it out to be. This was just sex, right? It was part of life as a gay man, and Levi was more than ready to discover it.

The rum and coke had been a good idea. It was doing a great job of melting away his nerves. The music helped too, loud, heavy, and pulsing through the floorboards. He hadn't gotten up enough courage to step out onto the dance floor, but another cocktail or two, and he'd be willing to try.

So many men. They were mostly in their twenties and thirties, he guessed, although he'd spotted a decent number of older guys too. All shapes, all sizes, and clearly men who loved to dance. Levi was content to lean against the wall and people-watch.

The heavy beat was no more, and instead Mariah Carey's 'Always Be My Baby' poured from the speakers, and then there were guys dancing close, moving in harmony to the music and one another.

And one of the dancers was walking toward Levi, beckoning with a crooked finger.

Oh shit.

He was maybe in his forties, his hair tinged with silver. He wasn't as muscular as a few of the men Levi had seen, but he obviously took care of himself. His black shirt was open at the neck, revealing a glimpse of dark hair, and—

Gleaming, sexy eyes locked on Levi's. "Dance with me." It wasn't a request.

As if in a trance, Levi took the proffered hand, and the guy led him onto the dance floor. They moved in time to the music, Levi's heartbeat thumping out its own rhythm when his dance partner looped his arms around Levi's neck. He couldn't brush away the feeling that he'd seen the guy someplace.

"Haven't seen you here before," the man murmured. "I'm Daniel, by the way."

"Levi. And this is my first time." His pulse thrummed as Daniel slid his hands to Levi's hips, holding him closer than Levi had ever been to another guy.

"I'm not usually this forward," Daniel confessed. "But I haven't been able to tear my eyes off of you all night." He stroked Levi's face. "I've got a thing for beards." He smiled. "You don't dance much, do ya?"

"Damn. And I thought I was doing okay," Levi quipped. To his surprise, Daniel clasped his hand and led him from the floor. When they reached Levi's previous vantage point, Daniel leaned against the wall.

"This is better." He studied Levi for a moment. "So where have you been all my life?"

Despite his racing heartbeat, Levi managed to laugh. "That sounds so cheesy."

Daniel chuckled. "But it worked. You loosened up a little. Relax, sweetheart. You look like a mouse caught in a trap, just waiting for the cat to pounce." His eyes glittered. "I don't pounce—unless you want me to."

Levi breathed easier. "I guess I'm a little out of my comfort zone."

"Yeah, I kinda got that part." Daniel inclined his head toward the bar. "Can I get you a drink?"

"A rum and coke?" Grammy always had a bottle in the house, not that Levi drank all that much.

"Great. I'll be a sec." Daniel narrowed his gaze. "You're still going to be here when I get back, right?"

"I'm not going anywhere," Levi assured him. He watched as Daniel made his way through the crowd, unable to resist a glance at his ass.

It was a very nice firm ass. Come to think of it, the rest of him was pretty nice too, and Levi couldn't help but wonder what lay beneath the clothing.

Maybe I'll find out. That thought was enough to send a wave of heat crashing over him, and his legs trembled. By the time Daniel returned with two plastic cups, Levi had gotten himself under control once more, and he took a few gulps of the dark liquid.

"This is good."

"Spiced rum," Daniel told him. "I always think when you mix it with coke, it kinda tastes like chocolate." He raised his glass. "To new beginnings." When Levi stared at him, Daniel smiled. "Your first time here. That's a new beginning, right?"

He nodded, and their cups met.

Daniel cleared his throat. "Okay, I'm gonna come clean. This might be your first time at Maine Street, but I've seen you plenty of times before tonight."

Levi stared at him. "I keep thinking I recognize you, but I can't place you."

Daniel nodded. "Picture me in blue…And here's another clue. 'Neither snow nor rain nor heat nor gloom of night stays these couriers from the swift—'"

He gaped. "Oh my God. You're our mailman."

Daniel grinned. "And we have a winner. Not that I expected you to recognize me. I've only been working that route for two months or so. Before that I was in Portland." He gestured to their surroundings. "This place is definitely an added bonus."

"Do you come here often?" Levi rolled his eyes. "Guess you're not the only one to come out with cheesy lines."

"To answer your question, I'm here every Saturday night. I work hard, but I like to play hard too." He leaned in. "So… tell me about Levi."

"Not much to tell."

"Everyone has a story. What's yours? What brought you here tonight?"

Levi swallowed. "I guess I came here with a purpose."

Daniel nodded. "Which makes you no different to anyone else in this place. We all came here with a purpose, whether that was to dance all night, drink, talk…" His dark eyes gleamed. "Some come here with other… pursuits in mind."

And there went his heart again. "Yeah?"

"Take me, for instance. Sure, I like to dance, drink and talk…and at the end of the night I don't go home alone. Not if I can help it."

Levi shivered. "I see."

Daniel stroked his beard. "I like the outfit, by the way. You're usually dressed more…"

"Conservatively?" Levi ventured.

Daniel gave a nod. "Not that I'm complaining. You always look good." He leaned in and pressed his lips to Levi's neck, his fingers easing under the cotton of Levi's tank top to brush over his nipple, causing goose bumps to break out on his bare arms. Daniel whispered, "Except *now* you look hot as fuck."

Sweet Jesus.

"Look who's talking," Levi croaked. Daniel was sex on legs.

Daniel straightened. "You know what? I think I want to dance some more. How about it?"

Levi opened his mouth to say that sounded perfect—and froze.

Noah was on the dance floor, surrounded by guys, and looking like he belonged there.

Levi's heart pounded. His mouth dried up.

I can't do this.

Daniel turned to follow his gaze. Noah was dancing closer to one guy, and they were talking. Then the guy took Noah's hand and led him out of sight.

Levi's ribs grew tighter, until it hurt to breathe.

"Hey." Daniel frowned. "What just happened?"

"I… I need some air." He pushed past Daniel

and headed for the door, through the congregation of men clustered around the bar, until finally he was outside, standing on the lower deck, where yet more men gathered to talk and drink. He stumbled over to the ramp that led to the street, and leaned against the railing.

A hand touched his back, and Levi almost leaped out of his skin.

"You okay?" Daniel stood beside him.

Levi took a couple of deep breaths. "Sorry. I didn't mean to leave like that. It's just…"

Daniel pointed to the street. "Come on, let's walk."

He blinked. "'Walk'?"

"You know, you put one foot in front of the other?" Daniel stroked Levi's back. "Somehow, I get the impression you don't want to go back inside, so let's go for a walk. And when you're ready, you can tell me what the hell freaked you out."

Levi took a moment to get his thoughts into some semblance of calm. There was something safe about Daniel. He seemed like a good guy, and he wasn't giving off any creepy vibes. Levi expelled a breath. "Okay."

They turned left on Main Street, then crossed over to Beach Street. Daniel seemed happy to let him remain silent, and that was fine by Levi. They strolled past the Betty Doon Motor Hotel, past the Aspinquid Resort, not stopping until they reached the bridge that went over to Ogunquit Beach. Instead of crossing it, Daniel took a left at River Road, pausing at the white railing running alongside it. A solitary bench overlooked the water, and he pointed to it. "Sit."

Levi did as instructed, and Daniel sat beside him.

Levi stared at the moonlight on the calm surface of the water. "I love this place," he said in a low voice.

Daniel took his hand, holding it with unexpected gentleness. "Okay. Who was he?"

Levi feigned innocence. "Excuse me?"

Daniel huffed. "I'm not blind, sweetheart. The guy you saw who made you take off like a bat out of hell. Who is he to you?"

Levi gave a shaky laugh. "That's a long story."

Daniel shrugged. "I've got nowhere to be right now but here. Share it."

So he did. He started with his crush on Noah back in high school, their friendship… Levi was shocked he could be so painfully honest. He left nothing out.

When he was done, Daniel didn't respond. He let go of Levi's hand and leaned forward, his elbows on his knees, gazing at the tranquil moonlit scene before them. Finally, he spoke, his eyes fixed on the horizon. "When I saw you there tonight, I wanted you. And I think if I'd asked you to come back to my place, you'd have come. But… I don't think you'd have done it for the right reasons." He turned to look Levi in the eyes. "Don't get me wrong. You tick all my boxes, and then some. But I'm not Noah."

"And Noah doesn't want me."

Daniel shook his head. "What you *mean* is, Noah doesn't want you in his bed. And that's all you can see right now, isn't it?" He narrowed his eyes. "Wanna know what it sounds like to *me*?"

"I think you're going to tell me."

"You and Noah have something special. A connection. And you should hold onto that. So stop thinking about what *you* want, what *you* need, and be what *Noah* wants, what *he* needs. Because if you do that, maybe you'll discover how to make it work between you two." He sighed. "I'm not saying it'll be easy." Daniel clasped his hands together. "I'm not one for commitment, but I think you are. You love Noah. If I felt about a guy the way you feel about him, I'd move heaven and earth to keep him in my life."

"Even if that means a life without a physical connection?"

Daniel smiled. "You're young. How many asexual people have you met?"

"Just him. As far as I know."

He nodded. "Well, in my forty-three years, I've met more than that. And while a few of them weren't into sex, a lot of them were. So stop confusing asexuality with abstinence, be there for him, and see where it takes you." He reached over and cupped Levi's cheek. "One place it definitely *won't* take you is my bed." He let out a heavy sigh. "Why did I have to be afflicted with scruples?"

Levi leaned in and kissed Daniel's cheek. "More people should suffer from the same affliction."

"Do you want to go back to Maine Street? He could still be there."

Levi shook his head. "I want to go home. I need to think." He got his phone out and clicked on Uber.

"Then I'll wait with you till I know you're safe." Daniel smiled. "And the next time you see me, say hi?"

"I will."

Daniel chuckled. "Actually, when you think about it… this could've been real awkward. I mean, with me delivering your mail and all. I don't think I could've looked your grandmother in the eye if we'd fucked. She's one sharp lady."

Levi knew exactly what he meant.

It's time to stop thinking about me, me, me. What do I need to do to make this relationship work?

That was easy—whatever it took.

K.C. WELLS

Chapter Five

"Is this better?"

Noah smiled at Jacob. "Much. I couldn't hear myself think down there." The upper deck was as full as the first floor, but at least there was a warm breeze, and the music was more muted. Men stood around, drinking, chatting, looking, kissing...

He wandered over to the railing and peered into the street below. Jacob leaned against the rail. "So..."

Noah knew what that drawn-out syllable meant, not to mention the expectant gleam in Jacob's eyes. "So?" Jacob hadn't been subtle on the dance floor, but Noah had ignored his advances. He knew little about Jacob, apart from his name, and the fact that he worked in a coffee shop in Ogunquit. He was cute, sure, and he was obviously on a mission to get laid, but...

Jacob pressed against him. "Wanna meet me in the restroom?"

Hell.

"It's a tad cramped in there, don't you think?" He'd done that once, and he wasn't anxious to repeat the experience. While the restrooms were clean, Noah didn't like knowing that on the other side of that thin wall, someone was probably getting off listening to *him* getting off. Except that was only half the story. Noah was trying hard not to feel pissed. He'd been having a good time dancing, and he'd liked Jacob's idea of going to the upper deck to talk.

Only, he doesn't want to talk, he wants to fuck.

But Noah didn't.

He stared into the street, trying to frame his imminent rejection into as polite a form as he could make it, when he spotted two men walking away from the bar. The shorter of the two glanced back at the bar, and Noah stiffened. *That's Levi. What the fuck?* The clothes were different, but Noah would know him anywhere. Not that he'd ever seen him at Maine Street. More than that, Levi hadn't shown any inclination to visit the bar. He studied the man walking at Levi's side. *Who's he? And where are they going?*

Not for the first time, Noah wondered how much there was about Levi that he didn't know. He could list Levi's favorite books, music, and movies, he could name Levi's comfort foods in a heartbeat, but as to what went on inside Levi's head?

Noah hadn't ever gotten that deep, but only now he was beginning to figure out that the reason for his lack of success lay with Levi. *It's as if he's always kept a piece of himself hidden away. But why? Self-preservation? Embarrassment?*

Maybe it was time for them to talk—*really* talk.

"We could always go back to my place," Jacob suggested. "I'm not sure if my roommate's home though."

It took a moment for his suggestion to register. "Hm? Oh. Right." He followed Levi with his eyes, watching as they turned onto Beach Street. *Are they going to the beach? At* this *time of night?* Then he remembered what else lay along Beach Street. The motor hotel. The resort. *Oh.*

Levi's walk took on a whole new meaning, and Noah wasn't sure how he felt about that.

"Your enthusiasm is overwhelming."

The comment dragged Noah's attention back into the moment. Jacob was smirking.

"I just struck out, didn't I?" He shrugged. "You win some, you lose some."

Oh, thank God. There had been a few guys who'd gotten nasty when he'd declined their advances, but word had soon spread. Maine Street was the kind of bar where everyone knew who was there and why, not that Noah was all that frequent a visitor. "I'm sorry. That's really not why I came here tonight. I just wanted to have a good time." He was pretty sure he hadn't been giving out signals that he was interested in sex.

Jacob bit his lip. "Damn. You're just my type too."

Noah gave him a sweet smile. "Look, it's not you, it's—"

Jacob held up his hand. "It's okay, all right? I mean, I've seen you around. I know you don't hook up with a lot of guys. I guess I was in a hope-springs-eternal kinda mood. No harm, no foul, right?" His eyes sparkled in the lights strung out over the deck. "Wanna go back and dance some more?" He grinned. "I need to expend some energy. And who knows, I might get lucky."

Noah chuckled. "Sure." Anything not to have to think about Levi—and the man he'd left with. Noah wasn't sure why he was so bothered by it. Maybe it was because he was worrying about Levi going off God knew where with a stranger.

Yeah, that was all it was.

Then Jacob tugged his hand and led him down the stairs to lose himself in the music that throbbed through the building.

Levi will be fine. He can take care of himself.
He hoped.

Levi lay in the semi darkness, hands laced behind his head, staring at the ceiling where the lights from passing cars could be seen. He'd just gotten into bed, but he wasn't ready to fall asleep. *Daniel nailed it. Everything was about me.* He'd been right about something else too—Levi didn't want to lose Noah.

He froze at the sound of a gentle knock, then the door opened. Grammy poked her head around it, then came into the room. Levi sat bolt upright. "Hey, what are you doing up? Are you okay?"

She came over to the bed, her fluffy apricot-colored robe pulled tight around her. "Heard you come in. And no, you didn't wake me up. I wasn't asleep." She frowned. "You were back earlier than I thought you'd be."

"You're complaining about me coming home early?" His heartbeat was climbing back down now he knew she was all right.

She cocked her head. "Did you have fun, wherever it was you went?"

Levi knew better than to conceal things from her. "I went to a gay bar."

Grammy arched her eyebrows. "I see."

"And it *was* fun—up to a point."

She came around to the side of the bed and sat on it. Grammy stroked the quilt. "I made this before you were born."

The randomness of the remark halted him in his tracks. "Really?"

"Mm-hmm. Your great-grandmother taught me. She was wicked talented." Grammy smiled. "She used to despair of me."

"Why?"

"I couldn't get my tongue around French."

He frowned. "Why should that make her despair?"

"She was from Montreal. I guess she felt French should've been in my blood." She cackled. "Looks like I missed out on that gene. Lord, when your great-granddad used to annoy her, she'd come out with a torrent of French, and he had no clue what she was sayin'. But darn it, she could quilt." She lapsed into silence. Before he could ask where she was going with this, Grammy looked him in the eye. "What's wrong, Levi? And don't even think about lyin' 'cause I'll know."

She would too.

Levi leaned back against his pillows, his stomach tight. "I suppose what it boils down to is, I love... someone, but I don't think they love me." It was easier leaving Noah's name out of it.

She regarded him in silence for a moment before nodding. "Thought it might be something like that. So..." He steeled himself for her questions. "What are you gonna do about it?"

He'd expected *What's his name? How long have you known him?* And because Grammy was as sharp as they come, *Is it Noah?*

"You gonna forget 'em? Walk away?" She cocked her head. "Or make 'em notice you?"

Despite the roiling in his belly, Levi forced a smile. "And how do you suggest I do that? Tell them how I feel?"

"Not if that's not how you wanna play it. Just... buy their chairs."

It was about then that Levi was convinced Grammy had lost the plot.

She narrowed her gaze. "An' don't you look at me like I'm linin' up for the funny farm. My mind is still as sharp as those kitchen knives downstairs."

"Sharper," he murmured.

Her lips twitched. "Glad we got that straight. Okay. I saw a movie a while back. *Phenomenon*, with that Travolta guy. You know, the one jigglin' his hips on the dance floor in that *Saturday Night* whatever?"

"Yeah, I've heard of John Travolta," Levi admitted with a smile.

"Fine, but the one who stuck with me in that movie was Robert Duvall. I always liked him. Your granddad used to tease me about him. Anyhow, he played the doc. Now, at the end of the movie, Travolta is dyin', an' folks are talkin' 'bout these... powers he'd gotten, but that's not the important part. The doc starts talkin' 'bout how Travolta's lady love is stickin' by him, 'cause he bought her chairs."

Levi couldn't recall the movie. "I don't think I saw this."

"She poured herself into makin' those chairs," Grammy explained. "An' although Travolta didn't need 'em, he bought 'em anyway, because they were important." She patted the quilt. "Before I started datin' your granddad, he turned up one day with a brown paper package tied up with string. It was full of fabric squares. All colors, different designs... but all quilting squares. He'd seen 'em in a store, an' thought I might find 'em useful." Her eyes shone. "He bought my chairs." She raised her chin. "So… this guy you love. What does *he* pour himself into? Because whatever it is, you need to show him you appreciate his passion."

"Even if I don't?"

Grammy rolled her eyes. "I'm not sayin' it has to become *your* passion too, okay? Differences are just as good as similarities. But have you ever taken an interest?"

She had him there.

"No, not really."

Grammy nodded. "Then maybe you should." She reached out and took his hand in hers. "I just want you to be happy, child."

"I know." Levi was no fool. *She knows exactly who I'm talking about.*

Grammy tightened her grip on his fingers. "Findin' love. That's what matters in this world. Not everyone who loves, gets to hold onto that love. So if there's anything you can do to hold onto yours, then you do it." She stilled. "You do everything you can." Then she relaxed. "Just don't twist yourself into knots over this guy. Let him do some of the runnin' too." She released his hand, and stood. "Now go to sleep." Grammy bent over and kissed the top of his head.

"You too."

She sighed. "Some nights the memories come thick an' fast, so many that sleep keeps its distance. This is one of those nights." Then she cupped her jaw and winced.

"Grammy?"

She rolled her eyes. "Jeannie Crummel, aren't I allowed to have a pain in my jaw without you panickin'?

And don't say you're not, 'cause I can hear it." She slid her hand to her neck and rubbed there. "A person my age is allowed to have a few aches and pains. It's in the Constitution."

Levi bit back a smile. "You find me the part where it says that, and I'll believe you." He narrowed his gaze. "Are you *sure* you're—"

"Levi Jeffrey Brown…"

He mimed zipping his lips. He knew that tone.

"Now turn off that brain of yours. No more thinkin'." She walked slowly toward the door, pausing at the threshold. "Leave the thinkin' till daylight. I always think best first thing in the mornin'."

"That's because your coffee kicks your brain into action."

She beamed. "An' *now* you know why I drink it. G'night, Levi." She left the room, closing the door behind her.

Levi shuffled down the bed. *She'd say if there was something really wrong, wouldn't she?* Then he gave an internal snort. *Yeah right.* But there wasn't a lot he could do, short of dragging her to a doctor's office, and not budging. Maybe she was right. Aches and pains came with old age. *Except she doesn't seem old to me.* His mind went over her words. *At least I know what Noah's chairs are. It wouldn't hurt to show some interest, right?* Then he realized he could do more than that.

He stretched out his hand to the nightstand, and grabbed his phone. His thumbs flew over the screen as he composed a text to Finn.

Hey. I know when you read this, it'll be Sunday, but can you call me when you have a minute? Need your help.

He replaced the phone on the nightstand, pulled the sheets higher, and closed his eyes.

Please, God. Tell me that guy Noah was with isn't important to him. Tell me I still have a chance.

Tell me I'm not too late.

Chapter Six

Sunday, June 20

The more Noah gazed at the space above his parents' garage, the more he realized he couldn't do the job alone. Okay, so he'd built the layout in modules that could come apart, and that meant the scenery layer could travel separately with only half a dozen wires to disconnect from screw terminals. But most of the pieces had been built in situ, and that meant not only were they too big to go down the narrow stairs, they were also too big to go up the equally narrow stairs leading to Grammy's attic. For one thing, there was the wiring to consider, and that was as big a job as the scenery, so being able to preserve as much of it as possible would be a big help when it came to reassembling.

He'd already removed anything not firmly attached, and so far there were dozens of book cartons ready to make the trip. But since the room where the layout had been assembled was a different shape to the attic, major segments would have to be rebuilt once he got them up there.

I'll need to move the layout in big chunks. That would necessitate a trailer with added cross arms so the sections could be carried lying upright. And the solution to the size problem would be to rent a scissor lift and get his friends over to help him load the pieces, one at a time onto the lift. Then it would be a case of out of the upper window of the garage, and once they reached Grammy's, they'd have to repeat the exercise, lifting the pieces and passing them through the window at the end of the attic.

It was going to be a logistical nightmare, but the alternative was leaving everything behind, and that was *not* an option. It would take careful planning, and that required time.

Then there was the problem of where to put everything. Did he wait until the attic was ready? He could see his dad getting impatient to get his floor space back. The book cartons would fit fine in the summerhouse—it was everything else that created a headache.

Maybe I should talk to Grammy. It was her attic, after all.

You're not going to Grammy's to ask about storage. You want to quiz Levi on what he was doing last night.

Yeah, he did.

Noah carried the boxes to the car, stacking them carefully, aware of his mom watching through the living room window. He hoped she'd stay there. He wasn't in the mood to discuss his plans. Besides, he hadn't been able to get Levi out of his mind. It wasn't just a case of him being at the bar—he had every right to go there, didn't he? No, it was more a case of how he'd *looked*. Noah thought he'd probably seen every item in Levi's closet, and not once had he *ever* seen him in skinny jeans and a tank top.

And oh my God, he looked good in them.

Noah closed the trunk and got behind the wheel. Grammy's house was only five minutes away. Out of courtesy, he pulled his phone from his pocket and dialed.

"Hey, Noah. What's up?"

"Grammy, would it be okay if I brought some boxes over?"

She chuckled. "How many are we talkin' 'bout?"

"They'll go easily into the summerhouse."

"I thought you had a ton of stuff."

"I do, but—"

"Get your butt over here. I'm in the middle of bakin', and I don't want them cookies to burn."

"On my way. Thanks." He disconnected.

As he drove along Post Road, Levi still occupied his thoughts. *What do I say to him? Do I come right out and tell him I saw him last night? Do I ask who he was with?* Except that felt rude. It was none of his goddamn business. By the time he pulled up outside Grammy's house, he'd come to a decision. He'd simply ask Levi how his Saturday had gone. If Levi wanted to tell him, that was fine.

And if he doesn't? Do I drop the subject?

He'd cross that bridge when he came to it.

Grammy opened the door with a smile. "Your timin's great. Just took the cookies out of the oven. I know you're partial to warm cookies." She looked past him to the car. "Ain't you gonna bring your stuff in here?"

"I need to talk to you about that."

She stood aside and he stepped into the house. The slow tick of the clock in the hallway was like an old friend. He'd grown up listening to it. Then he heard a muffled *thud* above their heads. "What was that?"

Grammy waved her hand. "Just Levi. He's doin' something. Come on into the kitchen."

He followed her into the sunny room, which was filled with the aroma of chocolate and spices. He inhaled deeply, and Grammy laughed. "Help yourself while I pour us some iced tea. Unless you want coffee?"

"Iced tea would be great." He took a cookie from the tray sitting on the stove.

Grammy opened the fridge and brought out the jug. She took two glasses from the cabinet and filled them. "Now then," she said as she placed them on the kitchen table. "What's goin' on?"

They sat, and he told her about the logistics of moving the layout. She listened, nodding here and there between sips of tea. When he was finished, Grammy put down her glass. "Something I want to show you." She got up. "Come with me."

Noah followed her upstairs, and she headed for her closet, which in reality was a bedroom she used for storing all her clothes. Noah had peeped in there a few times when he was younger. Grammy opened the door, and they went inside.

She surveyed the racks of clothes, the boxes, the trunks, and the mannequins. "Been meanin' to go through all this for a while. I got stuff in here I haven't worn since... well, before Levi was born. I'm not a follower of fashion, but even *I* would think twice about wearin' some of it now." She made a clicking noise with her tongue. "Seems to be a theme lately. The boxes in the attic, the clothes... I'm in need of a major declutterin'." She shook her head. "I used to laugh at folks in shows like *Clean House*, *Hoarders*, *Master the Mess*, but you know what? I'm just as bad as any of 'em. Well, it's time I did something about it." Grammy sighed. "Otherwise that boy will have an awful time of it when I'm gone."

"That's years away," Noah remarked.

She gave him a sweet smile. "None of us know

that, sweetheart. Now, you wanna put your trains in the summerhouse?"

He nodded. "They won't take up much room."

"That's just fine. And as for the rest of it, you wanna put it in here, or go with your plan of haulin' it through the attic window?"

"It would make more sense to hire a scissor lift and go in that way." He couldn't store anything in the bedroom. It was already bursting at the seams.

She nodded. "I agree. I'm glad the summerhouse won't be too full. It's a nice place to sit in the evenin'. Plus, Levi is forever takin' his laptop in there to work."

He stilled. "Grammy… could *I* maybe work in there sometimes?"

Grammy blinked. "Child, you can work anywhere you want in this house. You're family." She frowned. "Ain't you got no place to work wherever it is you're stayin'? Not that I know where that is."

He chuckled. "We're almost neighbors. I've got a unit at Wellington Manor."

She widened her eyes. "Jeezum crow, it must be noisy as hell there. All them summer complaints, with their kids runnin' around yellin'.… How do you expect to concentrate on your work?"

Thud.

Noah bit his lip. "Earplugs?"

Thud.

What was Levi up to?

Grammy pursed her lips. "Nope, it just won't do. You need quiet in your line of work." *Thud.* She raised her eyes to the ceiling and chuckled. "Not that it's peaceful here right this minute, but he'll be done soon enough. I hope. He's been at it all mornin'." She scanned the room. "I figure if we go through all this, we could lose maybe two thirds of it to either the trash or Goodwill."

"'We'?"

Grammy grinned. "You help me declutter, we fix this room up so it's comfortable—and then you move in."

What the— "I couldn't do that," he protested. She was already doing enough, giving him the space in the attic.

"Why not? If you wanna contribute to the bills, then fine. I won't expect you to cook—even Levi keeps out of my kitchen—but you'd have to clean up after yourself. Would your mom mind?" She peered at him. "Are things okay with you and your mom?" Before he could answer, she gave another eye-roll. "Jeannie Crummel, would ya listen to me. That was a damn stupid question. You moved out, so it stands to reason everything ain't hunky dory." Grammy placed her hand at his back. "Like I said, you're family, and you'll always have a place here."

Thud.

Noah peered at the ceiling. "What *is* he doing up there?" His mind was still reeling from her proposal. *Is she serious?* Then he dismissed the question. Grammy never did a thing without first thinking it through.

"Why don't you go take a peek while I make lunch?"

"Hey, wait a minute," he protested. "We're not done here."

She cackled. "Yes we are. You're gonna move in. No arguments."

"But... don't you want to run it past Levi? After all, it's his home too."

Grammy studied him for a moment. "Sure. But I

don't think he'll have a problem with it. Now go see him." And with that, she walked out of the room and down the stairs, humming to herself.

Grammy was a force to be reckoned with.

Noah left the room and went to the attic door. He pushed it open. "Levi? I'm coming up."

"What are you doing here?"

Noah climbed the narrow stairs and emerged into the attic. Levi stood on a stepladder, a nail gun in his hand. Then Noah looked again. Sheetrock covered the rafters. "Wow. You've been busy." He walked over to the foot of the steps.

"I'm almost done," Levi told him.

Noah chuckled. "Do you need a license for that thing?"

"Hey, I'm pretty good with—" The ladder wobbled, and Noah hastened to hold it steady. Levi gave him a mock glare. "That was your fault. You distracted me." He came down the steps and placed the nail gun on the wooden floor.

"Sorry. I thought Finn was going to do this."

"He was—until I called him this morning and said I'd do it. So he gave me detailed instructions, and then I drove to their place and picked up this deadly weapon."

Noah grinned. "I was about to say… Are you safe to be left alone with power tools?"

Levi glared. "That's what Finn said too. I'm doing okay, aren't I?"

Noah had to admit, he'd done a great job.

"I bought thicker insulation to go over the stuff Grandpa originally put up here, and I got rid of the wire netting. Plus, I spoke with an electrician this morning. He'll be here tomorrow. He agreed with me that one or two twenty-amp outlets would be plenty for your needs. And I've asked him to install recessed light fixtures with two switches, one at the bottom of the stairs, and one up here. That way, I can install a dimmer." Levi smiled. "I figure you'll want to show off your layout's night lighting, right?"

Noah stilled. "Well… yes, but… how did you know that? The lighting and the power, I mean."

Levi shrugged. "I did a little research."

He did all this for me? Warmth surged through him. Then he remembered he had to do a little research of his own. "You must have spent all your weekend on this." *Come on, Levi. Tell me no, you took a break last night and went to a gay bar.*

"I only started this today, although I was up real early." He fell silent, and in that moment Noah realized two things: Levi wasn't going to say a word about Maine Street, and Noah wasn't going to challenge him on that.

If he wanted me to know, he'd say something. If he wants it to be a secret, then I'm not about to embarrass him by mentioning it. The last thing Noah wanted was any awkwardness between them, especially if they were going to be living under the same roof.

Except Levi didn't know that part, not yet.

"Boys!" Grammy hollered from the foot of the stairs. "Lunch is ready. Noah, have you told him yet?"

Levi froze. "Told me what?"

"I came over to talk about transporting the layout," he said quickly. "I'm going to need help from you and some of the guys." He wasn't about to mention Grammy's latest idea.

I'll leave that part up to her. Despite her confidence, there was always the possibility that Levi wouldn't be happy with the prospect of Noah sharing his home.

I'm not even sure I know how I feel about it. Nervous, exhilarated, apprehensive… The idea had him in knots, and he had no clue why.

K.C. WELLS

Chapter Seven

Saturday, June 26

Levi glanced in Grammy's closet. *Except it's not that anymore, is it?* Amazing what a difference five days had made. Noah had come over every evening for dinner, and after, they'd gone up to the room. Grammy had supervised the proceedings, coming out with comments such as "Dear Lord, throw that in the trash," "What *was* I thinkin'?" and "Jeezum crow, if I wore those heels now, my ears would pop an' I'd get a nosebleed."

She'd also gone through the old-fashioned oak wardrobe in her room with a ruthlessness that had impressed Levi, although he'd commented if she got rid of so many clothes, she'd have nothing left to wear. Grammy had cackled. "Hey, lookit me, the modern woman. I'm creatin' a capsule wardrobe."

Noah had remarked that to his shame, he had no idea what one of those was.

And speaking of Noah...

I still can't believe she asked him to move in.

She'd told Levi if he objected, then of course she'd withdraw the offer. Except how could he do that and not look like a complete asshole? Not that he wanted her to withdraw it. Having Noah so close, in the room next to his... that could either turn out to be awesome—or torture.

And why haven't I asked him about Maine Street?

Except he knew why. Asking questions would reveal his own presence there, and Levi wasn't sure he wanted to do that. And there was also the very real possibility he wouldn't like Noah's response.

Much safer to remain ignorant.

He caught the sound of footsteps outside, and a moment later, Noah pushed the door open, carrying a big box. He came to a halt. "You taking a break?"

Levi chuckled. "Sorry. I zoned out for a minute. How many more boxes are there?" They'd already put five or six in the room, stacked against the wall. As yet there was no bed—Grammy had told them to leave that part to her—so Noah was to sleep in the guest room until it arrived.

"Three more. Then that's it." Noah put the box down. "That just leaves the layout, but Mom says my dad will have to wait till the attic's ready."

"About the attic… After lunch, I thought we might start bringing boxes downstairs a few at a time, and put them in the dining room. We can go through them in there. For one thing, it's warm up in the attic right now."

"What—you mean, you haven't installed AC yet?" Noah's eyes twinkled. "Just kidding. You've done an awesome job up there. Especially when you consider you haven't put a nail through your hand yet—or any other part of you."

Levi narrowed his gaze. "Don't think I didn't notice the first aid box that suddenly appeared. Your faith in me leaves a lot to be desired."

Noah held up his hands. "Hey, I'm just being practical. And who says it isn't up there for me? The number of times I've cut myself when I've been working on the layout… But bringing boxes downstairs makes a lot of sense."

Levi nodded. "That way, Grammy will be on hand to cast the deciding vote." His stomach churned.

Noah frowned. "Hey, what's wrong?"

"What makes you think something is wrong?"

He smiled. "Because I know you. So what went through your mind just now?"

Levi gazed at the remnants of Grammy's clothing. "It feels weird. Why is she getting rid of so much stuff?"

"She's thinking of you," Noah said in a gentle tone.

"Me?"

He nodded. "I know exactly what she's doing. My mom did the same thing after my grandpa and my aunt Lydia died. Mom was the executor for both of them, and it was up to her to clear out their houses before they could be sold." Noah sighed. "It was a job she'd dreaded doing. It was bad enough clearing Grandpa's place—Aunt Lydia was a hoarder. When she was done, Mom went on a decluttering jag. She kept saying we had too much stuff, that when they finally went, it would be up to me to sort through it all, and that she didn't want me to go through the hassle she'd experienced." He shook his head. "Dad would talk about buying something, and she'd yell at him that he wasn't allowed to bring one more thing into the house unless he got rid of something first. It was funny at the start, but she hasn't let up. It's gotten to be a mania with her." Noah's eyes were warm. "Grammy wants to make her passing as easy on you as she can."

"But she's got decades left!" Levi's chest tightened. "I hope."

"That's what I said to her too."

He blinked. "You... you talked about this with her?" He had no idea Noah and Grammy were so close. Then he reconsidered. *Why shouldn't they be? He's been coming here since he was fourteen.* Grammy treated all his friends as if they were family, and her generosity with them frequently blew him away.

"Yeah, last week, when she brought me up here." Noah cocked his head to one side. "You *are* okay with me moving in, aren't you?"

Levi rolled his eyes. "Will you just quit it? I said I was fine with it, didn't I? Last Sunday when Grammy asked me."

"Sure, but... you've been so quiet this week. I thought maybe you'd had second thoughts—or even *first* thoughts—and you didn't want to hurt my feelings or something."

The last thing Levi wanted was for Noah to feel awkward or uncomfortable.

"Okay, for the final time..." He looked Noah in the eye. "I'm happy you're moving in, okay? And I can't wait to see what you do with the attic." More than that, it was a new direction, one Levi hadn't seen coming, and he wanted to know where it would lead. His talks with Daniel and Grammy were never far from his mind.

Whatever you need me to be, Noah... I'm going to be that man. And I'll take as much of you as you're willing to give.

Sunday, June 27
Levi placed another box on the dining room

table. "You know, I just took a look up there. It doesn't feel like we've even made a dent."

Noah chuckled. "We're talking about a lifetime of accumulated stuff. It's going to take a while. We just need to keep at it, one box at a time." He glanced toward the living room, where Grammy sat in her armchair, her chin almost resting on her chest. "She hasn't kept much, has she?" he murmured. "A couple of photo albums that she'd forgotten about, and some books."

"At this rate, most of it will end up going." Levi opened the box and peered inside. "Ah. I can't see her wanting to give *this* to Goodwill." He removed a polished wooden chest, and placed it on the dining table. "This is beautiful. Why was it stuck in a box out of sight?" The varnished lid was inlaid with a single red rose, worked in different veneers.

Noah peered over at it. "Is that locked?"

Levi tried the lid. "Uh-uh." It was filled with bundles of pale mauve envelopes, each tied with a red ribbon. He picked the nearest one up, and thumbed through the bundle. "These are all addressed to Grammy, before she married Granddad. It's a different address too."

In the living room, Grammy coughed. "What?" She was there in a heartbeat.

"I thought you were asleep," Noah commented.

She snorted. "Sleep is for the weak." She stared at the envelopes in Levi's hand. "Don't open 'em."

"I wasn't going to," Levi assured her. "They're not addressed to me."

Grammy grabbed the bundle and stuffed it back into the chest. "These are *not* for your eyes."

Noah chuckled. "Oh, *now* I'm curious." He

grinned. "Just what is in them?"

"What's in 'em don't matter, 'cause you're not gonna read 'em." Her cheeks and neck were flushed as she pulled the chest toward her. "I'll take this."

Levi blinked. "Okay." He peered into the box, and a small journal caught his eyes. He picked it up. There was nothing written on the plain cover. He opened it to find a polaroid stuck on the first page. The photo contained a color image of what appeared to be a basement, furnished with a sofa and a couple of armchairs. Seated on them were six young men and a young woman. Levi looked closer at her. She had long hair, and she wore jeans and a white blouse. And there was something familiar about her...

"Grammy... is this you?" It had to be. Then he glanced at the young men around her, and his heartbeat quickened. *Are those two holding hands?* He grabbed Noah's arm, and when he had his attention, Levi pointed to the couple. Noah's eyes widened.

Grammy came to his side and stared at the photo. "Oh my..."

"That *is* you, isn't it? How old were you in this photo?"

She sighed. "Sixteen. This was taken in 1966."

Levi leafed through the pages of the journal, finding more photos of the young men and Grammy. "Who were these guys?" He returned to the first photo, and pointed to the two holding hands. "Especially these two."

She swallowed, then tapped the figure on the left with a slim finger. "That was my brother, Jeff."

He blinked. "You never said I have a great-uncle." Then he recalled her use of the past tense.

Before he could say anything else, she gave him

a sad smile. "That's 'cause you don't, not anymore. He died in Vietnam in '69. He was in the Air Force."

Levi peered closely at Jeff. "You looked alike." He could hear the pain in Grammy's voice. *No wonder she doesn't talk about him.*

Noah peered at the Polaroid. "So who were the rest of them?"

"Jeff's friends." Grammy stroked Jeff's image with her fingertips.

Levi studied the group. "They were all gay, weren't they?" He wasn't sure what gave them away, just small details, and it was only a feeling, but…

Grammy nodded. She tapped the photo again. "This was our basement. Mom and Dad set it up for Jeff. They wanted it to be his safe place, where he could bring his friends." Her gaze met Levi's. "Gay guys have it easier these days—yeah, I know that isn't always the case, but a lot of folks are more acceptin'—but back then, things were different. Maybe it was because Mom was from Montreal. She was more open to this kinda thing than my dad was." She gave the photo a fond glance. "So Jeff got to hang out with his buddies, in a place where he could be himself. So could they. Not that they ever got up to anything, you understand—at least, not while *I* was around. But I loved being with 'em."

Noah pointed to the guy holding Jeff's hand. "Who was he?"

She smiled. "Jeff's best friend, Wayne."

Noah bit his lip. "Seems to me they were more than friends."

Her eyes gleamed. "They were. I knew that after I saw them kissin' once when they thought they were alone, but I didn't need to see that to know they were in love."

"How old was Jeff when this was taken?" Levi asked.

"He'd have been twenty-one. Not long after this, he an' Wayne enlisted."

"And then they went off to fight in Vietnam." Noah shook his head. "That took guts. I'm not talking about fighting, I'm talking about being in the military—and in a same-sex relationship. They'd have to have been so careful not to get found out."

"Wayne died the same time Jeff did. And no, I don't think anyone ever guessed what they were to each other. They did a great job of keepin' it a secret."

"They died together," Levi murmured.

Grammy blinked back tears. "Yeah, they did. I don't remember all the details, but they were both caught up in some skirmish or other, and Jeff's helicopter got shot down. Wayne was with him." She swallowed. "August 15th, 1969."

What came to Levi's mind was the late-night conversation with her the previous week. "When you talked about finding love, and how not everyone who loves gets to hold onto that love…You were talking about Jeff and Wayne, weren't you?"

She nodded. "When I learned they were dead, I couldn't stop cryin'. Wayne had a younger brother, Robert—he was twenty-two when Wayne died—and he and I kinda consoled each other."

Robert…

Levi gaped. "That was Granddad."

"Yeah. We walked out together for a while, an' eventually he proposed—took him long enough—and we married in '71."

"How come you never told me about Jeff?"

Levi understood that the memories had to hurt, but he still couldn't believe this was the first time he'd gotten to hear any of this. It went a long way to explaining why Grammy didn't bat an eyelid at Levi's friends. *She grew up around gay guys.* If anything, it solidified his opinion of her.

Grammy was cool.

"It was a long time ago."

He stilled. "Oh my God. My middle name… Jeffrey…"

She smiled. "Yes."

Levi frowned. "Did… did *you* name me then?" It was a question he'd never thought to ask.

"I added the Jeffrey part. Levi was the name written in the letter I found in your crib when Amy left you on the doorstep."

Amy… Levi hadn't heard Grammy mention his mom by name in a long time.

"Would Jeff's name be on the Vietnam Veterans Memorial in Washington DC?" Noah asked.

She nodded. "Wayne's too."

"Did you ever go to see it?"

She shook her head. "Robert went, when it was first erected in the eighties. I couldn't." She bit her lip. "Not sure why. I told myself I'd seen the photos, and that was enough. Maybe 'cause I thought seein' it up close would bring back too many memories. But you wanna know something? I've always regretted it."

No way was Levi going to let her live a moment longer with any regrets. "It's not too late, you know."

She frowned. "Huh?"

"I'll take you there," he declared.

Grammy burst into a peal of laughter. "Child, I've gone my whole life not once gettin' on a plane. Not about to change that now."

Levi wasn't giving up that easily. "Then we'll drive. A two-day road trip. We can stay in a hotel on the way."

Grammy stared at him. "We're talkin' over five hundred miles."

"So? We'll split it up. We'll drive so far, stay in a hotel, carry on…" He locked gazes with her. "You *know* you want to do this." He had no idea why he wasn't going to let this drop. Maybe it was his subconscious. He knew Grammy probably had years left in her, but his niggles about her health lingered.

She needs to do this while she still can.

Grammy pursed her lips. "Lord, you remind me of me. Stubborn as a mule." Before he could respond, she held up a hand. "Okay. Fine. But I have a couple conditions."

"Okay." He'd agree to anything, if it meant she would undertake the trip.

"Number one. I pay for the hotel."

"Done."

"And number two—Noah comes with us."

Noah blinked. "Me?"

She nodded. "You an' Levi can share the drivin'. Plus, you'll be comp'ny for him. I never could stay awake in a car. Your granddad used to complain 'bout that every time he drove up the coast." Grammy gave him a beseeching stare. "Please, Noah? Do it for me?"

Levi smiled to himself. *He can't say no to her, any more than I can.* Grammy could fight dirty when she wanted something badly enough.

Noah heaved a dramatic sigh. "Well, when you put it like that… Fine. I'll come too."

She beamed. "Great. Then I'll start lookin' for

hotels." She glanced at Levi. "I just thought of another condition. We're gonna do this sooner rather than later, before it gets too hot. You got any objections?"

Levi snorted. "I wouldn't dare." He could arrange his schedule to fit around her plans.

"And I'll let my boss know," Noah added. "I'll just make sure I'm up to date before we go."

A road trip with Grammy—and Noah. *As if I'd complain about that.*

Grammy held out her hand, and Levi knew what she was asking for. He handed her the journal, and she placed it with the letters.

She has a chest full of memories there. Levi could understand her reticence. *How would I feel if someone wanted to rifle through* my *love letters?* Because that was the only thing they could be.

He'd never written one, and he had certainly never received one. The thought saddened him, until an idea filtered through his brain.

Write a letter to Noah. Tell him how you feel about him.

Okay, so Levi might never give it to him, but maybe the act of pouring his heart out onto paper might prove cathartic.

And maybe one day I'll find the courage to say it out loud.

Then something stirred in his memory.

But I did write such a letter—just once. Didn't I put all my feelings down on paper, a long time ago? He recalled sitting in the Wells High School library, maybe a month away from graduation. Noah had been seated opposite, his nose in a book, and…

Yes. He'd written a letter, one he hadn't been brave enough to deliver.

I wonder what happened to it.

Chapter Eight

Wednesday, June 30

Noah saved the file he'd been working on, and glanced at his phone. Time for coffee and a cookie. He shook his head, smiling. *Grammy is getting me into bad habits.* He had to admit, he'd missed his mom's cooking while he'd been staying at Wellington Manor. He'd never been much good in the kitchen, not that he had the chance now—it was Grammy's domain. But since the day he'd moved in, she'd insisted on a morning coffee break, accompanied by a cookie, or occasionally—heaven help his arteries—a cruller.

He raised his head at the sound of footsteps on the stone slabs outside the summerhouse. Levi paused at the threshold. He glanced at Noah's closed laptop, and smiled. "I take it my timing's good?"

Noah got up from the table. "Your timing's awesome."

"Great, because something just arrived that might interest you."

It took a moment for Levi's meaning to sink in. Then Noah grinned. "My bed's here."

Levi nodded. "The delivery men have just finished putting it together." He coughed. "And that's not all they brought."

Noah stared at him, his stomach churning. "Oh no. What else did she buy?" There was no way he could ever repay her for her generosity.

"You'd better come see."

Noah followed Levi into the house and up the stairs. They passed the two delivery men who were descending, and gave them a nod. Noah hurried into his bedroom, and came to a dead stop. "Oh wow."

An oak-framed queen bed stood against the wall, a matching nightstand beside it. Facing it was a chest of drawers, and by the window sat a comfy-looking armchair. The finishing touch was a desk and chair.

Grammy stood at the foot of the bed, surveying the room with a satisfied air. "*Now* it looks like a bedroom."

Noah's throat tightened. "Grammy… this is too much." He'd expected a single bed, nothing more.

She raised her hand. "Now, before you get on your high horse an' berate me for spendin' a ton of money on ya, you need to know a couple things. For one, none of this is new."

"Where did it all come from?"

She smiled. "My dear friend, Eliza Hampton. Her husband George died last year—God rest his soul—and her kids wanted her to sell up an' go live with them in Florida. She's been rattlin' around in that ol' house ever since he passed. So she said yes." Grammy chuckled. "She won't miss the cold, I know that much. Anyhow, two weeks ago after church, she mentioned she was gettin' rid of all the furniture. She wasn't gonna need it. Then you an' me got to talkin', and I realized I could help her out." She pointed to the rug on the wooden floor. It was thick, and done in fall colors. "An' that was my mom's. It's been rolled up in the attic for years, so I had Levi bring it down. I know what it's like to get out of bed on a cold mornin' and feel like your toes have frostbite."

Levi chuckled. "As if it's *ever* that cold in this house."

Grammy regarded Noah with bright eyes. "Well? Think you'll be happy in here?"

He beamed. "I'm sure of it." He glanced at the room. "This is amazing."

"I got lamps you can use. They're in my closet." She cackled. "That's one thing there's no shortage of in this house." She pointed to the desk. "An' when it gets too cold to work in the summerhouse, you've got a space here." Her eyes twinkled. "That's only so you don't have to work at the dinin' table with Levi. I know how he gets when he's concentratin', and I'll lay even money you're the same." She patted the footboard. "So when you've finished admirin' your new room, think you two could come downstairs? I wanna make sure we're ready for our road trip."

"We'll be ready," Levi assured her. "You're looking for a hotel, right? What else do we need to do, apart from decide on a date for it?"

"Maybe I'd like to discuss what sights we're gonna see? My first trip to DC, I wanna make sure I get to see everything worth seein'." She grinned. "I don't plan on makin' this trip twice. I figure once it's done, it's done." Grammy walked past them. "And there's a new batch of oatmeal raisin cookies, if anyone's interested," she called out as she went downstairs.

Noah laughed. "I swear, she's trying to fatten me up. At this rate, she won't need a turkey for Thanksgiving—she'll be able to stuff me." He was happier than he'd been in a long time.

Who wouldn't be happy? I have a home. A place where he felt secure, wanted…

The icing on the cake was Levi.

Thursday, July 1st

Noah gazed at the space surrounding him, trying to picture how it could look. The prospect sent flutters through his stomach, and an infusion of warmth. Few boxes remained, and that left a wide space crying out to be filled. Levi had skimmed the surface of the sheetrock with a thin layer of plaster, then applied another layer, this time of white paint. The lights had been installed, including the promised dimmer switch.

The attic was a blank canvas, just waiting for his first brush strokes.

"You up there?" Levi hollered from the foot of the stairs.

"Yup. I'm making notes."

Levi emerged from the stairwell. "Surveying your new domain?" He ambled over to where Noah stood, glancing at their surroundings. "Will you change the layout once you get it up here?"

"I think so. It would get lost in here. I did think about building new sections, and linking them with bridges, tunnels…"

"Great. Any thought to what you'd like to create? Maybe you could use a real place for inspiration."

That possibility had also crossed Noah's mind. What surprised him was Levi's level of engagement. "I've written down a few ideas."

"Me too."

Noah blinked. "Really?"

Levi nodded. "You don't have to take up any of my suggestions, but… Ever considered using Ogunquit as a source? Or York Beach?"

Noah bit his lip. "Last time I looked, there wasn't a railroad going through either of those."

"Yeah, I know, but think about it for a moment. There are so many places you could recreate in a layout. It would be amazing." His eyes gleamed. "Imagine making a model of Short Sands Beach? Remember how we used to go there when we were kids? Playing Skee Ball at the Fun-O-Rama? Buying Goldenrod kisses?" Levi widened his eyes. "We could make a model of the Goldenrod, with a tiny wrapping machine in the corner of the window. And the Nubble. You could even use real sand from the beach." He gestured to the attic. "I can see it now. Short Sands Beach, tiny lights strung between the lamp posts." He pointed. "Over there, you could have Ogunquit, right down to the Marginal. And connecting them, a bridge spanning the distance."

Levi's enthusiasm was infectious. "I like that. I could even include the zoo, the Leavitt…" Maybe some of the pretty white churches too.

"Would it fit in with your layout?"

"I'd make it fit," Noah announced. "And I like the idea of connecting different sections with track… bridges, tunnels…"

"We could even add a fairground, with a Ferris wheel, a carousel…" Levi frowned. "Are such things available for layouts?"

Noah laughed. "You need to remember, this is a hobby, okay? I'd have to spend a few hours working so I can pay for all this."

"So *we* can pay for it."

What the… Noah stared at him. "'We'?"

Levi nodded. "I want to help you build it. Then you can show me how to run the trains."

"Seriously?"

Levi smiled. "Of course. I can't even remember the last time I saw them running. How many different trains do you have now? What gauge? Do you prefer N gauge? Do you have any HO gauge trains?"

Noah gaped at him. "Okay, who are you, and what have you done with Levi?"

He chuckled. "All your trains are in the summerhouse, right? So why don't you show them to me? I'd really like that."

Noah narrowed his gaze. "You're not going to start snoring after three minutes? I'm just going by past experiences, you understand." *And leopards don't change their spots in one night.*

Levi sighed. "Yeah, that's all on me. But you're living here now, and this is a huge part of who you are. So… I want to know more."

Heat radiated through Noah's chest. "Then come see my treasures."

They went down the narrow stairs, continued to the first floor, and through the dining room to the backyard.

Grammy hollered as they crossed the patio, heading for the summerhouse. "Coffee's ready."

"With you in a minute," Levi shouted back. He opened the door, and Noah walked over to the table. Boxes were stacked along the sides, each marked with black pen to show their contents. Noah took a moment to pick out two, then brought them to the table.

He glanced at Levi. "So… we've been reading up on gauges, have we?" He couldn't resist smirking.

Levi coughed. "I *might* have leafed through a copy

or two of *Model Railroader*."

Noah laughed. "Ah, *that* explains it."

"Explains what?"

"I was looking for a particular back issue, and I couldn't find it." He opened the nearest box. "Well, in answer to your question, most of my trains are HO, but that's because I inherited them from Grandpa. When he was running them, N gauge was only just starting out. That's why I have separate layouts, one for Grandpa's trains, and one for the N gauge trains I've bought since I started on this."

Levi gazed at the model train nestled in packing peanuts. "Wait—is that the *Orient Express*?"

Noah nodded. He pointed to the dining car. "See those little lamps on the tables? They light up. And the sleeping compartments have these cute little beds."

"That's awesome. It looks just like the one in the movie."

Noah rolled his eyes. "Duh. That's the whole point."

"What's your most prized possession?"

Noah smiled. He replaced the lid on the book carton, then pulled the larger of the two boxes toward him. "This." He removed the lid and gazed at the model train, packed in its original box. "It's a model of the Union Pacific *Big Boy*, the largest steam locomotive ever built. This one was made in 1967, and it's one of the first models." He stroked the box. "The 4014 was the world's most powerful steam locomotive. This might be big, but you should see it take the curves. It can do that because the whole chassis is articulated."

Levi bent to peer at it. "Oh my God, would you look at that. You can even see the rivets. And it's got handrails, ladders, everything." He straightened. "I can't wait to see it in action."

Noah couldn't miss the note of genuine excitement in his voice, and it brought a lightness to him he hadn't experienced in a long time. "Well, the attic's done. All I have to do is organize a scissor lift, get some of the guys over, and then we'll get the layout up there." He'd have left the conversation there, but the question still hammered in his brain.

What's brought about all this sudden interest, Levi?

"Want to tell me what's changed?"

Levi frowned. "Huh?"

"With you. I mean, I love that you're showing an interest in my trains, but why now?"

Levi flushed, and he bit his lip. "Okay, I'll admit it got kind of intriguing—even addictive—once I started looking into it. I guess it just took a while for your passion to hook me too."

Noah chuckled. "What—like thirteen years?"

"Hey, better late than never," Levi remonstrated.

Noah wasn't about to argue with that.

"And like I said… it's a part of you, isn't it?"

Before Noah could respond, there was a rap on the wooden door frame. Grammy stood there, her eyes twinkling. "When you've finished droolin' over those trains, your coffee's gettin' cold. And while you've been jawin', *I've* found us a hotel." She grinned. "We're going Saturday. I figured that would interfere less with work. But we won't be back till Monday. That okay?"

Noah nodded. "That's fine by me. I've already cleared it with work."

"Where are we stopping?" Levi asked. Then he stilled. "Wait a sec. That means we'll be in DC on the Fourth."

She beamed. "Can you think of a better place to

spend it? And before you ask, I already checked. The Memorial is open on the Fourth. As for where we're stoppin', why don't you join me in the kitchen for coffee 'n' cookies, and I can show you all the details?"

Noah put the lid back. "Sounds good."

Levi gazed at the boxes. "And now I can't wait to see what else you've got in those."

As they walked back to the house, Noah's head was in a spin. *He means it. He* really *means it.*

What he couldn't deny was how awesome Levi's newfound interest made him feel.

Chapter Nine

Saturday, July 3

Levi glanced in the rear-view mirror. Grammy was asleep on the back seat, soft snores escaping her lips now and then. She'd fallen asleep before they'd crossed the Piscataqua River Bridge into New Hampshire, but then, she *had* been up with the birds, making sandwiches, bagging snacks, and filling a couple of Thermos flasks with coffee. Levi was sure they had enough food to last more than the two-and-a-half days their road trip would require, but Grammy never did anything in half measures.

Noah caught him looking and chuckled. "She may say sleep is for the weak, but this time she really is out for the count." He glanced at the map on his phone. "Not long now till we reach the Henry Hudson bridge."

"I'd better wake her for that. It's probably the nearest she's ever going to get to Manhattan." She'd never expressed a desire to visit New York City, at any rate. His stomach grumbled. "Besides, it's time we ate something." It was almost one o'clock, and they'd been on the road since seven. Noah had driven the first three hours, then they'd swapped. Traffic had been pretty much as Levi had anticipated, but he reckoned they'd reach Philadelphia by three. The thought made him smile. "She still hasn't told us which hotel we're staying in."

"I thought she did, the other day."

"Yes, but then she said she canceled, and booked us into another. She said it's a surprise." Grammy could be awful sneaky when she wanted to be.

"A hotel is a hotel, right? As long as my room has a bed and a shower, I'll be happy."

Levi chuckled. "She sounds so cute when she snores. Just don't ever tell her I said that," he added in a low voice.

"I've gotta say, I've seen her in a whole new light this past week." Noah twisted to gaze over his shoulder at her, then straightened in his seat. "I had no idea she was so cool. Not that I haven't *always* thought she was cool, you know? But learning about her brother, how she hung out with him and his friends…" He grinned. "Gay Great-uncle Jeff. I guess there really is a gay gene. But that part about how she and your granddad got together…"

Levi sighed. "I wish I'd known him. You know, that's something I've always envied about you."

"What?"

"You got to spend so much time with your granddad before he passed."

Noah smiled. "There was a time when I was growing up, when I think I was closer to Grandpa than I was to my mom and dad. Losing him…" His sigh echoed Levi's. "At least I'm surrounded by memories of him, every time I run his trains. Sometimes I close my eyes, and I can still see him, watching a train slow as it came into the station. I can still hear him too, hollering at me to 'make it go faster, boy!'"

"And next weekend, you'll think of him again when we get your layout into its new home." Seb and Marcus had promised they'd be there, along with Dylan and Mark. Between the six of them, Levi was certain they could accomplish the job.

"Does Grammy ever talk about your granddad?"

"Not much. I get to hear some of the things he said, and it sounds as if he was a funny guy." He paused. "I remember asking her once when I was little, how he died. I can still recall her answer." He swallowed. "She said he died of a broken heart."

There was a pause before Noah spoke. "Do you... do you ever think about her?"

It didn't take a genius to know who Noah referred to.

"What is there to think about?" he murmured. "I accept I had a mom, but that's as far as it goes. Grammy doesn't mention her, except when I ask questions, and I've only done that twice, once when I was little, and again when I was in high school. All Grammy did was give me the bare facts of what happened. And you know as much as I do. So do the other guys. It's not as if I've ever hidden the truth from you, right?" He set his jaw. "Besides, what's the point in thinking about her? She's probably dead by now."

"She might not be," Noah said in a quiet voice.

"No, she's dead, all right?" Levi declared. "I have to believe that."

"Why?"

Levi gaped at him. "Because what's the alternative? Believing she's still out there somewhere, but has never tried to find me? To contact her mom?" His chest grew tight.

Noah winced. "Yeah, that would cut pretty deep."

Before he could say another word, Levi turned his head slightly toward the rear of the car. "Grammy?

Grammy!"

"Wha? We there already?"

He forced a chuckle. "No, but we're crossing over into Manhattan. I thought you might want to see it."

"You kiddin'? You got any idea how many movies are set in New York? I've seen all I wanna see, thank you. But I do wanna eat. Are we stoppin', or are you gonna eat 'n' drive?"

"The latter." Levi wanted to make sure they got to their destination in good time.

Whenever Grammy deigned to tell them what their destination was.

"Want to tell me where I'm going?" Levi asked as they followed the loop onto N 15th Street. "Because right now, we're headed toward City Hall, and I'm pretty sure we're not staying there."

"10, Avenue of the Arts."

Noah typed the address into his phone, then let out a low whistle. "You have *got* to be kidding." He twisted to stare at Grammy. "We're staying *there*? Did you win the lottery, and just never got around to mentioning it?"

"Why? Where are we going?" Noah held his phone up, and Levi glanced at the screen. "That looks more like a bank or a courthouse than a hotel."

"That's 'cause it *was* a bank. Read that on the website," Grammy informed him. "And if we're gonna do this, we'll do it right."

"She's only gone and booked us into the Ritz-Carlton," Noah said. "It's a five-star hotel."

"It gets worse," she said with a grin. "We're stayin' here tomorrow night too."

"Grammy!" Levi had never known her to be so extravagant.

"Don't you Grammy me. This is my first visit outta state, and at seventy-one, that's a pretty poor state of affairs. So the way I see it? I'm pullin' out all the stops. And it's not as if we're gonna be eatin' soup and grilled cheese sandwiches for the rest of the month so I can pay for it neither." She gave him a hard stare. "Can you think of a better place to celebrate the Fourth, than in some swanky hotel with room service an' cute servers on tap?"

Noah chuckled. "You should know by now, Levi. You can't fight her."

Grammy cackled. "Boy talks a lotta sense." She grinned at Levi in the mirror. "I've also booked us a table in the restaurant, at seven. You boys did bring something to wear that ain't jeans, right? Like I told ya?"

Levi laughed. "You are one sneaky woman. And yes, I followed instructions." He'd assumed she wanted them to look smart at the memorial.

"I don't even want to know how much one room costs per night," Noah muttered. "But *three*? You'd have to have taken out a mortgage just to pay for them."

Grammy coughed. "Two rooms."

Levi blinked. "What was that?"

"I booked two rooms. I figured you two would be okay sharin'. Lord knows you've done *that* often enough when the guys sleep over."

That was true, but that didn't stop Levi's heart from skipping a beat. As he drove the car into the parking lot, he couldn't help thinking the situation was beginning to read like the plot of a romance novel. Forced to share a room…

She… she didn't do this on purpose, did she?

He always said Grammy was sharp. He wouldn't put it past her. Then he reconsidered. Maybe he was wrong in assigning ulterior motives to her—she was just being practical.

What he couldn't account for was his quickening heartbeat, the fluttering in his stomach. *How many times have I shared my room with him? Why should it bother me now?*

Then he stilled. *She would've booked a double room, right?*

Grammy came to a halt outside room 1004. "This one's mine." She glanced at the plastic card in the little paper wallet, then peered at the door with narrowed eyes. "There isn't a slot for it. Damn thing's defective."

Levi took it from her, and placed the card flat against the sensor. A green light accompanied the *click* of the door lock. "There. That's how you do it."

Grammy snorted. "Last hotel I stayed in, it had keys. You know, the metal kind, with a tag attached."

She arched her eyebrows. "And since when do *you* stay in enough hotels to know 'bout this?"

He chuckled as they entered. Outside her window

was the tower of City Hall, close by. A comfortable-looking armchair sat in the corner below a standing lamp, and there was a dark wooden chest of drawers on which stood a wide-screen TV. The queen bed had plenty of pillows.

He placed her small suitcase on the luggage rack. "What do you think?"

She shrugged. "It'll do at a pinch, I guess." Then she burst out laughing. "Just yankin' your chain." Grammy preened. "I'm gonna feel like the Queen of England." She walked over to the window and peered down. "Jeezum crow, this is high."

Noah chuckled. "It could be worse. This place has thirty floors."

She widened her eyes. "Lord, if you were on the top floor, it'd be like flyin'." Then she pointed to the clock face on the tower. "Won't need to look at my watch with that right outside, will I?"

"Are we next door?" Levi asked.

She handed him another paper wallet. "Nope. You're in 1009." When he frowned, Grammy rolled her eyes. "Well, what exactly do you think is gonna happen, that I'd need to bang on the wall an' holler for you?" Her eyes glittered. "Besides, I don't want you eavesdroppin', 'specially when a cute server brings me my hot chocolate."

Noah laughed at that.

Levi gave her a tight hug. "We've got a few hours till dinner."

She nodded. "After all them hours in the car, I wanna stretch my legs. Website says there's a walk near the river. Thought we might do that." Another gleam in her eye. "Then I'll be ready for my cocktail. Wait till you see the bar."

Levi smiled. "Now that I've seen this place, I understand why you said to bring something smart to wear." He grabbed his bag and walked toward the door, Noah following. "Give us time to freshen up, and then we'll come get you for that walk."

"Don't you hurry. I wanna check out the bathroom."

He was still chuckling when the door closed behind them. He headed for their room. "Can you believe this?"

Noah laughed quietly. "It's Grammy. I'd believe anything."

Levi stopped outside room 1009. "Well, at least we know what the room will be like." He opened the door, stepped inside—and came to a dead stop at the sight of a King bed.

His heartbeat quickened. *She didn't.*

Yup, she did.

Noah gazed at the pristine white comforter, four pillows, and two bed cushions. He turned to Levi, his eyes twinkling. "Great. I get to share a bed again with Levi the starfish."

Levi glared. "Hey. I do *not* hog the bed. And that thing is huge compared to my bed at home."

Noah nodded. "We could even put the pillows along the center, you know, like a wall?"

The first thought to enter Levi's head sent warmth surging through him.

And what if I wanted to hold you?

Noah put his bag on the couch at the foot of the bed. "Me first in the bathroom." He disappeared through the door facing them, then called out, "Wow, you should see this."

Levi chuckled. "I don't imagine it's all that

different from other hotel bathrooms."

"There's a tub, a sink, and a walk-in shower. And a separate toilet." There was a pause. "Damn, that smells good."

"What does?"

Noah poked his head around the door. "The hotel shampoo and body wash."

Levi rolled his eyes. "Will you just hurry up? It's been three hours since our last pit stop, and I need to pee too."

Noah flushed. "Oops. My bad." The door closed.

Levi stood at the foot of the bed. *We've done this loads of times, right?*

Then why did the prospect feel so different?

Chapter Ten

Noah had to admit, the hotel bar was impressive. Marble columns beneath a rotunda, with deep, comfortable chairs and sparkling lights, created an atmosphere of elegance and opulence. It helped that the bar's occupants weren't showily dressed—they were smart but not over the top—so he felt at ease in his suit. It was the one he'd bought for Teresa's wedding the previous year. Levi had brought his suit too.

He looks good. The navy suit fitted his slim body, and the lilac shirt and tie complimented it. No, he looked better than good. Then Levi caught him glancing, and Noah averted his gaze quickly to hide the flush creeping up his neck and over his cheeks.

"Did I miss some sugar or ice cream?" Noah turned back to find Levi rubbing his hand over his face. "Just checking."

Noah snickered. "Are you kidding? I think you took the pattern off the china, you were so focused on not leaving a smidge of dessert." Sarcasm and humor were an easy avenue to retreat into, one he seemed to be using a lot lately.

Anything, rather than let Levi see the mess in Noah's head.

He diverted his attention to Grammy. She wore a dress, something he'd rarely seen her in. It was dark blue, with a matching lace bodice and three-quarter sleeves. He glanced at her feet, and smiled. "No heels tonight?"

Grammy rolled her eyes. "I've got a lotta walkin' tomorrow. You think I'm gonna cripple myself tonight?" She peered at her watch. "And speakin' of tomorrow... We're gonna have to be at breakfast early in the morning." She winced, pressing her hand to her chest.

"Grammy?" Noah caught the note of panic in Levi's voice. "What's wrong?"

She glared at Levi. "Jeezum crow, can't a body suffer a little indigestion without you flyin' into a panic? I've got Tums in my room, all right?" Then she bit her lip. "Sorry. It's just that you take every little twinge as a sign that I'm about to meet my Maker. So let's change the subject. How long will it take to get to the memorial?"

"About three hours," Levi told her.

She picked up her purse. "Then I'm off to my bed. I suggest you two do the same." She stood, and they followed suit, Levi at her side as they walked out of the bar and toward the elevators. Noah was trying his damnedest not to think about going to bed, though he was at a loss to know why his stomach was fluttering, as if a bird had gotten in there.

It's just Levi, for God's sake.
We've shared a bed how many times?
What makes this time different?
Fucked if he knew.

They walked Grammy to her door, and she kissed them both on the cheek. "No stayin' up all night jawin'. Breakfast starts at six-thirty, and I aim to be walkin' out of this room by then. So set your alarms. Don't make me come bang on your door." Her eyes twinkled. "'Cause you *know* I would."

Levi chuckled. "Wouldn't put it past you. Goodnight, Grammy." He hugged her. "And no flirting with the servers when your hot chocolate arrives."

She snorted. "You're no fun." They waited until she was inside, then proceeded along the carpeted hallway to their room.

Once inside, Noah removed his coat, and went to peer at the AC. "Is it me, or is it warm tonight?" He adjusted the temperature, and the fans whirred into action.

Levi crossed the floor to the corner windows. "We don't get the view of the clock tower, but Philadelphia is pretty." He glanced at the tray on top of the chest of drawers. Two cups sat on it, along with coffee, tea, sweeteners… "Hey, there's hot chocolate. Want some?"

"Wait—we don't get a cute server to bring it?" Noah quipped. Levi turned to gaze at him, his eyes rolling, and Noah chuckled. "I'm fine, thanks." He loosened his tie and pulled it over his head. "Dinner was okay."

"Okay? That shrimp quesadilla was to die for. And I know Cast Iron Chicken looked weird on the menu, but it tasted great." He grinned. "It was worth it for the expression on Grammy's face when she tried the cilantro butter on her roasted corn. Talk about entertainment value."

"What was the big deal? I liked it."

Levi's eyes sparkled. "Yeah, but *you* don't think cilantro is, and I quote, 'the Devil's lettuce'. Apparently people either love it or hate it." He grinned again. "Looked as though you loved the churros with salted caramel ice cream."

Noah snorted. "So did you. Don't think I didn't

notice you trying to sneak a spoonful of mine once you'd eaten all yours."

"Guess the old Jedi mind trick didn't work."

Noah guffawed. "You mean, 'Hey, what's the guy over there eating?' Subtle, Levi, very subtle." He kicked off his shoes, then yawned. "All I've done today is drive, and go for a stroll along the river. Why do I feel tired?"

"No idea, but I feel the same. Maybe we both need an early night." Levi turned his back to Noah, and removed his coat.

"Same sides as always?"

"Hmm?" Levi twisted to glance at him. Noah pointed to the bed. "Oh. Sure."

Noah shrugged off his shirt and laid it over the arm of the couch, along with his tie. He undid his belt, removed his pants and socks, until all that was left were his briefs. He went into the bathroom, and grabbed his toothbrush.

"You do know tomorrow might be rough on Grammy," Levi said through the door.

"Uh-uh." It was about all Noah could manage with a mouth full of toothpaste.

Levi appeared at the door, meeting Noah's gaze in the mirror above the sink. "I don't think we'll be spending all that long at the memorial. Just enough to give her time to find their names." He leaned against the frame, his arms folded. "Did you see her sightseeing list? I told her we'd have to leave Washington by about four o'clock to be back here for dinner, so even if we get to the Vietnam Veterans Memorial before eleven, we're only talking five hours or so."

Noah rinsed. "What does she want to see?"

Levi counted off on his fingers. "The White

House—she said she doesn't want to go in it, though—the National Mall, the Washington Memorial, the Lincoln Memorial, the Capitol… She mentioned the Smithsonian, and I had to veto that one. Plus, she'll be exhausted."

"Which means she'll sleep on the way back here, and be full of beans by dinner time," Noah said with a smile. He hung the towel on the rail. "Bathroom's all yours." He brushed past Levi, close enough to feel his body heat, and went over to the bed. Noah climbed in. "What is it about hotel beds that always feels so good?"

"Seb says it's the high thread count in the cotton." Levi's chuckle drifted through the open door. "He'd know. Have you any idea how often those two go away for a weekend? Any excuse. Guess staying in hotels really does it for them."

Noah stretched beneath the white cotton comforter. "I know what he means. I could get used to this."

Levi strolled out of the bathroom and walked around to his side of the bed. "There was something I meant to ask. Did you and your granddad ever go see any of the abandoned locomotives at Eagle Lake up in the North Maine Woods?" He got into bed.

Noah blinked. "What do you know about them?" Levi was full of surprises lately.

Levi rolled onto his side, facing him. "I watched this great video on YouTube, all about the Maine two-footers, the locos that ran on two-foot gauges? There was some old film of them running." He smiled. "One line made me laugh. The guy narrating said the trains sat on the narrow gauge with… what was it exactly? … 'all the grace of a fat lady on a bar stool.'"

Noah mirrored Levi's position, his arm curled

under his head. "Grandpa took me up there when I was about seven or eight. That was when I was just starting to take an interest. We went back there a few years later before he died. It was quite a hike to get to them." He smiled. "You could still see tracks going through the woods. And then we came out of the trees and there they were. Two engines, most of them rusted away, but still awesome. There was rusted, jagged metal everywhere, so Grandpa said I wasn't to touch anything. All the boxcars were made out of wood, and they'd been sitting out there for ninety years."

"Did your granddad ever see the Downeast Scenic railroad?"

Noah shook his head. "They got it going again just as he went into the hospital, in 2010. I've always wanted to take a ride on it." He stared at Levi. "You really have been doing some research, haven't you?"

"The reason I mention it is… well… would you like to go see it? Ellsworth isn't that far from Aaron, and I'm sure he wouldn't mind if we stayed there. Then again, there are plenty of hotels over on Mount Desert." His eyes twinkled. "More chances for us to sleep under soft hotel sheets."

"You'd come with me?"

Levi's face lit up. "I'd love to ride on a steam train." Then he yawned, and seconds later Noah joined in. "I guess we should go to sleep. We can talk about this when we get home." He smiled. "Goodnight." Levi rolled onto his side facing the window, and switched off the light.

"Goodnight." Noah didn't move. He gazed at Levi's back, the comforter draped over his hips, the long line of his spine. Noah bet that if he stroked the smooth skin, it would be warm to the touch. He could smell Levi—a mixture of the hotel body wash and Levi's own scent that he hadn't noticed until recently. It was a comforting smell. Noah let his gaze drift lower to where the white cotton band of Levi's briefs lay snug.

Why he should pay such attention to Levi, Noah wasn't sure. Why now? All he knew was, he was aware of Levi in a way he hadn't been before.

Noah rolled, switched off the lamp, and lay on his back gazing at the ceiling, listening to the *whir* of the AC. He closed his eyes, waiting for sleep to wrap itself around him and drag him into its depths.

What came to mind was Levi.

So many memories… Levi had been a part of his life for so long, that not having him around would feel as though Noah were missing a limb. As an only child, Noah had gotten used to his own company, but all that had changed in high school, and Levi had been the catalyst. One minute they were introducing themselves, and the next, Noah found himself one of a bunch of great guys, with differing personalities, differing family backgrounds, and yet something tied them together.

Or rather, some*one*, because Levi was the heart of their group—Levi and Grammy. There was no one on earth Noah felt closer to, except maybe his parents.

Maybe.

Noah was certain the root of his confusion was that night at Maine Street.

I thought I knew him. Yet the sight of Levi in those tight jeans and tank top had stirred something deep inside Noah, something he couldn't quantify. He recognized the emotion that had surged through him as he'd watched Levi and the unknown guy walk away. *I was jealous.* But jealous of what? The idea that Levi was about to—

All speculation did was get his stomach in knots. *This is too good an opportunity to waste.* He'd put it off so many times, but he had to know.

"Levi?"

A wry chuckle met his ears. "I thought you were tired."

"Something I've been meaning to ask you for a while—well, two weeks, actually."

"Okay. Ask whatever it is. I'm not going anywhere."

Noah's heartbeat quickened. "The thing is… I was at Maine Street, and—"

"I know. I saw you. If we're talking two weeks ago, that is."

He froze. "You did?" Levi hadn't said a word.

"Yeah. You were dancing with some guy, and then you… disappeared someplace with him."

"We went to the upper deck—which is when I saw *you*, walking away from the bar toward Beach Street… with a guy."

There was a pause. "Looks as if we've both been keeping secrets."

Noah had worked out that much out for himself. "So… who was he?"

Levi rolled over, and there was just enough light to make out his features. "His name is Daniel, and he's a friend. In fact, you've seen him several times since that night."

Noah racked his brains. "Really?"

"Sure. He's our mailman."

"Seriously?"

"He told me that night." Levi's brow furrowed. "Why haven't you asked me about him before now?"

"Why haven't you mentioned him before?" Then

they chuckled. "You're right," Noah admitted. "We've both been keeping secrets. I've wanted to ask you about him… where you two were going…"

"We sat on a bench and talked. And when we were done talking, he put me in an Uber and I went home." Levi arched his brows. "Why? Where did you think we were going?"

To a motel? His place? Not that he could voice his suspicion, because whatever Levi chose to do with a guy was none of Noah's business. But there was a tiny part of him that swelled with relief to hear they hadn't ended up in Daniel's bed.

Why should that matter to me?

"And the guy I saw *you* with… Was he someone… special?"

"No… he was… he was just a guy I danced with. I mean, we just talked…" Noah's stomach clenched, and he had no clue why. Jacob wasn't special. They hadn't done anything, for God's sake, even though Jacob had wanted to.

Every time. Every goddamn time. Whenever things got complicated or uncomfortable, his usually excellent vocabulary dried up, and he became as articulate as Sylvester Stallone in those old *Rambo* movies his dad loved to watch over and over again.

"Hey, it's okay." Levi's voice was soft. "I get it. You'd rather not discuss this. That's fine. And you're right. We need to sleep." He rolled over once more.

Noah couldn't get over the impulse that swamped him. He wanted to pull Levi close, to fall asleep with his arms around him, to *keep* him close all night long…

What the hell is going on with me?

Chapter Eleven

Sunday, July 4

Levi had seen photos online of the memorial, but they hadn't prepared him for the quiet, contemplative park within a park. The polished black granite panels reflected their surroundings, rising to ten feet at the apex. The memorial was arranged in order of year: the east panel went from 1959 to 1968, and the west from then to 1975. At each of the sloping ends was a book containing all the names of those represented there, in alphabetical order.

Noah stood beside Grammy while she looked up both Jeff and Wayne. "Got 'em," she said in a low voice. "August 1969. Panel 20W. Gives the line numbers too."

Levi held out his arm. "Ready?"

She smiled, hooked one arm through his, and the other through Noah's, and they walked slowly along the west panels, joining many others on similar pilgrimages. The sunlight glinted on the polished surface, and Levi caught the sound of leaves stirring in the breeze.

Grammy pointed to the base of the panels. "Would you lookit that." Flowers had been laid, singly or in bunches, but there were other items too: folded flags, or little flags leaning against the granite, letters, photos, a pair of boots, and even a teddy bear. At the foot of one panel was a cigarette packet, with one cigarette poking from it. Visitors strolled by, but some stood in silence, older visitors saluted, while others bowed their heads in prayer.

As they neared panel 20W, Levi noticed a guy in a motorcycle jacket, his hand on the wall, head bowed, his long white beard resting on his chest. What made Levi's throat seize were the quiet sobs that shook the guy's body.

Grammy let go of their arms and went over to him, reaching up to lay a hand on his shoulder. "Hey," she said in a soft voice.

He jerked his head toward her, and straightened, wiping his eyes. "Sorry, ma'am."

"You got nothing to be sorry 'bout. Trust me, before long, I'm gonna be blubbin' too." She cocked her head. "Who you here for?"

He pointed to a name. "That guy saved my life." He swallowed. "Been telling myself ever since this place opened that I needed to come, but…" Another sharp bob of his Adam's apple. "I finally made it. But you know what? It should be my name there, not his."

"You don't know that," Grammy said in a firm voice.

His blue eyes met hers. "Excuse me, ma'am, but I do. See, one night fifty-two years ago, I got drunk. I mean, so stinkin' drunk that the next morning, my lieutenant said I wasn't to go on the mission." He pointed to the name. "He replaced me." The guy removed a folded flight cap from his pocket, and placed it at the foot of the panel. Then he stood, hands by his sides. "There you go, buddy. Sorry it took me so long to get here. Not a day goes by when I don't think about you. Now, maybe, I won't feel so guilty." He swallowed. "Maybe." He gave Grammy a nod. "Thanks for your kindness, ma'am."

She stepped closer and gave him a hug. He was larger than she was, and she had to stretch to get her arms around him, but then he returned the hug. "He sees you, okay?" she whispered. Then she released him.

He expelled a breath. "I believe you, ma'am." Then he walked off in the direction of the Lincoln Memorial, his back straight, head held high.

Grammy swiped her hand over her eyes. "Guilt can eat you up." She straightened, her gaze roaming over the panel. "There's Wayne." She pointed to where it was etched in pale letters, *WAYNE C BROWN*. A diamond followed the name. Grammy sighed. "That means his death was confirmed." She looked lower, and Levi knew the moment she found Jeff's name. Grammy stiffened. "Ah. There he is." Her voice croaked. She crouched, stroking the cool granite. "Hey you. I got here."

Levi gazed at the name of the great uncle whose existence he'd never known about. *JEFFREY L REED*. "We should've brought something to leave here," he muttered.

"I did," Grammy announced, rising. She reached into her purse, and removed a paper-covered flat object. She unwrapped it with care, and Levi's chest constricted. It was a picture in a frame, and he recognized it instantly. Jeff and Wayne sat on the couch, holding hands, and in the corner of the frame was a rainbow ribbon. Across the base was a tiny plaque, and he leaned in to read the words engraved there.

Jeff Reed & Wayne Brown. Joined in life, united in death, August 1969.

"When did you do this?" Levi asked.

Grammy smiled. "I had Noah copy that Polaroid

for me. He found me the frame, and the ribbon too. And then he found a local engraver, Adam, who did the plaque."

Levi stared at Noah. "You kept that quiet."

He shrugged. "That's because I was under orders. Grammy wanted it to be a surprise."

Grammy bent down once more, and stood the frame against the panel. "Couldn't have done this when they were alive. Hopefully now, no one gives a flyin' leap that two guys in the military loved each other." She rose, her head bowed, and Levi joined her, the three of them standing in silence.

Behind them, someone coughed, and they turned to find a guy in the dark blue dress uniform of the Air Force, his beret clasped in his hands. He looked to be in his late twenties. He gave Grammy a nod. "I heard what you said, ma'am. And I think what you're doing is awesome." He indicated the wall. "My granddad's name is here. I only found out this year that he was gay. No one in my family ever mentioned that fact, not until I… I came out. I asked if he'd had someone special in his life, and my grandma said yes, but she never knew his name."

"She knew he was gay when they married?" Grammy asked.

He nodded. "She said my great-grandparents kind of insisted they got married, because that was what you did back then. She knew though. My mom wasn't even born when he died." He pointed to the frame. "That's… that's beautiful."

"My brother Jeff, and my brother-in-law, Wayne," Grammy explained. She glanced at the photo. "I like to think they're watchin' us right now." Her eyes glistened. "And they'd be so proud to hear you, airman.

You came out with words they could only *dream* of utterin' in public." She smiled. "What's your name, child?"

"Robert, ma'am. Robert Weston. But everyone calls me Rob."

She beamed. "That's a good name. I'm pleased to meet you, Rob. Your granddad would be proud to see you in that uniform." And for the second time that morning, she hugged a stranger. Rob had to stoop to return it, being so much taller than she was.

Levi had to smile. *Grammy has so much love to give.* She'd shown it to every one of his friends.

Grammy released Rob and squared her shoulders. "Now I'm ready to go."

Levi gave Rob a warm smile. "Good to meet you."

"You too, and your partner."

"We're not a couple," Levi and Noah said in unison. Then they stared at each other. A moment later, they were laughing.

Rob flushed. "My apologies. I just assumed. You seemed so… comfortable with each other." He inclined his head toward the panel. "I'm going to stay here a while." He smiled. "Happy Fourth of July to you all."

"And the same to you," Grammy said warmly. She tugged their arms. "Let's give Rob here some space." They strolled back the way they'd come, heading toward the Lincoln memorial, with Grammy linking them. "Thank you, boys," she said in a low voice. "You were right. I needed to see this." She squeezed Noah's arm. "And thank you for all you did."

Noah kissed her cheek. "Anything for you, you know that."

"Can I say thank you too?" Levi met his gaze.

Noah's smile lit up his eyes. "You're welcome."

Levi gave Grammy a kiss too. "It took me until now to realize something. You did for me, what your parents did for Jeff, didn't you?" She said nothing. "You gave me—us—a safe space, where we could be ourselves. That's why my friends were always made welcome in our home, isn't it? Because of Jeff—and Wayne."

Her eyes glistened. "Darn it. You've made me blub again."

"But I *am* right, aren't I?"

She smiled. "Always said you were smart." She cleared her throat. "Okay. Next stop is the nearest restaurant. I'm starved," Grammy declared. "Don't forget, breakfast was five hours ago. And then we've got a ride on a bus."

Levi blinked. "Since when?"

Grammy rolled her eyes. "Since I booked the tickets yesterday. I wanna cram in as many sights as I can before we leave. Did you think I was gonna *walk* everywhere?" She gave him a pointed stare. "Well? Are we gonna eat?"

Levi laughed. "I'll bet you've even picked out the restaurant."

"As you're so fond of sayin'… Duh."

Noah chuckled as they walked. "You do know if you ever get married, she's going to plan the whole thing like a military campaign."

Grammy guffawed. "Lord, it's like you know me or something."

That's if she's still around.

Levi wasn't about to voice his concerns, but the bus tour had surprised him. Grammy walked *everywhere*. He told himself she was just ensuring she got to see all the sights in the time they had left, not to mention how hot and humid it was, but that small voice niggled.

And what if she's taking the bus because she doesn't think she's up to a long walk?

What if Grammy was hiding something about her state of health?

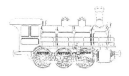

Levi lay on his bed, his hands behind his head. "I don't think I could eat another thing. In fact, I'm so stuffed, I'm amazed I made it to the room."

"I *was* going to ask if you needed me to roll you here on a luggage cart," Noah said with a smirk.

Levi snorted. "This from the man who just put away cheesesteak empanadas, half a roast chicken with truffle fries and grilled avocado, *and* a hefty slice of triple chocolate cake?"

"Which wasn't a patch on Grammy's, by the way."

"But where do you put it all?" Noah's build had hardly altered since high school.

Noah shrugged. "What can I say? I just burn it all off."

"But how? By running a marathon? I *never* see you work out. Unless you've got a home gym squirreled away in the closet…" He lapsed into silence.

Noah walked over to the window. "Wow. Look at all the fireworks." He glanced over his shoulder at Levi, his eyes twinkling. "Oops. My bad. I forgot… You're too stuffed to move."

As if Levi was going to let him get away with that.

He drew himself into a sitting position, then joined Noah at the window. Bursts of color lit up the sky, and the triple-glazing didn't muffle the sound of the bangs and whistles that echoed in the distance. "Wonder how the guys are celebrating tonight?" He grinned. "Well, we know what Seb is doing." The Gilbert clan had all decamped to Cape Porpoise, so Seb was probably coping with Marcus's relatives.

His phone vibrated on the nightstand, and he grabbed it. He smiled when he saw Finn's name. "Finn says Happy Fourth from him and Joel." Another text appeared. "Oh, and we need to keep July seventeenth clear. That's Finn's bachelor party."

Noah frowned. "Two weeks before the wedding? Why not any closer?" He rolled his eyes. "Why am I asking you?" He pulled his own phone from his pocket, and speed-dialed. "Hey. Just saw your text. Why isn't your bachelor party nearer to the wedding?" He listened. "Ah. Okay. Yeah. And where's it taking place?" Noah laughed. "Now *there's* a surprise ... Oh, okay, sure ... Give Joel my best ... And Happy Fourth to you both." He disconnected.

"Well?"

"Joel's bachelor party is the same night. Apparently, some of his guests couldn't make it any other time. And I don't need to tell you where Finn's party is being held, do I?"

Levi grinned. "Maine Street."

"Jackpot." Noah pocketed his phone. "Right now, Finn and Joel are on their deck with Nate, Laura, Carrie, Carrie's boyfriend Eric, and Joel's sister and her partner. They're setting off fireworks too."

Levi leaned against the window. "Do you think

Grammy's all right?" There had been a quiver in his stomach most of the afternoon as they'd toured Washington. By the time they were back in the car and heading to Philadelphia, his unease had subsided a little, but not entirely.

"Why? You think there's something wrong?"

Levi wasn't sure about anything. "It's just a feeling."

"What kind of feeling? And based on what, exactly?"

"You know what she's like. Full of energy from dawn till dusk. But lately… Is it me, or is she taking more naps?" He could be mistaken, of course.

"Maybe. I haven't noticed." Noah frowned. "That's not anything to worry about, is it? Her being a little more tired than usual?"

Levi stared at the starbursts lighting up the evening sky. "I don't know. I can't seem to shake the notion that… something's coming at us, from right around the corner." And whatever it was, it unsettled him.

Noah moved closer and put his arm around Levi's shoulders. "Hey. It's okay. It's been a long day, that's all. A long, emotional day."

That much was true. Grammy had been in a thoughtful mood after the memorial, and that had lingered all the way back to the hotel.

Levi leaned into Noah. "Thanks."

"For what?"

"Being here. Being my rock when I needed one."

Noah's arm tightened around him. "Anything for you." His whisper tickled Levi's ear. "After all, we're a couple, remember?" He chuckled.

Levi's chuckle echoed his, but it felt forced to his

own ears.

I wish we were.

"Happy Fourth of July, Levi."

He raised his head to meet Noah's gaze. "Happy Fourth."

Now all he had to do was get through one more night sharing the same bed.

Chapter Twelve

Wednesday, July 7

Noah closed the door to the summerhouse, and headed along the path. It wasn't time for lunch yet. Levi had shut himself in the dining room, a sure sign he needed to concentrate on his work. Grammy had gone to the church, where she and some other ladies were arranging flowers for a wedding that weekend. And Noah had spent the morning in the summerhouse, working on his accounts.

He paused at the edge of the patio, drinking in the sights and smells. The regal lilies that grew tall against the fence were in bloom, creamy petals with purple veins underneath, and pollen that was almost orange. Bees flitted about the flower heads, and their fragrance wafted through the yard. Noah had opened the door and windows while he worked, allowing the scent to filter into the summerhouse. It was a far cry from the unit at Wellington Manor, and not for the first time, Noah reminded himself how truly lucky he was.

"Good morning, neighbor."

Noah started. Mark peered over the fence separating the properties. Noah raised his hand. "Hey."

Mark cocked his head. "That *is* right, isn't it? Dylan said you'd moved in with Grammy and Levi."

He nodded, then inclined his head toward the summerhouse. "How's this for a workspace?"

Mark smiled. "Beautiful. Want to see mine?"

"I wouldn't want to bother you."

He chuckled. "I wouldn't have suggested it otherwise. I was about to make myself some tea. You could share a cup. I'd like the company too."

"Sure." Noah walked over to the loose fence panel, and Mark lifted it out. Noah stepped into the yard, and caught his breath. "Wow. You've been busy since we were all here that day." The flower beds were neat, with shrubs that would fill them in time. Honeysuckle climbed over trellis standing on either side of the French doors.

Mark flushed. "I bit the bullet and asked Grammy for advice."

"I'll bet she had plenty to give."

He laughed. "She said how refreshing it was to find a man who not only asked for advice, but followed it too." Mark pointed to a circular patio constructed of warm beige stone, on which sat a round table and four chairs. A deep green parasol shaded it. "Take a seat. I'll be right out with the tea. You okay with chamomile?"

"Yeah, that's fine." Noah sat beneath the parasol, surveying Mark's garden. Lavender and rosemary provided yet more scents, and he had to admit, the fragrances were soothing. When Mark returned with a tray containing a delicate china tea pot and two cups and saucers, Noah smiled. "You didn't have to go to all that trouble. I'd have been okay with a tea bag in a cup."

Mark shuddered. "My grandfather would have called me a slob. This was his china tea service. I like using it. Kinda reminds me of him." He sat facing Noah, and poured.

"So, have you had any clients yet? For the

massage therapy, I mean."

Mark shook his head. "I'm almost ready. The therapy room got its last coat of paint this week, and the massage table arrived Saturday. Finn installed the French doors, and then added magnetic catches so if I want them open, they won't bang around in the wind. I like the idea of bringing the garden into the room. That was the whole point of planting the lavender, honeysuckle, rosemary, and roses." He smiled. "When the breeze catches them, it's heavenly." Then he snickered. "The screen doors are there so something *else* doesn't come in from the garden. Otherwise, my clients would need a transfusion after their massage."

Noah sipped his tea, added a sugar lump, then stirred it. "So you don't miss your... former career?"

Mark chuckled again. "No. I mean, I'm still involved in the industry to a point—I promote friends' websites, and occasionally I help them out with shooting—but as for missing being a porn actor? No." He patted his stomach. "I think I've put on a little weight since I stopped working out every day, but Dylan likes it." His eyes sparkled. "Not gonna argue with that, am I?"

Noah beamed. "Sounds as if him moving in with you has worked out well."

Mark's smile lit up his face and reached his eyes. "I don't think I've ever been this happy." He gave Noah a searching glance. "How about you? Have you settled in okay? And what's this I hear about you roping in me and Dylan to help you move some trains? Just how big are they?"

He laughed. "You're helping me move the layout. That's the scenery part. The trains are already here."

"Will this be before or after the wedding?"

"Oh, before. I'm not gonna wait till August." Noah gave him a speculative glance. "So… where are you all going for Joel's bachelor party, or is it a deep dark secret?"

Mark guffawed. "Hardly. We're having dinner at an Irish pub in Portland. Joel says the food is great, and they've got plenty of space upstairs. I think there'll be seven or eight of us. Apart from Joel, Marcus, Nathan and me, the only other guest you might know is Eric."

Noah blinked. "Joel's ex's boyfriend? Isn't that a little… weird?"

"Joel doesn't think so. He says they get along really well." His eyes twinkled. "At least they have something in common." Mark leaned back in his chair. "When you've had your tea, I'll show you the therapy room. By the way, any time you want a massage, just holler."

"I've never had one," Noah admitted.

"Then that's something we need to change. Massages are great when you've been hunched over a laptop." He smiled. "I'm glad we've got this chance to talk. Usually, there are so many of us."

"I think we've reached our limit now," Noah observed.

"So you're not about to turn up at the wedding with a partner in tow? Hey, so could Levi, if it comes to that." Mark grinned. "You guys seem to prefer gatherings for announcing such things."

"I'm not seeing anyone. And Levi isn't." Noah's stomach clenched.

Thankfully, Mark changed the subject. "So how is it working out, living next door?"

"It's great. I have an awesome room, space to work, an attic where I can run my trains… what more could I ask for?" It sounded idyllic. It *was* idyllic.

Then why aren't I doing a happy dance?

Mark regarded him with a thoughtful stare. "And you're sharing a house with your best friend. You left that part out."

Noah couldn't speak. His throat seized, and his chest tightened.

"Is everything okay between you two?"

He took a drink from his cup to get his throat working. "Why do you ask?"

"Just a feeling."

"Levi and me, we get along just fine."

Mark said nothing for a moment. "I'm glad to hear it." Another sip of tea, then he replaced his cup on its saucer with a sigh. "Okay, I'm only going to say this once. I know we haven't known each other all that long, but if there's ever a time when you need a friend—another one—my French doors are always open." He smiled. "For a massage, a chat, or just a cup of tea. And if you don't want me to share whatever it is we discuss with Dylan, I won't."

Noah swallowed. "Thanks." He nodded toward the house. "Want to show me your new room?"

Mark beamed. "Step this way." He stood, and Noah followed him toward the doors.

Levi is *my best friend. And since I moved in, we've only gotten closer.*

Then why was his head in such a mess?

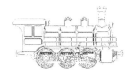

Friday, July 9

Noah stood in the shade, peering at the screen on his camera. "I think that's all of them. I've got pics of the Goldenrod, Fun-O-Rama, the Nubble, Wild Kingdom, the Leavitt…"

"Then can I make a suggestion?" Levi asked.

Noah rolled his eyes. "Don't you think we've got enough?"

Levi chuckled. "I was *about* to say…." He pointed to the building behind them. "Want to grab a bite here?"

Now that he mentioned it, Noah *was* feeling hungry. "Sounds good."

"I don't know what the food is like."

He grinned. "I do. Inn on the Blues was one of my haunts when I needed to get away from the noise. They do a wonderful lobster mac-and-cheese."

Levi's eyes widened. "Sold."

Noah led them up the wooden stairs to the upper deck, where Stacey stood behind the bar. She raised a hand in greeting. "Hey, Noah. Good to see you. Grab a table, I'll be right over."

He scanned the tables next to the railing, and headed for the one at the corner of the deck. "This'll do." Lisa, one of the servers, deposited two menus on the table, along with the cocktails list.

Levi peered at it. "A blueberry lemon drop?"

Noah smiled. "Fabulous cocktail. It's got blueberry liqueur, limoncello… The raspberry margarita is great too."

Levi laughed. "Hey, I'm driving, remember?"

"Then you can have a sip of mine."

Levi snorted. "Wow. Thanks."

Stacey wandered across, and Noah ordered their

food and drinks. Levi gazed at the beach below, with the strip of land to the left, crowded with houses. "When I was little, I wanted to live there. I thought it would be awesome to have the ocean outside my bedroom window."

Noah chuckled. "When I was little, I asked my mom if we could live next to a railroad. You can guess how that request went down. My second option was to live in the Nubble. I said we could have Brown's ice cream for dessert every night."

That earned him another laugh. Then Levi sighed. "Life was so simple then."

Noah gazed at him. "Is yours so complicated now?"

He huffed. "It is when I'm trying to write a speech for the wedding. I know you said you'd help me get ready, but I still have to come up with ideas for it."

"There must be plenty of embarrassing stories you can relate about Finn. Hell, even *I* know a few."

Levi coughed. "Yeah, and *those* are the ones I'm going to avoid." They both chuckled.

"I got to see Mark's new therapy room a couple of days ago," Noah told him.

"What's it like?"

Noah smiled. "It's gorgeous. The walls are done in a really pale green—really calming—and there are wooden shelves for all the oils, towels, candles…"

"'Candles'?"

He nodded. "All kinds. And he's got speakers so he can play music in the background. Then there's the massage table. One end of it has a padded hole where you can poke your head when you lie face down. He's got plants too. There's a beautiful peace lily in a pot by the door."

Levi let out a contented sigh. "Makes me want to go book a massage right now."

"Mark said I could have one whenever I wanted. I might take him up on that." He leaned on the railing, staring at the horizon. "Do you ever go for a swim in the ocean?" The waves didn't appear to be too rough, but he knew that wasn't always the case.

"Sometimes… when I'm feeling masochistic." Levi's eyes sparkled.

Noah gazed at him. "You trimmed your beard."

Levi stroked his chin. "It was starting to look scruffy. I thinned it out a little too. Grammy made a comment the other day. She said it looked as though I was chewing a cat."

Noah snickered. "Sounds like something she'd come out with." Their drinks arrived, and Levi cast longing glances at Noah's dark purple cocktail. Noah pushed the glass toward him. "Go on. You know you're dying to try it."

Levi grinned. He took a cautious sip. "Wow. That's delicious." He rubbed his chin again. "Grammy has a bottle of limoncello in her liquor cabinet… And I bet I could find blueberry liqueur someplace."

Noah burst into laughter. "You're going to make your own version? I'll be your guinea pig."

Levi put his elbows on the table, then rested his chin on laced fingers. He closed his eyes.

"Feeling sleepy?"

Levi smiled. "Listening to the waves on the shore. It's soothing."

Noah took advantage of the opportunity to study him. Levi wore his warm brown hair swept up from his forehead, his brow smooth. His fingers were long and elegant. He wasn't tanned, but neither was he pale. His lips were pale pink and tantalizing, and Noah wondered how it would feel to take that full lower lip between his teeth and tug on it gently. Through the thin white cotton of Levi's tee, he spied the dark discs of his nipples, pushing against the fabric.

What came to mind was Levi on his back, Noah leaning over him, teasing those taut little nubs with his fingers and tongue…

Noah stilled, grateful that Levi still had his eyes closed. Because Noah was certain his cheeks reflected the heat surging through him. For the first time in his life, he was aware of a need to touch, caress… He was aware of his own heartbeat, the hairs rising on his nape… Nerve endings stirred and tingled. A pleasurable shiver trickled through him.

This was new.

This was strong.

This was intense.

Noah remembered to breathe, restoring a measure of calm. He recognized the emotion that had him in its grip, and it both exhilarated and excited him. His mind raced, searching for answers.

It's kind of fitting that the first person I find myself wanting is my best friend.

Then his heart sank.

But not if Levi doesn't want me.

A cough shattered his internal musing, and he jerked his head toward the sound. Stacey stood, holding a tray with their food. She smiled as she placed the dishes before them. "Enjoy." Then she walked off.

Levi sniffed. "That smells great."

Noah unwrapped a fork from a napkin. "Mark asked if we would be bringing guests to the wedding. I told him I wasn't seeing anyone." He waited, praying for confirmation that Levi was just as single.

Levi smiled, but didn't respond.

"You know, it's just occurred to me that we never talk—"

"Are you kidding? We talk all the time."

Noah gave him a mock glare. "Let a guy finish a sentence? I was *going* to say, we never talk about... stuff like that."

"Stuff like what?" Levi took a mouthful of mac and cheese, and rolled his eyes heavenward. "Oh my God, this is good."

"You know... boyfriends... dating..."

Levi blinked. He picked up his glass of soda and took a long drink. "Maybe because... I'd have to actually go on a date before I could talk about dating."

Noah froze. "Wait—you've never..." He'd had no idea.

Levi's face flushed. "And to be honest, I sort of got the impression that you didn't *want* to discuss personal stuff."

Maybe Levi had nailed it. Maybe Noah had instinctively avoided engaging in personal conversations because he didn't want to hear about Levi's love life.

Levi's sex life.

Then the full import of Levi's words hit home.

No. It couldn't be true. There was no way Levi could still be a virgin.

"Noah."

He met Levi's gaze. "Hmm?"

Levi looked him in the eye. "Whatever you're thinking... the answer is yes. And now we're going to eat our mac and cheese, and not mention this again. Okay?" That flush hadn't receded.

"Okay." Noah swallowed a mouthful of

blueberry lemon drop, his mind still racing.

Why? How? What the fuck?

A simple trip to take photos had turned out to be a day of revelations, and Noah reeled from it.

Chapter Thirteen

Saturday, July 10

Levi placed the glass of water on the nightstand, then ran his hand over Grammy's brow. She frowned. "Will you quit that? I'm fine, all right? I don't have a temperature, if that's what you're checkin' for. I just need a nap. Gimme an hour, and I'll be turnin' somersaults." She smiled, the skin crinkling around her eyes. "Stop worryin', child."

He bent and kissed her forehead. "It's what I do."

Grammy cupped his cheek. "I know, sweetheart, and I love you all the more for it. Now, if you wanna do something useful, go to my bathroom an' bring me a couple of Tums. That lunch is repeatin' on me."

He did as instructed, dropping them into her outstretched hand, then walked to the door. When he stepped into the hallway, Noah was waiting, his brow furrowed.

"How is she?" he asked as Levi closed Grammy's bedroom door.

Levi sighed. "She says she's fine, but then again, that's what she always says."

"So why does she seem so tired sometimes? That's not like her."

"You noticed that too?" Then he realized it was a dumb remark. Noah noticed everything, and he loved her as though she were his own grandmother.

"I've been watching her more closely since you mentioned it in the hotel. And yeah, I think you're right. There *have* been more naps lately."

"There's something else. For the last few weeks, she's complained of pain in her neck and jaw. Then there's the indigestion. That's not like her. Grammy has the constitution of an ox."

Noah cocked his head to one side. "And what did Google tell you?" He rolled his eyes when Levi gave a start. "Oh come *on*. I know you. When did you Google her symptoms?"

"Last night." He'd put it off, mostly because Grammy insisted there was nothing wrong, but the accumulation of aches, pains, and fatigue had become too much to ignore.

"And?"

Levi swallowed. "I think she needs to see her doctor. I know her last physical was okay—at least, that's what she told me—but I still want her to get checked out." *And soon.* The results of his search had been a shock. *I know she's not going to live forever, but I'm not ready to lose her yet. She's only seventy-one, for God's sake.*

"Levi?" Noah's hand was gentle on his arm. "What is it? What do you think is wrong with her?"

He didn't want to say the words, as if voicing his fears would somehow talk them into existence. *But if I'm right, we need to act sooner rather than later.* "It could be coronary heart disease. Her symptoms are textbook."

Noah frowned. "My uncle had that. He had chest pains and a tingling in his arm. She hasn't had those—has she?"

Levi sighed again. "Apparently the symptoms are different in women. It's a more gradual thing. Trust me, I've done a lot of reading on this." He'd spent most of the night on his laptop, unable to sleep.

"Need a hug?"

Levi smiled. "Always." Noah drew him close, wrapping his arms around him, and Levi drank him in, breathed him in, letting Noah's scent and warmth surround him.

Damn, he feels good. Noah might be a string bean, a tall, lanky guy who could get blown off his feet by a breeze, but right then he felt strong, and Levi needed that strength. He didn't want to let go. And judging by how long Noah held him, he felt the same way.

"Better?" Noah murmured.

Only if I could stay like this forever. "Yeah." The doorbell rang, Noah released him, and Levi cursed whoever had just brought their hug to an abrupt end.

The kind of hug you remember. The kind that makes you feel good, hours after it happened.

"You expecting anyone?"

Levi headed down the stairs, Noah behind him. "Nope, unless Grammy has ordered more quilting supplies." She'd started planning a new quilt for Noah's bed. "She keeps talking about turning the guest bedroom into a craft room, but she won't, not when the guys visit as often as they do." He went to the front door. When he opened it, he found a young woman and a young man standing there. "Hello. Can I help you?"

The young woman swallowed. "Oh my God." She glanced at the young man, then back to Levi. "I didn't expect to find you here. And now that I see you…"

Levi frowned. "Have we met?" He took a good look at the pair. The girl was maybe nineteen or twenty, with long black hair and blue-grey eyes. A multicolored bag strap lay snugly across her chest. There was something familiar about her, but he couldn't put his finger on it. The boy had maybe the same age and coloring, only his eyes were a deeper shade of blue. It felt weird talking on the doorstep, but he wasn't about to invite two strangers into his home until he knew more about the purpose of their visit.

"No, we haven't," the girl confirmed. "In fact, until recently, we never even knew you existed. I wasn't sure we had the right address, but as soon as I saw you, I knew this had to be the place. There was no mistaking you." She hesitated. "Linda Brown does live here, doesn't she?"

He jumped at Grammy's name. "Yes, but—"

"Can we come in?" the young man demanded. "We've been driving for over four hours, we've got a lot to talk about, and we can't do it out here." His words were blunt, but Levi didn't miss the bob of his Adam's apple, the tremor that went through him.

The young woman fired him a glance. "I know you're nervous—so am I—but that was rude. Apologize."

He swallowed. "I'm sorry. I had no right to speak to you like that."

Levi arched his eyebrows. "Apology accepted, but could you please tell me who you are?"

The young man drew himself up to his full height. "I'm Elijah Johnson, and this is my sister Amelia. Linda Brown is our grandmother, so that makes you our half-brother, Levi."

What. The. Fuck?

"I think you've made a mistake." His voice shook. But even as he said the words, realization began its slow crawl into his brain. *Look at him.* Levi wasn't stupid—he just didn't want to accept the possibility.

"I brought proof," Amelia told him. "I didn't want you to think we were a couple of weirdos. But it's a long story, and could I please have something to drink?" She glanced at her brother with a half-smile. "I didn't trust him to get us here in one piece. I've seen how he drives."

Elijah rolled his eyes.

Levi couldn't move. Couldn't speak.

Then Noah was at his side. He gave them a polite smile. "Hey, I'm Noah White. I live here too. I think you'd better come inside."

Levi didn't *want* them inside. He wanted this not to be happening. A nudge snapped him back. Noah looked him in the eye. "We need Grammy. Now. I'll take care of your… guests, while you go get her."

He nodded, unable to get words past the rock in his throat. He hurried toward the stairs and climbed them, two steps at a time, his heart thumping, his breathing ragged. When he reached Grammy's bedroom, he paused. Maybe it would be better to wait until he'd had a chance to speak with—

The door opened, and Grammy stood there. "I heard voices. We got comp'ny?"

"Yeah, but—" Levi took a deep breath. "I think you'd better prepare yourself for a shock."

She stared at him for a moment, then nodded. "Then I'd best go downstairs and see what's up. Whatever it is can wait till I'm in my chair. Who was it said shocks are better absorbed with the knees bent? Think I heard that once on a horror movie." Then she paused. "Is it… bad news?"

"Not bad… just…" He shook his head. "You need to hear this."

Grammy narrowed her gaze, then headed for the stairs. Below, Levi could hear murmurs of conversation, and he was thankful for Noah's cool head.

His was a mess.

He followed her into the living room, and almost ran into her when Grammy came to a sharp stop. "Oh dear Lord." She stared at Amelia. "Don't have to ask who *your* mom was, do I?" She grabbed the doorknob, the skin stretched tight over her knuckles.

That was all it took to make Levi's heart plummet and his stomach clench.

Then it is *true.*

Amelia and Elijah sat on the couch in the window. She flushed. "She… she always said I was the spitting image of her when she was younger. I guess she was right."

Grammy walked a little unsteadily to her armchair, then eased herself into it. "No doubt whatsoever."

"What… what should we call you?" Amelia asked after a moment's hesitation. It was obvious to Levi that she was the more confident of the two. Elijah, for all his abruptness on the doorstep, had lapsed into silence now they were in the house.

"You call me Grammy, like everyone else who comes here." Grammy rested her head against the back of the chair. "You must know, I've got a ton of questions."

"And I'll try to answer them, if I can," Amelia responded. "But you need to understand something. Until last week, we had no idea you existed."

Levi gazed at Amelia. "*Now* I know who you remind me of." He glanced at Noah. "Remember the photos of Grammy when she was sixteen?"

Noah nodded. He spoke to Amelia. "I'll go get you both a soda. Grammy, do you want anything?"

"A brandy." She gripped the arms of the chair, as if she was afraid of falling off it.

Levi blinked, and when Noah gave him a questioning glance, he nodded. Noah walked out of the room, and Grammy cleared her throat. "So… what are your names? How old are you? Where do you live? And… where's your mom?"

"I'm Amelia, and this is my twin brother, Elijah. We're twenty. We live on Mount Desert Island. And… Mom died two months ago."

"I see."

Levi's breathing hitched, and pain lanced through his chest. "Well, *I* don't. Because if what you're saying is true, my mom has been alive all these years and didn't *once* bother to come home and see how her son was doing. Her *only* son." He glanced at Elijah. "Except now it appears I wasn't." He couldn't repress the bitterness that laced his voice. He'd believed her dead, and he could cope with that. He'd never known her, after all. But *this*…

Then Amelia's words finally registered, and rage bubbled up through him. "Wait a minute. You only found out about me and Grammy *last week*? She never told you she had a son?"

"Levi…" Grammy's voice quavered. "Now is the time to listen, all right? I have questions, same as you, but let 'em talk."

Talk? Levi didn't want to hear another word, not when everything that came out of Amelia's mouth stung his skin like shards of glass, piercing it, working their way into his flesh, inching toward his heart.

Noah returned with a tray containing cans of

soda, two glasses filled with ice, and a small glass of brandy. Levi took the latter and gave it to Grammy, who drank it in a couple of gulps. Her hand shook, and she kept her gaze focused on Amelia and Elijah as Noah handed out the beverages.

Levi took the empty glass from her, then sat on the small couch. Noah joined him, his arm at Levi's back. He leaned closer. "You okay?" he murmured.

Levi didn't trust himself to speak.

Grammy sighed. "Okay. How did your mom die? Not that I don't already have a pretty good idea…"

"Cardiac arrest. Dad said her heart was damaged." Amelia swallowed. "She was only forty-eight. But it wasn't until Dad gave us the letter she wrote him that we learned about the… the—"

"The drugs," Elijah blurted. "Then it all made sense. Why she was always telling us not to touch them. I mean, she drummed it into us. That's what damaged her heart, wasn't it? All that stuff she used when she was our age?"

"*Before* she was your age," Grammy said in a quiet voice. "I'm amazed she made it to forty-eight. I've been waitin' all these years for a knock at the door, waitin' for a couple of cops to be standin' there, tellin' me they've found a body, and it was Amy."

Levi found his voice again. "And *I'm* amazed she got to forty-eight and didn't make it back here *once*," he ground out. "You know, to see how the baby she left on a doorstep was doing? I mean, who does that? Who leaves a baby in a crib on a doorstep in freaking *September*? I wasn't even *two weeks old*, for Christ's sake." Noah's hand was gentle on his back, but he shrugged it off, his anger shifting from simmer to a rolling boil.

"Levi…" Grammy gazed at him, and his chest

tightened to see the love in her eyes. "I know, child. It hurts."

"Oh, Grammy, hurt doesn't *even* begin to describe what I'm feeling."

"You're not the only one who's hurting, all right?" Elijah blurted. He glared at Levi. "We lost our mom, in case you missed that part."

"Yeah, I got it. I'm just having a hard time getting past the my-mom-didn't-give-a-fuck-about-me part." Blood pounded in his ears.

"Levi." Grammy's voice was like a knife.

Noah was pale. He gave Levi a beseeching glance. "Hold it together, okay? You and Grammy need to hear them out. I can't get close to knowing how you're feeling right now, but…" He took Levi's hand in his, and this time Levi didn't break the contact. "You can do this, all right? You can be *stronger* than this."

Levi's vision blurred as he tried to fend off tears. His chest ached.

"Listen to me, sweetheart." Grammy spoke more softly. "No one in this room understands what you're goin' through more than I do, okay? We want answers. But Amelia and Elijah have come here lookin' for their own answers. They've just found out they have a whole other family. So I'm askin' you to step up to the plate for a while, because child, we need to hear this, an' you know it." Her voice shook.

Levi struggled to breathe evenly, clutching Noah's hand like a drowning man holding onto a life preserver. Little by little, his usual calm seeped back. He addressed Amelia and Elijah. "I'm sorry. It's just that it's been such a shock."

Amelia nodded, her eyes glistening. "Tell me about it."

"Mom said in her letter she'd have been dead years ago, if it hadn't been for my dad," Elijah croaked. "My dad said meeting him was the best thing that could have happened to her." He wiped his eyes, and Amelia put her arms around him.

She glanced at them. "We're still pretty raw. We thought we were doing okay, until the letter. Then… it was like she'd died all over again. And coming here… We thought we'd find our grandmother. We didn't expect to find you here too." A phone buzzed, and Amelia blinked. She picked the bag up that she'd put on the floor, unzipped it, and removed the phone. "It's my dad. Oh God." She held the phone to her ear, wincing. "Hey, Dad… Yes, I know I took the car without asking… yes… yes, I know that too…" Elijah gave her hand a squeeze, and she smiled. "Yes, he's with me… where?… well… we're in Wells." She closed her eyes. "Yes, I know you said not to… but we just wanted…" Amelia listened for a moment. "But we only just got here."

"Amelia." Grammy straightened in her chair. "You an' Elijah can stay here tonight. I'm not lettin' you drive all the way back to Mt Desert, not in the state you're in. Besides, we have a lot to talk about." She leaned forward. "You can tell your dad you're stayin' with your grandmother. I'm sure he won't mind bein' without you for one night. After all, he's had you both for the last twenty years. One night doesn't sound like a lot to ask."

Amelia's breathing caught. "Dad, did you hear all that? … Okay… yes, I promise…we'll see you tomorrow." She ended the call, then lowered the phone. "We… we didn't tell him we were coming here."

"That much I worked out for myself," Grammy said in a dry tone.

Maybe there was something to that stuff about absorbing shocks better with the knees bent after all—Grammy appeared to be rallying.

Levi was nowhere near that point.

She got to her feet. "I'm gonna check the freezer, make sure there's plenty for dinner." She met Levi's gaze. "Can you and Noah go get the guest room ready? Put the foldin' bed in there too, in case Amelia and Elijah don't wanna share." She didn't break eye contact, and Levi knew she expected him to put aside his anger, hurt, and betrayal—at least until he reached the sanctuary of his room.

Except another emotion was taking hold of him, a wave of sorrow that made him feel so tired when he thought about how his life might have been.

"We'll talk some more later." Grammy walked over to the couch. "In the meantime, you're welcome in my home."

Amelia was on her feet in a heartbeat, her arms around Grammy, a sob tumbling out of her. Then Elijah joined her, and Grammy had her arms full. Judging by the way her shoulders shook, Levi knew she was crying too.

Noah squeezed his hand. "Let's leave them to it, okay?" he whispered. "There'll be plenty of time for questions later. Looks like you all have a lot of catching up to do."

That had to be the understatement of the century.

Chapter Fourteen

Noah didn't have to glance at his alarm clock to know it had been hours since he'd climbed into his bed. His head was full of Levi.

He was so quiet tonight. Which was understandable in the circumstances, and easier to deal with than the rage that had engulfed him upon learning of Elijah and Amelia's origins. He'd said little during dinner, and Grammy, bless her, hadn't tried to drag him into the conversation. She seemed to be coping reasonably well, and asked lots of questions about where they lived on Mount Desert. Their father owned a hardware store, and they'd grown up on the island. Levi had shown little interest, and appeared to have retreated into himself.

That had been enough to make Noah's stomach clench. This wasn't like Levi, but then again, there hadn't been any events in his whole life to match the one that had just crashed into them.

A gentle tapping on his door startled him. Noah threw back the comforter and padded across the room. When he opened it, Levi stood there in his shorts and a tee.

Noah took one look at the misery etched on Levi's face, and pulled him into the room. "How did you know I was awake?" he whispered as he closed the door.

"I didn't," Levi replied in a low voice. "I just

hoped."

Noah led him to the bed. He switched on the lamp on the nightstand and got back under the comforter, propped up by pillows. Levi leaned against the footboard, his legs crossed. Noah studied his tight expression. "Have you had any sleep?"

Levi shook his head. "You?"

"Nope." He tilted his head. "How much did you take in of tonight's conversation?"

"I think I stopped paying attention pretty early on in the proceedings." That bitter edge to Levi's voice sent Noah's heart plummeting. Then he crumpled before his eyes, his cheeks glistening, and Noah couldn't bear the distance between them.

He threw back the comforter once more. "Get in."

Levi didn't hesitate. He scrambled over the bed and got beneath the covers, and Noah covered them both. He lay on his back, his arm outstretched, and Levi pressed his body against Noah's side, his head on Noah's shoulder. Noah held him, aware of the tremors that coursed through him. "I've got you," he murmured. "Let it all out."

His words apparently opened the floodgates. A moment later, hot tears dripped onto his skin, and Noah's heart ached for Levi.

"Why didn't she want me? Why did she never come back for me?" Levi choked out. "And why does it hurt so much?"

Noah stroked his hair. "Because grief hurts."

Levi craned his neck to stare at him, the light catching on his tear-stained cheeks. "I can't be grieving for her. I never knew her."

"This is a different kind of grief. You're grieving

for the life you *could've* had, if things had been different. You listened to Elijah and Amelia, and you saw two people who'd grown up with a mom who loved them, cared for them. And it hurts."

"God yes," Levi croaked, and then he clung to Noah, shaking as he wept. Noah said nothing, but he held Levi close, stroking his hair, his shoulders, his back, waiting for the tears to ebb. And when they finally did, Noah couldn't help himself. He kissed the top of Levi's head.

"Go to sleep," he whispered. "I've got you." He left the light on, and lay there, holding his best friend, his brother from another mother…

The mother who, although she was dead, was bringing Levi pain.

I love you, Levi. And if there was anything I could do to take this pain from you, I'd do it.

Levi's breathing changed, becoming more even, and Noah knew he was drifting into sleep. His own breaths were in sync, and he could feel Levi's heartbeat.

It wasn't long before he too was asleep.

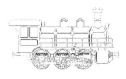

Sunday, July 11

Levi opened his eyes to find Noah lying on his side, looking at him. "Have you been awake long?"

Noah shook his head. "I can hear Grammy downstairs."

Levi sat up in bed. "I'm sorry. I had no right to unload all my shit on you. And it's not like I don't have a bed of my own."

"Excuse me?" Noah narrowed his gaze. "You unload as much as you want. It's better than bottling it all up inside. And so what if you shared my bed? Wouldn't be the first time, right?" His expression softened. "You needed me last night. You think I *minded* being there for you?" He smiled, then leaned over and pressed a soft kiss to Levi's forehead. "And *because* I'm such a good friend, you can hit the bathroom first. It might get a little busy later." His eyes twinkled. "Maybe we should ask Finn for a quote on how much it would cost to add a couple of bathrooms. We could easily lose some of the space in here."

Levi widened his eyes. "Hey, if anyone gets a bathroom, it'll be me."

Noah laughed. "This all supposes Grammy likes the idea. But you'd better get your ass out of this bed and into that shower. It won't be long before she's hollering for us to help with breakfast."

Levi's thoughts went to the occupants of the guest room. "I guess I'd better knock on their door."

"Leave them to me. You go take that shower." Noah smiled. "Not that I'm complaining about the way you smell. You always smell good first thing in the morning."

It wasn't until he was out of the door and creeping along the hallway that Noah's words sank in.

He notices how I smell? Levi was acutely aware of how Noah smelled—he hadn't expected Noah to be paying similar attention.

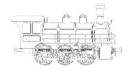

Levi went into the kitchen to get more coffee and juice. From the dining room, he could hear Amelia's clear voice, praising Grammy's cooking. He leaned against the sink, drawing in a couple of deep breaths, shame flushing through him.

I'm better than this.

All his life, Levi had been the peacemaker, the intermediary, but faced with their two guests, his ability to see both sides of a situation appeared to have deserted him. Noah had been the one so far to engage them in conversation, to ask questions, trying to pull Levi in.

They're my family—my new family. Why should this be so difficult?

He already knew the answer to that. His mom's—betrayal? Was that the word he sought?—decision not to seek him out was proving a huge hurdle to get over.

Footsteps behind him made him stiffen, but he relaxed when Noah joined him.

"Grammy wanted to know if you'd gone to Colombia to get the coffee beans."

Levi forced a chuckle. "Sorry. Guess I zoned out for a minute there." He went to the fridge to grab the carton of juice, while Noah set up another pot of coffee. As he walked toward the door, Noah stopped him with a hand to his arm.

"It's going to be okay, you know."

Levi swallowed. "Eventually."

Noah didn't let go. "Hang in there, okay? They're leaving after breakfast."

And then I can breathe again.

Levi hated the tightness in his chest that had been evident since he'd sat down at the dining table. He hated the way his stomach churned when Elijah talked about his mom—*our mom*—and when Amelia showed Grammy photos of their home. Levi had hardly given them a second glance, and now that he thought about it, his reactions felt mean-spirited.

This isn't their fault. They had no idea we existed.

Such thoughts didn't make the situation any easier.

Levi gave Noah a tight smile. "I'd better get the juice in there, before Grammy asks if I've gone to Florida for the oranges." He headed for the dining room, forcing himself to breathe evenly.

I can do this.

Grammy glanced at him as he retook his seat at the table. "Amelia was tellin' me she and Elijah both study at UMA in Augusta."

Levi blinked. "I went there to study Computer Science."

"Grammy told us." Amelia inclined her head toward Elijah. "Eli's studying that too, and I study music."

Eli snorted. "We couldn't be more different, could we? I don't have a musical bone in my body, and Amy panics if her laptop won't let her login." Amy glared at him.

Grammy stilled. "You prefer Amy to Amelia?"

She flushed. "My dad calls me that. I guess it stuck." She peered at the upright piano against the wall of the dining room. "Did Mom ever play that?"

Grammy nodded. "My parents bought that in 1960, when I was ten years old. They wanted me to learn."

Levi stared at her. "I never knew you could play the piano." The gleaming oak Kimball Upright Console and its bench had been there as long as he could remember.

She cackled. "That's 'cause I can't. I was a hopeless case. My piano teacher, Mrs. Goldman, despaired of me. She said I played like I was wearin' boxin' gloves."

Noah winced as he placed a fresh pot of coffee on the mat at the center of the table. "Ouch." He sat next to Levi.

She snickered. "Paints a picture, don't it? But it wasn't a complete waste of money. Jeff played beautifully. So maybe there's a musical gene in there somewhere. Anyhow, when I married your granddad, she gave it to us, for when we got kids." She swallowed. "Your mom could play too. I still remember watching her climb onto that bench for the first time. She had to have been five or six. It wasn't long before we knew something special was goin' on. She could hear a tune and play it back note for note." Another sharp swallow. "That child could've been something."

"She used to play for us when we were little," Amy said in a quiet voice. "I could sit for hours next to her, just listening."

"Do you play?" Levi asked.

Amy blushed, and Eli chuckled. "Does she play. She's awesome."

"Would you play something for us?" Grammy pointed to the bench. "I think there's some music left in there."

Amy got up from the table and went over to the piano bench. She opened it, and her eyes sparkled. "Debussy, 'Clair de Lune'. Mom used to play this for me. It's my favorite piece."

Grammy's eyes glistened behind her glasses. "It was hers too."

Amy removed the sheet music and sat on the bench. She pressed the keys almost tentatively. "It needs retuning."

"And how. Maybe I'll get onto that, seein' as there's someone in the family who can play the damn thing." She peered at Noah. "How 'bout you?"

He smiled. "My limit is 'Chopsticks.'"

"Eli's too." Amy laughed. "Sounds like he inherited his piano-playing skills from Grammy." That earned her a laugh. She propped the sheets up on the beautiful lattice-work stand, then began to play.

Levi's breathing hitched at the sound of the first lilting three notes, and then he lost himself in the beautiful music. Amy's hands flowed over the keys, sinuous and fluid. He glanced at Eli, and loved his rapt expression.

Eli caught him looking, and smiled. "She's great, isn't she?" he whispered. "She's been playing since she was six years old."

"She's amazing." Levi wasn't musical, but he admired those who were.

Noah touched Levi's knee, and he turned his head to find Noah staring at him, his eyes wide. *Look at Grammy*, he mouthed. Levi peered at her, and his throat seized. Grammy gazed at Amy, tears trickling down her cheeks, her hand to her chest. Levi grabbed a Kleenex from the box on the sideboard and handed it to her.

"Thank you." Grammy wiped her eyes as Amy

finished playing. "Child, that was… beautiful. Lord, you remind me of your mom. It could've been her playin'." She gave a loud *sniff*.

Amy's phone rang on the dining table, and everyone jumped. Amy got up from the bench and grabbed it, retaking her seat. "It's Dad again." She touched the screen, then held it to her ear. "Hey, Dad. We just finished breakfast … Yeah, we're leaving soon…" She lapsed into silence with a look of intense concentration. Finally, she smiled. "Okay, Dad. I'll let them know. See you soon." She disconnected, then replaced the phone on the table. "My Dad—his name's Tim Johnson, by the way—said to tell you that any time you're over our way, feel free to stop by. He'd love to meet you. He also said you might like to read Mom's letter."

Before Levi could react, Eli piped up, "Noah said last night at dinner that you've got a friend in Bar Harbor?"

"Yes, Aaron," Noah confirmed.

"Well, next time you visit him, why not come see us?"

Levi opened his mouth, but Noah got in first. "Actually, Levi and I are planning to visit the Downeast Scenic Railroad in Ellsworth soon. That's not far from Mount Desert."

Levi blinked, amused to find his suggestion had become a certainty.

Amy's face lit up. "No, it isn't. Let us know when you'll be there, and I'll make sure we're around."

"We'd better get going," Eli said gloomily. "You know how busy the store gets on the weekend." He glanced at Grammy. "We help out when we're not in school."

"I'm sure he can't do without you," Grammy said warmly. She got up from the table. "I'll go fix a bag for you to take with you. Some sodas, cookies, fruit…"

"You don't have to do that," Amy protested.

Eli glared at her. "Are you crazy? Did you *taste* those cookies?"

A moment later, Grammy burst out laughing. "I got another fan, I see." She left the dining room.

"You *will* come see us, won't you?" Eli asked, his face anxious.

Levi wasn't about to make promises he wasn't sure he could keep. "We'll try."

Noah nudged him, then gave Eli a smile. "I'll make sure he does better than try."

Eli's face glowed. "He's lucky to have a boyfriend like you."

Levi was thankful not to be drinking at the time.

Noah coughed. "A nice thought, but no, we're not boyfriends."

Before Levi could digest his statement, Amy closed the lid on the piano, then rose. "We'd better get ready. Thanks again for letting us stay. I know it must have been a huge shock."

"I hope you're not in too much trouble with your dad," Noah remarked.

She bit her lip. "He's used to it." She tugged Eli's elbow. "Bathroom. I'm not stopping every hour like we did on the way here."

"Then don't drink the soda," Eli retorted. He flashed them a grin before leaving the dining room, Amy close behind.

Levi regarded Noah with a hard stare. "*We're* visiting the Downeast Scenic Railroad, are we?"

"Hey, you're the one who suggested going there.

I'm just agreeing with you."

Levi didn't break eye contact. "And one more thing… Us being boyfriends is a nice thought?"

Noah flushed. "Anyone who gets to be your boyfriend will be a very lucky man. If that isn't a nice thought, I don't know what is."

"Noah? You got a minute?" Grammy hollered from the kitchen.

"Coming," he yelled, then hurried from the room.

Levi stared after him. In all the years Levi had known him, Noah had never uttered something so… sweet.

He liked it. Liked it a *lot*.

K.C. WELLS

Chapter Fifteen

Sunday, July 11

Aaron went into the kitchen to put on another pot of coffee. From the living room came the buzz of voices. He'd expected most of the gang to turn up, but the arrival of Joel, Marcus, and Nathan had been a surprise. To be honest, he wasn't sure why they'd come.

Ben stuck his head around the door. "Got any snacks? I've been sent to ask."

"Gee, no, I didn't think of that." Aaron rolled his eyes. "After all these years, I know better than to not provide food." He inclined his head toward the cabinet. "In there. Chips—and yes, I bought Cheez-its." Ben grinned. "There's a bag of tortilla chips too, and ranch dip and guacamole are in the fridge."

Ben grabbed two large bowls and proceeded to empty the bags of chips into them. "Where's Dean?"

Aaron chuckled. "Stupid question. He's painting. Not that he was going to be here anyway. He doesn't exactly approve."

Ben huffed. "Neither do Joel, Nathan, and Marcus."

"Then why did they come?"

Ben's eyes glittered. "To keep an eye on us, I think. At least, that's what Finn and Seb told me. Apparently, they think we might plan something over-the-top."

Aaron grinned. "Wow. It's like they know us or

something." He had to admit, he'd had second thoughts about the whole intervention idea. *We shouldn't interfere.* He doubted Levi would appreciate them trying to push the two men together. But then Seb had called to check if they were still going to meet, and Seb definitely thought it was worth doing.

It seemed Marcus wasn't on the same page. Aaron had to smile at that. Seb needed a keeper, and Marcus was good for him.

Ben carried the snacks into the living room, and Aaron followed with the coffee. "Okay, have you come up with anything while I've been gone?"

Nathan bit his lip. "Didn't Ben tell you? He thinks he's found the perfect solution."

"Oops. Forgot the dip." Ben scooted back into the kitchen.

Aaron placed the coffee on the table. "Help yourselves." He sat in the armchair. "So what's Ben's plan? Or do I not want to know?"

Finn chuckled. "He thinks we should write each of them an anonymous letter, telling them how the other one feels about them."

Aaron gaped. "What—are we still in high school? Because that's the kinda dumb thing he would've come up with back then." He stared at the others. "Tell me you weren't seriously considering it."

Marcus smiled. "Don't worry. That's why Nathan, Joel and I insisted on coming. *Someone* has to be the voice of reason."

Seb snorted. "What he *really* means is, they didn't trust us to come up with something sensible." He grinned. "They might have a point."

Ben put the dip and guacamole on the coffee table. "Well, does anyone have any better ideas? That *is* why we're here, isn't it? To brainstorm ways to get those two to see what's right under their noses."

"I'm still not convinced this is a good idea," Joel said, his voice quiet. "If they're meant to be a couple, then why not leave them to find their path in their own time? Rather than pushing them together. I can see so many ways such an action might backfire."

"I agree with Joel," Shaun announced, grabbing a tortilla chip and loading it with guacamole.

"And we discussed this at Grammy's party," Ben added. "We're only talking a little push. It's not as if Noah doesn't have a sex life—he told us he did, last summer." His eyes twinkled. "All we're doing is presenting him with a new partner."

"They've been friends forever," Finn piped up. "We just want them to see each other in a different light—see that they're *made* for each other."

"Then maybe what we need is a bit of orchestration." Dylan smiled. "And I *do* have an idea how we might do that, if anyone's interested."

All eyes were on him.

"Well, don't stop there," Ben declared. "Share!"

"Look, it's the bachelor party on Saturday, right? That sounds like the perfect opportunity. We get all of us onto the dance floor, and with a little… choreography, we engineer it so that they're dancing close to one another. A word in the DJ's ear, a slow song or two—"

"And a judicious push so they end up in each other's arms," Seb interjected. "I love it."

"And what if they don't *want* to be pushed into each other's arms?" Nathan speculated.

Ben stared at Aaron. "You tell us—will they?"

Aaron's heartbeat quickened. "One of them

definitely will."

"Then it's settled. That's our plan." Seb leaned against Marcus. "Now all we have to do is make it appear as natural as possible."

Marcus burst out laughing. "Impossible if you have anything to do with it. Subtlety is *not* in your vocabulary."

"I still think it's a bad idea," Joel commented.

Finn gave him a hard stare. "Then isn't it a good thing you won't be there to see it? *You'll* be having your mature, fun-free dinner with Marcus, Nathan, Mark, Eric, and the rest of your buddies." He patted Joel's cheek. "Don't worry. Someone will film it."

Joel gave him a mock glare. "Fun-free? You have *no* idea what I have planned for my bachelor party."

"Are we talking male strippers?" Marcus asked with a gleam in his eye.

Joel coughed. "No."

"Female stripper?" Nathan ventured.

"Definitely not."

"Entertainment that can't be mentioned here, because they're *way* too young for such a thing?" Marcus appeared to be enjoying himself.

Joel stared at him. "Now I'm dying to know what kind of *entertainment* you had in mind."

Ben burst out laughing. "'Fess up. It's just dinner, isn't it?"

"There's nothing wrong with that," Joel retorted.

Finn leaned in and nuzzled his neck. "Nothing at all," he murmured. "Your party, your night. And sitting down to a meal surrounded by friends sounds perfect." Then he grinned. "Not as perfect as dancing your feet off, surrounded by hot guys, but you can't have everything." He glanced at the others. "So that's what we're going with? Setting up a couple of slow songs and seeing if Levi and Noah bite?" There were nods, and frowns from Nathan, Joel, and Marcus. Finn rolled his eyes. "You didn't have to come today, y'know. You could've stayed at home if you wanted to be blissfully ignorant."

"Maybe we felt we *needed* to be here," Marcus observed. "You know, to make sure you didn't concoct some outlandish scheme? After all, we're older than you, we've seen more of life than you have, we—"

"Oh, *now* I get it." Seb rolled his eyes. "You wanted to give us the benefit of some old guy wisdom, is that it?"

Marcus narrowed his gaze, but his lips twitched. "Are you calling me old—again?"

"Maybe?"

"Fine. You keep that up, and you know where my hand's going to be when we get home later."

Seb's eyes sparkled. "Promise?"

Aaron choked. "Okay, that was *way* TMI. And definitely not a picture I want in my head."

"Guys?" Nathan frowned. "Is that really the best you can come up with? Although I should add, I have no idea what *I'd* try to do to get two obviously reticent people's heads out of their asses."

"Leave them be," Marcus commented. "If they're *that* concerned about Levi and Noah's future together, they could always try this newfangled idea all the young people are doing these days. I believe it's called 'talking.'" He smirked.

Seb nudged him with his elbow. "I think *you've* talked enough. Especially if you want me over your—"

"Seb!" Shaun, Dylan, and Aaron chorused.

Finn cleared his throat. "Guys? We have news."

He and Joel laced their fingers. "The house is finished —well, almost. There's just the plastering and painting to be done."

"That's awesome." Ben's face glowed. Then he beamed. "Especially since it means you can start on Wade's house next."

Shaun chuckled. "Getting tired of keeping the noise down at his mom's place?"

Ben raised his eyes heavenward. "You have *no* idea. I mean, I love Mary and Gramps, but yeah… we need our own space." He waggled his eyebrows. "If only to say goodbye to my bitch of a landlady." That raised a few chuckles.

"Will it be ready by the wedding day?" Dylan asked.

Finn nodded. "In fact… here's a date for your calendars. We've booked the U-Haul for Wednesday, July 28. Anyone who wants to help with moving day will be welcomed and fed. We have all the stuff at Joel's house, plus what's left of mine in storage."

Marcus got his phone out and tapped the screen. "Added. We'll be there."

Seb blinked. "Oh, *we* will, will we?"

"Why—you got someplace else to be?" He peered at the others. "Anyone else staying the night of the wedding at a hotel? There are a ton of them around Freeport."

Dylan nodded. "We're staying at Hotel 44 North. It has a pool."

Seb gaped. "So are we."

"And us," Ben added. He snickered. "Whoa. We might end up next to some of you."

Marcus's eyes gleamed. "That does it. I'm bringing a gag." Ribald chuckles erupted.

"None of you mentioned coming here to Levi or Noah, right?" The last thing Aaron wanted was word of this little committee getting back to them.

Everyone shook their heads.

"I wonder how Levi's getting on with his speech?" Shaun mused.

Aaron had been wondering the same thing. He flashed Finn a grin. "You're a braver soul than I am. Just think of all the stories Levi could share."

Joel arched his eyebrows. "Oh really? This might prove educational."

"Lord, I hope not," Finn muttered.

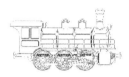

Levi was at the French doors, gazing out at the yard. Noah stood for a moment, taking in the sight. Watching Levi surreptitiously had become his favorite pastime of late. There were times when they were both working that he'd glance over, loving the look of intense concentration as Levi peered at his laptop screen.

Right then he was watching Grammy, and judging by the way he held himself so stiffly, all was not well on Planet Levi. Noah walked over to him, and put his hand on Levi's back. "You seem to have the cares of the world on your shoulders."

Levi turned his head. "Look at her, sitting out there under the tree Granddad planted. Now she really *does* carry the cares of the world."

Noah stared at Grammy, the late afternoon sun

creating dappled shadows over her as it filtered through the canopy of leaves. "Has she talked about Eli and Amy since they left this morning?"

"Nope, not a word. Not that I tried to bring the subject up. I figure if she wants to discuss it, she'll make the first move." Levi sighed. "I've got other stuff to occupy my mind."

"Such as?"

Levi bit his lip. "My speech?"

"Have you written it yet?"

"Yeah, I tried to make it funny. But it's not the speech that's the problem, it's my delivery."

Noah cocked his head. "Okay, while she's out there, come up to my room. Bring the speech. This calls for a little one-on-one coaching."

Levi raised his eyebrows. "Really?"

"Sure. It's just like reading lines. You have to work on your timing, your inflections…"

Levi snorted. "No, what *I* have to work on is opening my mouth and not putting my foot in it. I get so tongue-tied, so embarrassed."

A glimmer of an idea caught light in Noah's head. "Then we won't practice with the speech."

He blinked. "Then what *are* we going to work with?"

Noah grinned. "Trust me. If you can say *these* lines, you can cope with anything."

Levi narrowed his gaze. "Color me intrigued."

Noah crooked his finger. "Then come with me." He left the dining room and headed up the stairs, Levi following. Once inside his room, Noah grabbed his Kindle from the nightstand, and swiped through his books, searching for a title. He grinned when he found it. Noah clicked on it, and did some more swiping to find the perfect bit.

"Right. Stand at the foot of the bed," Noah instructed. "Imagine you're standing at the top table, or whatever they call it, about to give your speech." He grinned. "By the way…. Imagining your whole audience is naked? Really does help."

Levi shook his head. "You were always such a paradox in high school."

"Me?"

"Yes, you. On the one hand, you were the guy who acted as though math was the most interesting class *ever*, but when you got on stage, you were this whole other person."

Noah smiled. "That's what I liked about it. I didn't have to be me. I could be someone else." He tilted his head. "It meant a lot to me, knowing you were out there, watching."

Levi flushed, a tide of red rising from the neckline of his tee. "So what is it you want me to read?"

Noah handed over the Kindle. "Here." Then he climbed onto the bed and sat back, legs stretched out in front of him.

Levi peered at the screen and blinked. Blinked again. "Are… are you seriously asking me to read this?"

"You don't have to start on that page if you don't want, but anything from that chapter should be good to help you work on inflections. You're trying to make it sound more like a piece of theater than part of a book."

Levi swallowed. "I guess you know what you're doing, but…" He met Noah's gaze. "I had no idea you even *read* stuff like this."

"You learn something new every day." Noah folded his arms. "Go for it."

Levi's Adam's apple bobbed, and he licked his

lips. "Okay then…" Another swallow. *"He rolled his body on top of Tommy, his face inches away, and rotated his hips, letting Tommy feel his hot, hard cock. "And you still want this, don't you?"*

"Lord, yes," Tommy moaned softly, pushing up with his hips, his dick already starting to fill. "I want this."" Levi paused and cleared his throat. "You sure about this?"

"Absolutely. If you can read this, you can do anything."

"So… what is it about?"

Noah stroked his chin. "The basic plot is a virgin trying to persuade a bartender-cum-porn star to punch his V card. Which is what is about to happen in this chapter."

Levi lowered his gaze to the screen, then jerked his head up, his eyes wide. "They… they're gonna have sex? Just how graphic does this get?"

Noah grinned. "You're about to find out." He pointed to the Kindle. "Keep going."

Levi took a deep breath. *"Mike chuckled. "I guess you do at that." He pushed a knee between Tommy's thighs and spread him wide, then dropped his head to Tommy's shoulder. "But not half as much as I want to be inside you," he whispered."*

"Now read it again," Noah instructed. "But slower this time. Get some emotion into the words."

"Emotion? You don't know what you're asking," Levi remonstrated. "The only emotion I'm feeling right now is full-on lust."

Noah smiled. "And you're so busy dealing with it that you have no time to be embarrassed. Now… Read. It. Again."

Levi did as he was told, re-reading the passage three times before he scanned the page for another. He shivered as he read "*Tommy grabbed a pillow and hugged it as Mike's tongue renewed its acquaintance with his hole, circling it, licking, sucking, pushing inside him once more. Oh God, the sounds Mike was making…. Tommy panted, pushing back to get more, wanting more of that tongue that was fucking him, driving him out of his mind. His cock rubbed against the comforter, already hard as nails, the skin sensitized. When Mike spread him wider, stretching his hole and pushing farther into him, Tommy cried out, the sound loud and harsh.*" Levi raised his head from the Kindle. "I don't know about practicing for the speech—this is really turning me on."

It was turning Noah on too, but it wasn't the text—it was imagining himself as Mike, rimming Levi's virgin ass, hearing the sounds pour from Levi's lips, watching him writhe as Noah loosened him up—

"Keep going." Noah sat cross-legged, a pillow in his lap, his hands clasped together and resting on it, not so much for comfort but a means of hiding his erection.

Levi read the passage again, slowing in the more sensual parts, and speeding up when the action gained more heat. When he got to the orgasm part, he read it with feeling, the words flowing far more easily. "*Mike broke free of the kiss and arched, gasping, filling him all the way. "Oh fuck, Tommy."*

And suddenly Tommy was there, coming, coming so hard, the feeling white hot as it raced through his body, through every vein and artery, bursting out of him in a thick arc that hit Mike squarely on the chest.

Mike lay on him, letting Tommy's body support him, stroking over the damp skin of his chest. He raised his chin and looked Tommy in the eye, his breathing ragged.

"That was… amazing.""

Levi lowered the Kindle. "I second that."

"Then I'll third it," Noah added. He beamed. "You did great. Now do it all again." He couldn't wait to be alone, to wrap his hand around his aching cock.

And I'll be thinking about Levi.

Levi chuckled. "You just want to hear me read about hot sex."

Noah rolled his eyes. "Duh." They both laughed. Levi went back to the start, and Noah had to admit, he nailed it, sounding so much more confident and at ease.

Noah was definitely *not* at ease. The reading session had proved one thing to him without a shadow of a doubt—he wanted to make love to Levi.

He wanted to be Levi's first.

Chapter Sixteen

Tuesday, July 13

Noah stepped out onto the patio and breathed in the fragrances surrounding him. That was what he loved most about Grammy's garden—it was a sensory delight. The brief morning shower had heightened the smell of the grass, and the afternoon sun had soon dried the slabs. Levi and Grammy had gone shopping, and Noah had the house to himself. He was grateful for the chance to be alone for a while.

Having Levi so close was messing with his head.

"Good afternoon, neighbor. Thanks for the text about moving the train layout."

Noah smiled to see Mark's face above the fence. "Is that okay? I know it's the day after the bachelor party, so I don't expect anyone to be up too early. That's why I suggested Sunday afternoon. Shaun said he and Nathan would help too."

"Yeah, that's fine." Mark peered at him. "Everything okay?"

Noah was stumped for an answer. "Yes? No? Maybe?" He sighed. "There's stuff going on that I can't discuss—that's Levi's business—but… yeah, things are kinda weird right now." And while he didn't want to talk about Eli and Amy, he had to talk to *someone* about his confusion. "You got a minute?"

Mark smiled. "For you? Always. Come on over." He lifted the fence panel. "You want some tea?"

Chamomile tea sounded perfect right then. "Please."

Noah stepped over the concrete base board and into Mark's yard. Mark walked toward the house, and Noah headed to the patio. He sat in one of the chairs beneath the parasol, and took a deep breath. The more he thought about it, the more he realized Mark was exactly the sounding board he needed.

Mark returned with the pot of tea and two cups. "Now," he said as he set the tray down. "Suppose you tell me what's on your mind."

"I guess the crux of it is… I'm confused."

"What about?"

Noah huffed. "This whole situation is so ironic."

Mark's eyes sparkled. "Maybe if I knew what situation we're discussing, that might make more sense." He poured the tea.

"You know when we all met up at Aaron's house at Easter?" Mark nodded. "Well, I got there the day before. I had a lot on my mind, and I needed to talk to someone." Noah gave a half-smile. "Rather like today, I guess. Anyway, Aaron and I chatted about what was going on in my life, and finally we got around to Dean." Noah sipped his tea. "I gave Aaron some advice. I told him not to get stuck on labels, to go with the flow, be open to new experiences."

"All of which sounds like good advice—which he followed, judging by what happened at the party. So where does irony come into it?"

"Because that made me seem as though I knew what I was talking about. I thought—then—that I knew who I was. Now?" He swallowed another mouthful of tea. "I'm not so sure anymore."

Mark leaned back. "Okay, I'll bite. Who *were*

you?"

"I was Noah the asexual, who hooked up with guys because he wanted to get off, not because he was sexually attracted to any of them."

"So they were a means to an end? Nothing wrong with that." Mark smiled. "And I do know where you're coming from. I've worked with a few ace performers."

Noah blinked. "Really?"

"Sure. Okay, while there are some aces who don't have strong feelings about sex, or are even repulsed by it, there *are* some who find enjoyment in it." He smiled. "Like you."

Noah heaved a sigh of relief. "Yeah, like me. I haven't had that many sexual partners—I'm just as happy to make do with a hand or toys." His face grew warm. "Sorry if that was too personal."

Mark chuckled. "I'm probably the one person in your band of friends who is all but impossible to shock when it comes to talking about sex." He bit his lip. "Except maybe Seb." They both laughed at that. "So… back to you. What's changed?"

Noah could answer that with a single word. "Levi."

Mark frowned. "Levi's changed?"

"No.. It's more… the way I see him. I… I think about him… a lot."

"Not seeing what the problem is—*oh*." Mark stilled. "I guess that depends on *how* you think about him."

"Uh-huh. And I don't know why I should suddenly start thinking about him… like that."

Mark cocked his head. "You're living under the same roof. You see a lot of each other. Of course he's on your mind more." He drank a little tea. "Can we go back a sec? To where you were talking about labels? There's a story I'd like to share, that I think might be relevant to your present situation."

"Sure."

Mark put his cup down. "Okay… Back when I worked for a studio, I did a couple of scenes with four or five guys over a weekend. It was one of those fuck-fest shoots, where they rented a house, crammed as many guys into it as they could, then had us fuck all over the place—couples, three-ways, an orgy or two… Anyhow, on the second day of the shoot, I got talking with this one guy, and he confessed the scene he'd done with me that morning had been one of his best ever."

Noah grinned. "Seb would argue every scene you've ever shot is your best one."

Mark put his hand to his chest. "Oh, what it is to have fans…"

They chuckled. "So I asked this guy why it had been so good. *You* know… if it was something I'd done, I wanted to know so I could do it again. He told me he was ace, and that most of the time, he didn't feel a connection with his fellow porn actors, so he retreated into his head to replay a fantasy or two. He said it helped with his performance. *Then* he said he hadn't had to do that with me. When I asked him why not, he said it was because we'd met the night before the shooting started, we hadn't fucked, but we'd talked… and talked… and talked. We really got along. So when we finally got to do our scene, it made the sex so much better." Mark smiled. "He was good at his job, but he couldn't just flip a switch. If he didn't connect with someone on an emotional level, then he had to rely on his own resources." He met Noah's gaze.

"Asexuality is a pretty big umbrella term, and it covers a

lot of width on the spectrum. And none of us are a fixed point on that spectrum. Change is inevitable." Mark smiled once more. "So someone who considers himself asexual might look again at his circumstances, and decide a better label might be… demisexual. Because that decision really *could* flip a switch."

Noah sat still, his thoughts tumbling through his mind. Demisexual? He knew the term—he'd just never thought it could apply to him.

Except now that Mark had said it, the term made perfect sense. *Why didn't I see this?* Easy answer—there was too much else going on in his life.

"And if it makes you feel better, you're not alone," Mark added. "I've been around longer than you, and you know what I've discovered? A lot of demi people start out thinking they're ace. It's not until they meet their person that they realize they're demi." He studied Noah. "You and Levi have been friends for years, right? And you've never thought about him sexually."

He coughed. "Not exactly." When Mark arched his eyebrows, Noah sighed. "If I'm honest, there *were* brief… pangs, I suppose you'd call them, in the past— moments when I had feelings for him—but I guess I logicked my way through them. I told myself those feelings didn't fit into the box I'd created for myself." He shrugged. "It was easy to dismiss them, but now…"

"You can't dismiss them any longer," Mark surmised.

Noah shook his head.

"Think about it," Mark continued. "You already had a rock-solid friendship. Then your circumstances changed, you moved in with him and Grammy…." His gaze grew thoughtful. "I'd guess there have been other changes too. Something has created an even deeper emotional bond between you."

Noah's breathing caught. "Yes." *So much yes.*

Mark held up his hands. "You don't have to tell me what's happened to create that bond. That's none of my business. But to sum up… you're in love with your best friend—not that you haven't loved him like a brother for years, but now it's different. And you're just waking up to the realization that you want him to be *more* than your best friend." His eyes glittered. "So what's stopping you?"

Noah swallowed. "You've just described *my* half of the equation. What about Levi's?"

Mark gave another tilt of his head. "Has he shown any indication he feels the same way?"

"No… maybe?" Half the time, Noah was certain he was reading too much into Levi's responses, his glances… seeing what he *wanted* to see.

"I can't help you there," Mark declared. "The only way you're going to discover how he feels is to talk to him. Are you ready for that conversation?"

"Noah?" Levi's call sent the birds on Mark's feeder rising into the air with a flurry of wings.

"They're back." Noah inclined his head toward the fence. "I'll be right there," he hollered.

"Then I guess we're done talking. But you and Levi haven't even started yet." Mark smiled. "By the way, I think it's wonderful."

"What is?"

"Falling for your best friend. Dylan and I were friends before we ever fell into bed, but that connection only grew stronger. You and Levi… you already have a really good foundation on which to build a relationship. This is just the next step." He leaned forward. "But I *will* leave you with something to think about. You like sex, you said. You enjoy it. So imagine how much better it's going to be when you're having sex with someone you share a deep emotional bond with." His eyes gleamed. "Because I can tell you from experience— there is *nothing* like it."

"Noah?" That was Grammy.

Mark got to his feet. "You'd better go before she sends out a search party." He squeezed Noah's shoulder. "Now, stop worrying, and follow your own advice—go with the flow."

Noah stood. "I'm crap at following my own advice. Thanks, Mark."

"Anytime." He walked with Noah to the fence, and waved to Grammy who was standing at the French doors. Noah stepped through the gap, and Mark replaced the panel.

Grammy gave him a broad smile. "I'm making eggplant Parmesan tonight. I know you like that."

"I love it."

She disappeared into the house, and like a rabbit popping out of a magician's hat, Levi stuck his head around the door. "Keep Thursday free."

"Why? What've you got planned?" Noah went toward him.

He grinned. "How does a trip to Ellsworth sound? A ride on a restored diesel locomotive?"

Noah beamed, his anxiety pushed aside. "Sounds great." Then he thought about it. "And maybe you have a drive over to Mount Desert in mind too?" It seemed an awful long way to go for a short train ride, and they did have Eli and Amy's address.

Levi's smile faded a little. "Yeah. You okay with that?"

"Sure. Are we doing the round trip in one day, or staying someplace?" Levi had talked about a hotel when he'd first proposed the idea, but there was always the possibility Mr. Johnson might ask them to stay at the house.

"We'll come home Friday, if that's okay. I'm sure we can find a room over there."

"Levi…" Noah lowered his voice, in case Mark was still outside. "It'll be okay."

Levi's face contorted. "I have so many questions."

"I know. But whatever you discover…" Noah looked him in the eye. "I'll be there for you, all right?"

Levi's face glowed. "Thanks. Don't think I could even contemplate doing this without you." He went back inside.

Noah stood for a moment on the patio, mulling over his talk with Mark.

Not sure I'm ready for that conversation yet.

Chapter Seventeen

Thursday, July 15

"Well?" Levi demanded. "Was it worth getting up at the crack of dawn for?" They were sitting in the green open-top passenger car, chugging leisurely through woodland to the accompanying sounds and smells of the restored locomotive pulling them along. As soon as they'd arrived at Ellsworth, they'd grabbed a bite of the sandwiches Grammy had thrust into their hands as they left the house, and then they'd walked up the winding ramp leading to the train.

He'd loved every second of it, but the icing on the cake had to be Noah's rapturous expression. It had been a no-brainer he'd choose the open-top car: it was way too nice a day to be inside.

Noah let out a sigh. "My grandpa would've loved this."

"I'm sure he's watching, maybe a little jealous, but you *know* what he's saying." Levi smiled. "'Make 'em go faster!'"

Noah laughed. "You know it. I want to do it all over again." He studied Levi. "What about you? Did you like it?"

Levi nodded. "I was trying to imagine what it would've been like, when all we had were steam trains."

"Somewhere I have a list of heritage railroads in the US. There's more than you might think, and a few of them are in Maine. I always wanted to visit the Wiscasset, Waterville and Farmington Railway in Alna."

Noah smiled. "I think we need another road trip. Think Grammy would come along too?" Then his face fell. "Damn. We're pulling into Ellsworth. So soon?"

"We can buy another ticket if you want." Right then Levi would have done anything to keep that beautiful smile in place.

"Sweet thought, but you can have too much of a good thing—"

"Not according to Seb," Levi interjected.

Noah laughed. "Yeah, well, you might have a point there. But don't we have someplace else to be?" He cocked his head to one side. "You do want to meet Eli and Amy's dad, don't you?"

Levi nodded, his stomach churning. "I sent Amy a text last night, telling her we'd be in Ellsworth. That was as far as I got before she texted back to say we had to visit. They're both helping out in their dad's store today."

"Then let's head over there, and after that..." Noah gave him a kind smile. "We'll play it by ear, okay?"

Warmth flooded through him. "Thanks for coming with me."

"To ride on a train? Are you kidding? You couldn't keep me away."

Levi leaned into him. "And for having my back when we see them."

"Always."

The sincerity in Noah's voice was a balm to Levi's troubled mind.

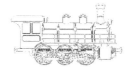

"That looks like the place." Noah pointed. "That sage green building. The sign says Johnson Hardware."

Levi turned off Main Street and onto the wide driveway leading to the parking lot. The store had a low, sloping roof, and along one side was a veranda, together with netting that protected the plants. Three baskets filled with colorful flowers hung above the white lattice veranda, and off to the left, a plastic-topped pergola covered the ground where trellis panels leaned against the side of the store, and ceramic flowerpots in all sizes and colors stood around. Three steps led up to the main door, and as they pulled into a space, Levi saw Eli descending them, carrying a large cardboard box. He waved when he saw them, and hurried toward a dark blue truck. By the time they'd killed the engine and gotten out of the car, Eli had deposited his load and come over to where they stood.

He smiled. "Amy said you were coming. I've gotta make a delivery, but I won't be long. Go on in and take a look around. Dad's out back, but Amy's at the register." Eli stilled. "I'm glad you came." Then he went back to the truck, got in, and drove away.

Levi and Noah climbed the steps and entered the store. The first thing Levi saw was a large cardboard box sitting on a counter, and inside it was a grey cat, asleep.

Levi smiled. "I wonder how much they're asking for the kitty."

"Maybe the kitty isn't for sale," Noah mused. "It

might be an employee. You know, in charge of security." His eyes sparkled with humor. "Would *you* want to mess with a kitty's claws?"

Levi spotted Amy at the register, dealing with a customer. She looked up and beamed at them. "Hey." Amy turned her head toward the rear of the store. "Dad? Can you come out here?" Then she turned back to them. "How was the train ride?"

"Awesome," Noah replied. He gestured to the store. "This is pretty impressive."

"This is Dad's second hardware store. His first is in Augusta, but he started this one not long after we were born."

A tall, broad-shouldered man with short greying hair walked toward them. His eyes widened when he saw Levi, and he swallowed. "You have to be Levi." He extended a hand. "Tim Johnson."

Levi shook it. "And this is Noah White, one of my closest friends."

Tim gave Noah a nod, then brought his attention back to Levi. "I'm a little busy right now, and I can't easily get away from the store, but Amy will show you how to get to the house, and I'll be home in time for dinner. You *can* stay for dinner, can't you?" Another swallow. "We have so much to talk about."

"You're not going back to Wells tonight, are you?" Amy frowned. "Dad, they can stay with us, right?"

"It's okay," Levi protested. "I was going to find a hotel room."

Tim bit his lip. "At the height of the season? I doubt you'd find much."

"They can have my room," Amy said. "I'll share with Eli. It's only one night." Her eyes twinkled. "I'm sure I can survive one night."

"*You* might—I'm more concerned about Eli," Tim said with a chuckle.

"Please, don't put yourselves to any trouble on our account," Levi remonstrated.

"It's no trouble," Tim assured him. Behind him, a phone rang, and he sighed. "No rest for the wicked." He turned to Amy. "When Eli gets back, have Pete take over at the register, and you two take our guests to the house."

Amy kissed his cheek. "I'll have dinner ready for when you get home."

Tim smiled. "Good girl. There *is* one thing though—take the General with you?"

She laughed. "What you *really* mean is, don't leave him here with Pete. How can a grown man be scared of a little kitty-cat?"

Tim sighed. "They just don't like each other, never have. And if Pete finds he's on his own in the store with the General, I'll never hear the end of it. So make an old man happy, and give me some peace?"

"Sure, Dad."

With a final nod to Levi and Noah, he hurried toward the door at the rear.

"Is that the kitty's name—the General?" Levi inquired.

Amy smiled. "Yeah. Don't ask me why. My mom named him, but that was sixteen years ago. He's pretty old for a cat. We let him do what he wants—at that age, he's earned it."

"How far is the house from here?" Noah asked.

"Less than ten minutes, right along Main Street. The house backs onto Echo Lake. As soon as Eli gets here, you can follow us in the truck." Just then, another customer came into the store. Amy gave them an apologetic glance. "Sorry. Let me deal with them, then we can go."

"No need to apologize," Levi told her. "We'll go say hi to the General."

They walked over to where the cat stretched and yawned, revealing sharp teeth. Levi stroked its sleek head, and was rewarded with a rumbling purr.

"Tim seems okay," Noah murmured, rubbing slowly along the General's spine.

"Yeah, he does." Levi glanced at him. "But I have to be honest… I'm nervous, not so much about meeting him, but more about what he's going to share with me." His stomach clenched. "I know so little about Mom. But what also concerns me is Grammy."

"What did she say to you this morning as we were leaving?"

Levi sighed. "She told me whatever I learn, she wants to know too." He gazed at Noah, his heart heavy. "She's one of the strongest people I've ever met, but what if… what I find out is more than I think she can bear?" His throat tightened. "And what if it's more than *I* can bear?"

"You're stronger than you think. And you know who you get that strength from? Grammy." Noah locked gazes with him. "I'm here for you—for both of you."

Levi had never been so grateful to have his best friend at his side.

The house was beautiful, a light, airy property nestled amid trees. Its white cedar shakes-covered walls reflected the sun, and inside was just as bright. There were few doors on the first floor, and archways gave an impression of space.

Amy and Eli had given them a tour, and Levi had to admit, it was a lovely place to grow up. Echo Lake could be seen from the upper windows, above the canopy of trees, the sunlight sparkling on its calm waters. Eli showed them his paddle boards, and Levi had to smile.

"You'd like our friend Aaron. He's into water sports too."

Eli's face shone. "He's the park ranger you told us about? Cool."

Tim returned earlier than expected, having left Pete, a local man who also worked at the store, in charge. Amy poured iced tea for them all, and they sat in the living room, where bay windows looked out toward the road running by the house. The General was curled up in Eli's lap, and Eli stroked him now and then.

"I guess you have a lot of questions," Tim began. "We do too, but I think they can wait." He got up from the couch and went over to the varnished writing desk in the corner. He opened the flap, removed a long envelope, and re-closed it. Tim walked over to where Levi sat. "Your mom left this with a lawyer, only to be given to me when she died. Unfortunately, there was a delay in getting it to us." He tapped the envelope against his upturned palm. "This is the original. I had a copy done for you to take home with you. I figured your grandmother would want to read it too." He handed Levi the envelope. "It was addressed to me, but you need to read it."

Levi gazed at it, his heart pounding.

Noah leaned in. "You wanted answers. They could be in there. But you'll never know until you open it." His hand was at Levi's back, firm and comforting.

Just do it.

Levi opened the envelope and slid the folded paper out. He took a deep breath and unfolded it.

My dearest Tim,

If you're reading this, then all the stupid things I did so long ago have finally caught up with me. I'm not going to talk about those things. I was a different person then, and I regret letting myself get sucked in.

There are other things I regret too.

Not marrying you, *though. That was the best decision of my life. You came along after the overdose, after I'd hit rock-bottom and climbed up out of the hole I'd dug for myself… after I got myself clean. You knew I was an addict, and yet you supported me… loved me. I regret that my addictions took such a heavy toll on my body – they robbed me of more time with you, Eli, and Amy.*

My biggest regret? Not making an attempt to see my parents—and my son, Levi.

Yes, you read that right. I have a son. He was born September 4th, 1993, and when he was a couple weeks old, I realized having me for a mom was the worst thing that could happen to him—he didn't deserve that—so I went to my parents' house and left him there, in a crib on their doorstep.

Yes, I'm ashamed of myself. It was a big enough mistake abandoning him—I made it worse by never going back. I told myself he was better off without me, that my parents would take good care of him… And as the years went by, I'd think about going back, only to dismiss the idea. He didn't need an addict for a mom, so I allowed my fears of ruining his life to determine my future.

This letter is my attempt to exorcise those fears.

I didn't go to my dad's funeral—I saw his obituary, weeks later—and that was the one time when I was sorely tempted to return to Wells. But I didn't. I told myself I didn't have a son.

I'm nothing but a coward, Tim. I didn't even tell you about Levi.

Well, enough is enough. I can't let my stupid fear affect Eli and Amy. Because somewhere, they have a half-brother. I don't know if Levi still lives with my mom—her name is Linda Brown, and I'll leave her last known address at the end—or if he's moved on. It's possible. He could have gone to college, moved to another state... I don't want to rob them of the opportunity to get to know Levi, even though by staying away, I robbed my mom of her only daughter.

So many regrets, Tim—and so much gratitude. I've had years of happiness, of family life, with you and the kids. And you did make me happy, sweetheart. Never doubt that. But now I need you to do something for me.

Find my mom? Find my son? Let them know how sorry I am that I was such a fool. I still believe Levi will have had a better life without me. My one hope is that you can make them understand. I never forgot them, not for a second. But I ruined my life, and I saw no reason to ruin theirs.

Kiss the kids for me. Love you.

Amy.

Levi dropped the letter to his lap, tears sliding down his cheeks.

Oh Mom.

Chapter Eighteen

Levi wiped his eyes and straightened his shoulders. "I'm sorry for your loss." In the midst of his own grief, he recalled it hadn't been that long since his mom had passed. That made their hospitality all the greater—they had to be feeling pretty raw right then.

"Can I see it?" Noah asked, almost timidly.

Levi glanced at Tim. "If it's okay with you, could Noah read it? He's as good as family." Tim gave a nod, and Levi handed over the letter.

"Thank you for the condolences." Tim's voice quavered. "I do appreciate you never knew her, so I have no idea what you're going through."

"What was she like?" It was the question Levi had never dared ask Grammy, for fear of upsetting her. "All I know about her so far is that she played the piano." *And took drugs. A lot of drugs. Don't forget that part.*

As if he could. What he'd learned about her at an early age had colored his thinking, so much so that it had almost driven a wedge between him and Seb last summer. It had taken Levi time to overcome his own prejudices, forget what he knew, and see Marcus the way Seb saw him—a warm, caring guy who plainly loved Seb to death.

Noah lowered the letter. "Wow. Talk about a bombshell."

Tim nodded as he took the letter from Noah. "We were still reeling from her death, and then *that* arrived." He folded it, and Levi gave him the envelope.

"She was a quiet kinda person," Amy observed.

Eli snorted. "She wasn't quiet when the General crapped in her slippers."

Noah winced. "Ew. And *this* is why I never wanted a pet growing up—I heard too many horror stories from other kids."

"She took the cat for his shots," Tim explained. His eyes sparkled with humor. "Apparently, he objected to that." He glanced toward the rear of the house, and his gaze grew fond. "She loved being out on the water. We have a small rowboat, and a couple of canoes. I'd take her out on the lake to watch the sunset." His Adam's apple bobbed.

"I remember her reading to me," Eli remarked. "I think that's my first memory of her, hearing her voice while I was going to sleep."

"I'm sorry for *your* loss too," Tim told Levi.

Before he could respond, Amy stood. "I'd better finish dinner, or we'll be eating at midnight at this rate." She left the room, and Levi was certain her hurried exit was so they wouldn't see her crying.

"And I need a shower," Tim added. "I won't be long." With a nod to them, he followed Amy out of the living room.

Eli cleared his throat. "Seeing as we're all getting a little choked up about this, I'm gonna change the subject, and ask if you'd like to see where you're sleeping tonight. Only, please bear in mind it'll look better once Amy's cleared all her shit out of it."

"I heard that!" came from the direction of the kitchen.

Levi was grateful for his attempt to lighten the mood. "That would be good, thanks."

Eli lifted the cat and placed him gently on the seat cushion. "Follow me, guys."

They climbed the stairs to the second floor, where the ceiling sloped. Eli headed for one of the four doors, and they stepped into a large room filled with light. The white wrought iron-framed bed with its scroll work headboard was covered with a pink-and-white quilt.

"This is pretty." Levi went over to the bed and gazed at the quilt. It was a simple pattern, beautifully executed.

"Mine's blue-and-white. Mom made them."

"Looks like the apple really didn't fall far from the tree," Noah commented. Eli gave him a puzzled glance. "Grammy makes quilts too."

"Oh wow." Eli's face glowed. Then he bit his lip, a flush rising to stain his cheeks. "By the way, now that I've got you on your own… Can I apologize for what I said when we stayed with you?"

"You already did," Levi said with a smile. "Forgiven and forgotten."

Eli shook his head. "I'm not talking about how rude I was when we first met. And yeah, I *was* rude. But no… I wanted to apologize for making that assumption. You know, that you two were an item."

Levi waved a hand. "It's okay. Noah and I have known each other since we were fourteen."

Eli beamed. "That's so cool. And I guess it was an easy mistake to make. You do kinda… fit together."

Tell me something I don't know. There were days when Levi felt as if he was a puzzle, almost completed, and Noah was that one missing piece.

"Do you have anyone?" Noah inquired. "Maybe someone you met at school?"

Eli's flush deepened. "No, not yet. I can't wait till I'm twenty-one. Not long now."

Levi arched his eyebrows at the randomness of the comment. "You that keen to go to a bar?"

"Not just any bar." Eli straightened. "Happy Endings, in Bangor. About an hour's drive from here, but it'll be worth it."

Noah's eyes twinkled. "It's a gay bar, isn't it?" Now that he mentioned it, Levi was sure he'd heard Ben or maybe Nathan talk about it.

Eli gaped at him. "How did you know?"

"Lucky guess?"

"I made it to my first gay bar recently," Levi said. "In Ogunquit."

Eli blinked. "Then you *are* gay?" Levi nodded. Eli arched his eyebrows. "Does it run in families?"

Levi chuckled. "It does in ours."

"Did you go to Maine Street?" Eli asked.

"You've heard of it?"

"I Googled it. When we stayed the night at your place, I was *this close* to sneaking out and driving there to take a peek. Not that I could go in, of course, but it looks like it's a great bar."

"It is," Noah confirmed. "One of my favorite places to go dancing."

"In fact, we'll be there Saturday night," Levi added. "For a friend's bachelor party." An idea took root. "Tell you what... Next time you visit, we'll go there—providing it's after your birthday, of course."

"Really?" Eli's smile lit up his face.

"Sure. Besides, I have a bunch of people to introduce you to." It wasn't until that moment that it had sunk in. Levi had a *gay* brother. He could just imagine Grammy's reaction when she learned that snippet of information.

He suspected the words *Jeezum crow* would be in there somewhere.

"Dinner's almost ready," Amy hollered. "Eli, set the table, please?"

"Coming." Eli gestured to the door. "The bathroom's across the hall. I'll bring you some towels after dinner. And if you need anything, just ask." He glanced at the bed. "You two okay sharing? There's a folding bed someplace…"

"It's fine," Levi insisted. "I just need to make a call before we eat."

Eli nodded. "Okay." He headed for the door.

Noah followed. "I'll go down and see if I can make myself useful."

Levi couldn't resist. "Hey, if they don't need you, you can always keep the General company. Just don't take your shoes off."

Noah narrowed his gaze. "Funny man." He went out of the room.

Levi took his phone from his pocket and speed-dialed. "Hey, Grammy."

"You still on Mount Desert?"

"Yes. We're staying tonight with Tim, Amy, and Eli. Oh, and the cat."

She cackled. "That don't come as a surprise. Your mom loved cats. When Tinkerbell died, she was heartbroken."

Levi stilled. "You had a cat? How come we never had one when I was growing up?"

Grammy snorted. "Because that damn cat scratched up my furniture, that's why. Once bitten, an' all that." She paused. "Well?"

Levi knew what she was asking. "I read the letter

she wrote to Tim."

"And do I get to see it?"

"Tim says he's made me a copy."

"Good." Another pause. "Do I *wanna* read it?"

"That's a dumb question, Grammy, because you're going to read it whatever I say."

"You know it." Then she sighed. "Except that's not true. I'm kinda in two minds about this, but... I'll trust your judgment."

He reflected for a moment. "Yeah, you do need to read it. It won't give you a lot of information, if that's what you're looking for, but... she wrote about you and me."

He caught the hitch in her breathing, the stifled sob. "Okay." The word came out as a croak.

"Levi!" Noah called out. "Dinner."

"Sorry, Grammy, I have to go." He hated breaking off when he could hear so much emotion in her voice. "Want me to call you later?"

"No, that's fine. Go spend time with them. And tell them they're welcome to visit any time."

He said goodbye and finished the call. Levi glanced at the quilt. *Mom, you and Grammy lost out on so much.* He could imagine them quilting together, choosing fabrics, designing... His throat tightened at the picture in his head.

What he needed right then was a hug—a Noah hug.

Noah left the bathroom and crossed the hallway to their room. The house was quiet: everyone had gone to bed just before ten, Tim apologizing for not staying up, but he had an early start in the morning. Eli and Amy had surprised Noah with a hug before they said goodnight, but then Noah reasoned Levi had told them he was as good as family.

Funny how life works out. When Noah was six, he'd asked his parents if they could buy him a baby brother. Not that he remembered this demand—it had become one of those stories they trudged out at family gatherings. *Do parents get lessons on how to embarrass their kids?* But as the years went by, it had become obvious there were to be no siblings. When he'd reached high school, Noah had found himself with a whole *set* of brothers, who he'd quickly learned would be there for him if needed.

Best of all, Levi had found *him.*

He opened the bedroom door and saw Levi sitting on the bed, some kind of large book open in his lap. As he drew closer, Noah realized it was a photo album.

"Where did that come from?"

"Amy brought it while you were in the bathroom." Levi raised his chin. "I look like her," he murmured.

It didn't take a genius to work out he was talking about his mom.

Levi patted the bed. "Come take a look." Noah joined him, and Levi turned back the stiff pages. "This is the first one." It was a wedding photo, dated July 18, 1998.

Noah studied it. "I see what you mean." Levi shared his mom's coloring, and Noah got why Grammy had been so shocked the first time she laid eyes on Amy—she and her mom could have been sisters.

Levi turned the pages, revealing photos of his mom and Tim in different seasons: dressed in warm clothing, surrounded by snow; walking through woodland, a carpet of vibrant fall leaves almost reaching their calves; his mom in the boat, the sunset lighting up her face; and a summer photo, where she'd been heavily pregnant and looking as if the heat was about to kill her.

"Screenshots of a life," Levi muttered. He pointed to a photo of two babies in their cribs, placed side by side. "'Amelia Linda and Elijah Robert Johnson, born September 5, 2000.' Wow. They even share my birth month." The twins were so small, their little faces scrunched up and reddened, Eli waving a tiny clenched fist.

"She gave them her parents' names too," Noah said in a low voice. He peered at another photo. "Is it me, or does your mom not look so good in some of these?"

"Maybe she was right when she said the drugs had taken a heavy toll."

Noah stared at her drawn face. "Do you think she knew all along that she wouldn't—as Grammy says—make old bones?"

Levi swallowed. "Possibly. I do think Tim took great care of her. Sunday would've been their twenty-third wedding anniversary."

"Unlucky for some." Noah though back to her letter. "Do you wish you knew what happened in those missing five years between leaving you with Grammy and marrying Tim?"

Levi shook his head. "No. We know there was an

overdose. Maybe that was the close call she needed. I don't want to know how far she fell—what matters is, she climbed out of the hole she'd gotten herself into." He let out a sigh. "Then she met Tim. I'm glad about that, but… it still hurts." He gazed at Noah with stricken eyes. "I'm finding out about this woman who was nothing but a name all my life so far, and now she's so much more—and I wish I'd known her. I understand she was scared. Hell, we *all* get scared. Trust me, I know."

It wasn't an emotion Noah ever connected with Levi, and it sent a trickle of unease through him. "What scared you?"

Levi closed the photo album and set it aside on the bed. "Wrong tense. It's more a case of what *scares* me…"

That trickle became a torrent. "Can you tell me?"

Levi studied him for a moment before speaking. "Maybe I can do what my mom never could—get over my fear."

Oh God. "Now you're scaring *me*." Then Noah's breathing hitched when Levi leaned in and kissed him lightly on the lips. He froze, unsure if he'd dreamed the impulsive, intimate gesture.

Levi pulled back and stared at him, his eyes wide. "Fuck. I shouldn't have done that."

No, no, no. That was the *last* thing Noah wanted to hear. "Then why did you?" He covered Levi's lips with his fingers. "No—wait. Before you tell me…" He looked Levi in the eye. "I'm not complaining, Levi, okay? I'm… shocked, sure, but… I'm not unhappy you kissed me."

Levi caught his breath. "Then… can I do it again?"

Noah smiled. "As if you have to ask." Then Levi's hand was on his cheek, the other on his neck as he leaned in again, only this time Noah was ready for him. Their lips met, and Noah's heart did a happy dance to hear the sigh that escaped Levi's lips.

I don't want this to end.

Noah cupped Levi's nape and returned his kiss, savoring the feel of Levi's beard against his skin, the soft scrape of his mustache on Noah's upper lip, the way Levi's fingers traced the curve of Noah's cheekbone...

At last Levi broke the kiss, and Noah stroked his beard. "*Now* tell me why."

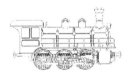

Levi swallowed. "Because I love you." He still couldn't believe he'd summoned the courage to do what he'd dreamed of doing for so long.

Noah smiled. "I love you too, but—"

"No," Levi interjected. "You don't get it." He had to make Noah understand. "I love you like you were my own brother, that's a given, but... I've loved you since I was fourteen years old. Meeting you?" He forced a smile. "That was how I *knew* I was gay, beyond a shadow of a doubt. Because I looked at you, and... you turned me inside out."

Noah gaped at him. "All this time... and you never said..."

Levi let go of his face, and took Noah's hand in his, gazing at it. "I've been too scared to. I didn't want to screw up what we had."

Noah lifted Levi's chin with his fingertips, and Levi stared into his warm eyes. "Then maybe I need to repeat myself." He didn't break eye contact. "I love you too."

It took a moment for the truth to sink in, and when it did, warmth radiated throughout Levi's body, his heartbeat raced, and his smile wouldn't quit. Right then it didn't matter what their relationship would look like—he knew it wouldn't be as he'd imagined—what was important was that they were *finally* on the same page.

Levi beamed. "I don't want to sleep. I want to sit up all night and talk, kiss…" Because if that first kiss was anything to go by, Levi was never going to get enough of them.

Noah chuckled. "We picked a great night for revelations." He sighed. "I want us to come here again, but we won't get another invitation if we keep everyone awake with our chatting. So… can we put off this conversation till we get home?"

Levi's heartbeat was still racing. "Only if you promise to fall asleep holding me… the way you did almost a week ago." His cheeks were warm. "Waking up with your arms around me… I wanted to tell you how amazing that felt, but I couldn't."

"I think that can be arranged."

Then his heart thumped as Noah popped the buttons on Levi's shirt, moving lower until he reached Levi's jeans. "Let me," Levi said quickly before unzipping them. He rose to his feet, shivering as Noah undressed him without a word, leaving him in only his briefs.

Noah gestured to his own jeans and tee. "Want to

return the favor?"

Levi smiled, and moments later they stood facing each other. This time Levi didn't look away, but drank in the sight of Noah's smooth chest, his slim waist, his long legs.

"Are we going to stand here all night ogling each other, or are we going to get into bed?" Noah bit his lip. "It's not as if you haven't seen me in my briefs before."

Levi found his voice. "Sure I have, lots of times—but this is the first time I'm seeing you after telling you I love you, and… it feels different." He shivered. "I don't want to forget this."

"I won't let you," Noah assured him. "I'll keep reminding you, so often you'll probably get sick of it."

"No way."

Noah drew back the quilt and the sheet beneath it, and they climbed into bed. Levi lay on his side, pushed back against Noah's chest, and sighed when Noah enveloped him in his arms. "Is this real?"

Noah's breath tickled his ear. "God, I hope so." He chuckled. "I also hope I'm not going to bed with Levi the starfish." Levi jerked his elbow, and it landed on Noah's belly. "Hey."

"How come you're so much calmer than me about all this?" Levi demanded. "I'm finding it difficult to lie still."

"Maybe I'm just a calm person," Noah said in a low voice. Then he chuckled. "I hate to break it to you, but this cool calm exterior is an act. I'm dancing inside. But *one* of us has to be the calm and collected one."

It felt good to know Noah wasn't impervious.

Levi turned his head. "Kiss me goodnight?"

Warm lips pressed against his, Noah's hand

cupping his jaw. When they parted, Noah smiled. "Goodnight, Levi."

"Goodnight." Levi reached over to switch off the lamp, and the room was filled with the blueish hue of moonlight. He lay there, surrounded by Noah's scent and the smell of lavender emanating from the bedding. Noah's breathing became more regular, his arm more of a weight across Levi's body.

As if he cared about that.

He loves me.

It was everything he'd dreamed of—well, almost everything.

I'll take whatever he has to offer. Levi wasn't going to make demands. If Noah was happy with the way things were, then so was he.

Chapter Nineteen

Friday, July 16

"Do you have to go?" Eli pleaded as they headed for the front door.

Levi chuckled. "If we keep you away from the store a moment longer, your dad will have my balls for earrings, and seeing as we want to come back, the answer is yes, we have to go." It was almost eleven o'clock, way later than he'd intended leaving. Tim had left for work after breakfast, and Amy had followed him an hour later. Eli claimed his dad could do without him for a while longer. What touched Levi was the fact that Eli wanted them to stay.

Levi wanted to stay too.

He'd awoken in Noah's arms, and it had taken a moment to recall the previous night. Then those arms had taken on a whole new meaning. *I'd be happy to wake up like this every morning.* He'd sung while showering, and he'd heard Noah laughing across the hall. Levi couldn't help it. He was freaking *happy*, and he didn't care who knew it. It was all he could do not to stare at Noah throughout breakfast, because every time Levi looked at him, he wanted to smile.

He loves me.

They had to be the best words ever.

Noah cleared his throat, and Levi knew he'd zoned out—again. Noah patted Eli's arm. "Thanks for the walk around the lake. You were right, it's beautiful."

He glanced at Levi before adding, "I can see why your mom loved it."

Eli's smile faltered. "Yeah, she did." He straightened. "Did you mean it? About taking me to Maine Street?"

Levi nodded. "You'll be twenty-one in early September, right?" Eli nodded. "Then the first weekend you get, come visit, and we'll go out Saturday night." He'd organize as many of the guys that could make it to join them.

"But that's *weeks* away," Eli exclaimed. "Can I come visit before then?"

"Of course." He knew Grammy wouldn't mind.

Noah smiled. "Our friend Aaron usually has a cookout at the end of August. I'm sure he'd be okay with you and Amy coming along, once you've been introduced." He chuckled. "At least you won't be staying the night. It's first-come-first-served when it comes to grabbing a bit of floor to sleep on."

"You two could stay here," Eli proposed.

Levi liked that.

Eli let out a sigh. "You'd better go, I guess, otherwise Dad will have *my* balls for earrings." He walked them to their car, and as Levi unlocked it, he gave them both a hug. "Safe trip back to Wells. Give my love to Grammy. And tell her she makes the best cookies in the world."

Levi wanted to leave Eli with a smile. He glanced at Noah. "Is it okay if I… share a little?"

Noah's eyes shone. "I was going to ask you the same thing. Sure."

"Share what?"

Levi placed his hand on Eli's shoulder. "Remember that comment you made at my place? You know, the one where you made an assumption...?"

Eli flushed. "Of course I do. But I already—"

"I think you should repeat it. Now." That bubbling feeling was back, surging through him, and he couldn't contain it a moment longer.

"I don't understand."

Levi smiled. "But you will—if you repeat it."

Eli scrunched up his eyebrows. "I *think* it went something like... You said you'd try to visit, then Noah said he'd make sure you did better than try. And then *I* said you were lucky to have a boyfriend like Noah."

Levi beamed. "Yes, yes I am."

It took a few seconds for his words to register, but he could see the moment they sank in: Eli's eyes widened, and he grinned. "No *way*! But I thought you said—"

"Circumstances change," Noah said, his eyes twinkling. "So do people." His gaze met Levi's.

Levi wasn't sure he fully understood that remark, but seeing Noah's contented expression brushed his curiosity aside.

Eli hugged them again, only this time he held on for longer. "I'm so happy for you both." When he released them, he was still grinning. "Is it okay to tell Amy and Dad?"

"Sure." Levi was already working out the best way to tell Grammy. Not that he thought his revelation could come as any great surprise—someone had to get up real early to get a march on Grammy.

"Come on." Noah tugged his elbow. "We've got a long drive. I'll let Grammy know we're leaving."

He nodded, and got behind the wheel. Noah joined him, and they backed away from the house. They waved at Eli when they reached the road, and then they were heading north.

Levi glanced at Noah beside him, and Noah laughed. "You've been doing that all morning. I'm not going anywhere. It wasn't a dream."

He bit his lip. "Am I that obvious?"

"Yes, but it's cute, so you're forgiven. You can look at me that way as much as you like, but I'd prefer it if you didn't while you're driving." Noah was grinning too.

Levi had a feeling he'd still be smiling when they reached Wells.

As soon as Levi opened the front gate, the door opened and Grammy stood there. "Wasn't sure if you were gonna make it back in time for dinner."

"We stopped for a bite in Camden."

Grammy smiled. "Did you see Ben?"

"Yeah. He asked us to stop by. He had an idea for tomorrow night." Levi was still giggling about that.

Grammy narrowed her gaze. "Mm-hmm. I smell shenanigans." Then she cackled. "Poor Finn." She stood aside as they entered, and Levi inhaled the glorious smells wafting from the kitchen.

"You made mac and cheese?" There was another aroma he couldn't place.

She smiled. "It's your favorite, isn't it? Only, I added a little extra somethin', after a comment Noah made a few weeks ago."

Noah frowned. "*I* did?"

She nodded. "I went out this morning to Mike's Fish Market just down the street. Got there as they opened."

The other odor suddenly made sense. "*Lobster* mac and cheese?" Levi was trying hard not to drool.

Grammy beamed. "Surprise. And there's plenty for a salad for lunch tomorrow. You'll need a good lunch inside you, if you're gonna be dancin' all night. Now go wash up, and I'll put dinner out."

"Wait." Levi reached inside the inner pocket of his jacket and withdrew an envelope. "This is for you."

She took it, studied it for a moment, then left it on the hall table next to the potted gardenia.

"Aren't you going to read it?" Levi inquired.

"In my own time," she replied. "Don't you go rushin' me." She pointed to the stairs. "Go wash your hands. And if you wanna change out of them clothes, there's time."

They climbed the stairs, pausing at the top. Noah pulled Levi to him, and they kissed, a slow well-hello-again kind of kiss that was exactly what Levi needed. He wanted to ask Noah about where they'd be sleeping that night, but this was not the time.

I hope he wants to share my bed.

"So… when do we tell her?" Noah murmured. "Because you're not planning on keeping it a secret, are you?"

"After dinner." Levi grinned. "Don't want her choking on her lobster mac and cheese, now do we?"

Noah stroked his cheek. "Have I told you lately that I love you?"

Levi bit back a smile. "Isn't that a song title? And have I told *you* I love it when you kiss me?"

"I have plenty of them." Noah leaned forward

and whispered, "And they're all for you." A cough from below made them spring apart. Noah chuckled. "Later." He planted a light kiss on the tip of Levi's nose, then disappeared into the bathroom.

"Hey! You snuck in before me!" Levi protested.

Noah's laughter made his heart sing. "See? *My* Jedi mind tricks work. I got you off-balance with the old kiss-on-the-nose routine."

This was a different Noah, a lighthearted, playful Noah, and Levi couldn't wait to see more of him.

Levi pushed his plate away with a sigh. "That was delicious."

"Glad you liked it." Grammy picked up her water glass, drank what was left, then set it down. She leaned back in her chair, her elbows resting on the arms. "So what's Tim like?"

"He's a good guy," Noah said. "A hard worker too. He started a hardware store in Augusta, then opened a second on Mount Desert."

"And their house is beautiful," Levi added. "It's right by Echo Lake." He paused. "I saw a photo album. Pictures of Mom." His chest tightened. "I think he made her happy."

"So he goes on the Christmas card list?"

When Noah blinked, Levi had to chuckle. "Ah, something you don't know yet. Grammy keeps a list of people who always get a Christmas card. If you get crossed off the list, then you *really* did something to piss her off." Grammy rapped his knuckles with her spoon, and he yelped. "Ouch."

"Language? Since when do you speak like that around me?"

"Sorry, Grammy." He'd noticed the envelope was still on the hall table when he'd come downstairs, but wasn't about to say anything. *It's her choice.* "And yes, he goes on the list."

She smiled. "That tells me a lot." She narrowed her gaze. "Okay… now suppose you tell me what's goin' on between you two?"

No. There was no *way* she could have guessed. "What do you mean?"

Grammy rolled her eyes. "I'm no dubber. You two have been squirmin' ever since you sat at the table. You keep lookin' at each other, then peekin' at me to see if I'm watchin'—which I *was*, of course. And I don't think you've stopped smilin' since you walked through that door. So start talkin'."

Levi took a deep breath. "You remember the night I went to that bar? The night we talked, and you gave me some advice?" She nodded. Levi glanced at Noah. "Well.. I suppose you could say I bought his chairs." He smiled when Noah gave him an inquiring glance. "Tell you later."

Grammy's mouth fell open, and her eyes widened. "You two are… how does Seb put it… an item?"

Levi grinned. "Always said you were a sharp lady."

She broke into the most beautiful smile Levi had ever seen her wear. "Hallelujah!" She got up from her chair and came over to where he sat, her arms wide. "Well, stand up so I can hug ya! And you too, bean pole. Get over here."

He laughed as Grammy seized him in a tight embrace. Then Noah received the same exuberant treatment. When Grammy released him, her eyes glistened.

She wiped them with the back of her hand. "Don't you mind me. You have no idea how happy I am to hear this—and to see the pair of you." She beamed. "You're both lit up like my Christmas tree." Then she smacked them on the arm. "About damn time you got your heads outta your asses."

"Excuse me?"

She rolled her eyes. "Lord, I must have the patience of a saint. The number of times I've been dyin' to say something. Because if ever two people belonged together, it's you two." Her eyes gleamed. "Of course, you wouldn't *be* together if I hadn't given you a little push in the right direction."

"Grammy... what are you talking about?"

She grinned, and Noah gasped. "Oh, you sneaky, *sneaky* woman."

Grammy cackled. "And I always said *you* were sharp."

Noah turned to Levi. "The attic... letting me put my trains up there... getting us to clear that bedroom out so I could move in... We've been set up."

Grammy waved a finger. "Nope. All I did was make you see what was right under your noses." She took Levi's hand. "That night when you told me you loved someone, but you thought they didn't love you...I hoped you were talkin' 'bout Noah. 'Cause this was something I'd prayed for."

"For how long?" Noah demanded.

She shrugged. "A while."

"Define 'a while.'"

Grammy bit her lip. "You were maybe seventeen or eighteen. I wasn't blind. I saw the way Levi looked at you—always when you were lookin' in the other direction, mind you." She put her arms around them. "When nothing happened, I thought I'd got it all wrong. Then it came to me. I had to leave it in the hands of the Lord, 'cause all things happen accordin' to *His* timin', not ours. It was then I started prayin'."

"And the day after we talked, you asked him to move in." Levi frowned. "You'd already told him he could use the attic."

"That was part one of my plan." Her eyes sparkled. "I figured the Lord might need a helpin' hand, 'cause it was obvious you two were more than He could handle on His own." She let go of them. "And now I'm gonna get us some of my homemade chocolate ice cream. This is a celebration." Grammy left them and went into the kitchen.

Noah wrapped Levi in his arms. "I've never been a great believer in God," he murmured. "I might have to rethink that."

Levi had been having the same thought. "I've never seen her so happy."

"God knows she needed a little of that, after Eli and Amy's bombshell. I guess you did too."

Levi closed his eyes and breathed in Noah's scent. "All I needed was you."

They still had so much to learn about each other, but it was a journey Levi was happy to embark on. He had questions, but he wasn't about to ask them.

Let's get used to being us for a while.

Noah undressed, his mind pulled in different directions. He kept glancing toward the door, wondering if Levi was going through the same mental gymnastics.

Why don't I find out?

He pulled on a tee—just in case he should meet Grammy in the hallway—and headed for Levi's room. He gave a gentle tap on the door, and Levi opened it, dressed in his briefs.

"Come in," he whispered. Noah stepped inside, and Levi closed the door. He chuckled. "Why am I whispering?"

"I just wanted to ask if you felt like sleeping alone tonight."

Levi smiled. "And I was about to knock on your door with the same question. I sleep better when you're there." He pointed to the bed. "Your usual side?"

Noah walked over to it and stripped off his tee. He paused, his hands on the elasticated band of his boxers. He only ever slept in them when Levi was around.

Levi flushed. "Take 'em off if you'd rather sleep in the buff. It's not as if I haven't seen you naked."

Noah chuckled. "The last time you did that was in the locker room."

Levi grinned. "You haven't changed all that much, have you?"

His heart hammering, Noah pushed down his shorts, his dick soft. Levi looked him up and down, and

Noah smiled. "Well? Have I?"

Levi swallowed. "You got a little bigger, I think."

Noah had a feeling he wasn't referring to his height. He got into bed, lay on his side, his head propped in his hand. "Are you getting in?"

Levi stared at him, then quickly removed his briefs before clambering onto the bed and diving beneath the sheets. Noah switched off the lamp, listening to Levi's uneven breathing.

There was a space between them.

"Are you going to stay on your side, or do you want to snuggle?"

A second later, Levi was lying beside him, his hand on Noah's chest, his head on Noah's shoulder. "I was waiting to be asked."

"You don't ever need to do that." Noah kissed his head. "I'm a snuggler too."

"Thank God."

In the silence that followed, Noah waited for Levi to bring up the subject of sex. He was aware of the gentle push of Levi's cock against his thigh, but Levi didn't speak of it, or draw attention to it in any way.

He's nervous.

Noah was *not* going to push him, but he knew that at some point they would need to discuss it.

And we have a lot to discuss.

"Goodnight, Levi." Noah kissed his forehead.

"Goodnight, Noah." A pause. "Still feels like a dream."

He smiled in the darkness. "A wonderful dream."

Chapter Twenty

Saturday, July 17

"What's taking them so long?" Noah asked. Music pumped through the doors of Maine Street, and judging by the number of guys who'd gone in while Levi and Noah had been standing there, it was going to be packed inside.

Levi grinned. "Relax. They'll be here. We just need to make sure we're all here before Dylan arrives with Finn." He pointed to the street. "Here come some more of us." Ben, Wade, and Aaron got out of a taxi, and farther up the street he caught Seb's laughter. Shaun had texted to say he was on his way.

Ben waved at them, holding a large brown paper bag. "I've got everything." He laughed. "This is gonna be *so* much fun."

"Let's hope Finn sees it that way," Wade said with a smile.

"Where's Dean tonight?" Levi asked Aaron.

"He stayed home. I told him he'd be welcome to join us, but we've got guests at the moment. His brother and sister-in-law are visiting."

"I'm only sorry Joel and the others have to miss it," Seb piped up. He held up his phone with a wicked glint in his eye. "This'll have to do."

Levi's phone vibrated, and he glanced at the screen. "It's Shaun. He'll be here any minute."

"Just make sure to take some really

embarrassing video footage," Ben flashed Seb a grin. "The sort of thing we can show to their kids." He gave a mock glare. "You know, the kind someone usually takes of *me* dancing." That raised a few chuckles.

Levi's phone buzzed again. "Right on cue. Dylan says they just reached Ogunquit."

Another car pulled up, and Shaun got out. "Made it," he said as he approached them. "Had to find another Uber, because mine canceled on me."

Noah pointed to Beach Street. "There they are." Finn and Dylan walked toward them, and Finn was laughing.

"Hey, why aren't you all inside?" Finn demanded as he reached the little group. He performed a turn. "Will I do?" He wore black jeans and a plain black tee.

Seb shook his head. "You *could've* taken me up on that offer to loan you one of my tees for tonight."

Finn laughed. "No fear. I've seen your tees. I don't want to stand out tonight. I'm just here to have a good time and dance my feet off."

"Oh, that's a pity," Ben said with a sigh.

"What do you mean?"

"Because we've all been waiting for you to arrive so we could get you ready for your party." Ben's eyes sparkled.

Finn stilled. "Oh God. Should I be worried here?"

Wade laughed. "To quote one of my mom's favorite movies—Be afraid. Be very afraid."

The friends formed a circle around Finn, who seemed increasingly nervous. "Guys? What are you doing?"

Levi grinned. "We'll leave this to Ben, seeing as all of it is his idea."

Ben snorted. "Didn't hear you saying 'no no no' when I told you about it. So hush." He straightened. "I was watching a documentary on BritBox the other week, about what the Brits call a Hen night—their version of a bachelorette party. Anyhow, the bride-to-be gets to dress up. She wears a tiara, a wedding veil, a sash…"

Finn's eyes bulged. "I am *not* wearing a tiara and a veil, guys!" He narrowed his gaze. "And before anyone else comes up with the idea, high heels are out too."

Everyone laughed.

"Aw, would we do that to you?" Ben batted his lashes.

Finn stroked his bearded chin. "Let me think— hell yeah."

Ben reached into his paper bag. "We thought we'd keep you in character, so…" He pulled out a carpenter's tool belt.

Finn laughed. "Okay, that's not too bad. I can cope with that."

Seb took it and fastened it low around Finn's slim hips. "That's where it belongs." He grinned. "Should I give his jeans a tug, so he's showing his crack? Gotta look the part, right?"

Finn glared. "No, you shouldn't."

"We're not done yet," Ben told him. "Now we need to fill it with a few wedding essentials." He reached into the bag once more, and brought out a handful of packets of lube.

Finn chuckled as Ben stuffed them into one of the pockets on his belt. "I'll never say no to lube."

"And this is for those times when you want it to last all night." Ben held up a box of Viagra.

Finn snorted. "Yeah right. Someone wasted their

money."

"Hey, just remember you're marrying an older guy. He might need a little... help." Seb's eyes gleamed.

"Sure he will—maybe when he's in his seventies. And somehow, I doubt he'll need them even then." There was a touch of pride in Finn's voice.

Levi grinned. "Hey, Ben. A tool belt needs tools, doesn't it?"

"Why yes, thanks for reminding me." Ben reached into the bag and removed a very long, slim, pink dildo, complete with sucker cup on its base. "For when Joel's not around."

"Speak for yourself," Seb retorted. He dug his elbow in Finn's ribs. "Talk to me about all the things you can do with Joel *and* a dildo."

Finn shuddered. "Not sure I want to know."

"And for emergency use only." Ben removed another dildo, only this one was twice as thick, and had a button on its base. "This sucker vibrates. And before you ask, they're both brand spanking new." He grinned. "Hear what I did there?"

"Is that it? Are you done?" Finn demanded as Ben slotted the two dildos through loops on his belt.

"Not quite." Ben shoved his arm all the way into the bag, then withdrew, holding a bag of—

"Dog treats?" Finn gaped. "Why are you giving me dog treats?"

Ben snorted. "They're not for you—they're for Bramble, for those nights when you wanna... distract him." He stuffed them into the front pocket. "And finally...your hat. Except it's not so much a hat, more a... fascinator. You know, those things rich women wear on their heads at the racecourse? I saw them this year, at the Kentucky Derby." He grinned. "Gotta say, this one was all Joel's idea."

Finn narrowed his eyes. "He *knows* about all this?"

Ben chuckled. "Of course. He said something about how… tactile you get when you two go dancing. You know, your hands kinda invariably stray a nudge too far now and then? So we found the perfect fascinator for you." He held up a dark green velvet stuffed octopus, its tentacles curling upward. A piece of elastic had been attached to its underside.

"No way," Finn choked as Ben perched it on top of his head, adjusted it until it was slightly askew, then looped the elastic under Finn's chin.

Ben stepped back to admire his handiwork. "Guys? I think we're ready." A spatter of applause erupted, and he took a bow. A few of them got out their phones and took pictures.

Finn stared at the circle of friends. "You're serious? You really want me to go in there like *this*?" When everyone nodded, he glared at them. "You just wait. Because when it's *your* bachelor parties, I am *not* gonna forget this." Then his lips twitched. Twitched some more, until finally he burst into laughter. "All right. If I'm only gonna do this once…" He paused. "Just so we're clear? I'm not gonna wear an octopus all night."

"If you make it past five minutes—and photographic evidence—we'll consider your ordeal over," Ben told him.

"Thank God." Finn squared his shoulders. "Okay, let's get in there." And with that, he strode through the open door, and a caterwaul of cries filled the air.

"Now that's what I call making an entrance,"

Levi murmured to Noah as they followed Finn inside, Levi and Noah bringing up the rear. "Ready to dance the night away?"

"You bet. Remember what we said." They'd decided not to share their news. After all, this was Finn's night. Noah had suggested they kept apart while dancing. "You know what they're like," he'd said. "We don't want to give them any ammunition."

Levi wasn't going to argue with that, especially when just the *prospect* of dancing close to Noah had an effect on certain regions of his anatomy. "You stick to one side of the dance floor, and I'll be on the other."

Noah leaned in and whispered. "As long as you don't stick to your side of the bed tonight." He straightened, and then there was no more conversation as the music's thumping beat swallowed them up.

Levi's heart was thumping too. *What does he mean?*

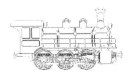

Seb met Aaron at the bar. "I've set it up with the DJ. So we're ready."

Aaron nodded. "Then you, me, and Dylan will go dance with Noah, and Ben, Finn, and Shaun will be on Team Levi." He still wasn't convinced this would work, but they had to do something—Levi and Noah had been apart all night.

Finn joined them. "Is it time?" He wore a huge grin. "I'm havin' *such* a good night."

"What did you do with the octopus?" Seb inquired.

"Handed it to the bartender for safekeeping." He glared. "You know, some of the guys out there keep tryin' to steal my dildos, not to mention my lube." He blinked. "Well? Is it time to work a little matchmaking magic on those two?" He squinted at the dance floor. "Which one of 'em is mine?"

"Levi." Aaron chuckled. "Are you sure about this? You're not exactly sober, and we need subtlety on this mission."

He gave Aaron a look of drunk indignation. "I can do subtle. Watch me." And then he made his way through the throng of gyrating men to where Levi was dancing with Ben and Shaun.

Aaron shook his head. "This is all going to go tits up, I can see it."

Seb tugged his arm. "Then we'd better get over to Noah. We've got about five minutes before I give the DJ the signal."

"Five minutes? They couldn't be farther apart if they tried."

What they needed was a miracle.

Aaron and Seb hurried to join Dylan, and then all three of them did their best to draw Noah deeper into the crowded floor. He saw Shaun and Ben doing the same, and grinned. *This might work after all.* Noah was clearly enjoying himself, moving to the beat. Then all eight friends met in the center of the floor. Seb glanced toward the DJ and raised his arm. A moment later, Troye Sivan's 'Lucky Strike' poured from the speakers, and Seb gave Noah a push toward Levi just as Ben shoved Levi to meet him. The two men collided, and

Seb gave the nod for the others to fall back.

Okay. That's it. Enough.

Time to see if there really was magic in the air.

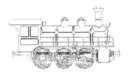

Levi grinned at Noah. "You thinking what I'm thinking?" he said into Noah's ear.

Noah rolled his eyes. "They're not exactly subtle, are they?"

Levi's eyes twinkled. "Want to have some fun?"

"What did you have in mind?" Noah couldn't be mad at their friends for their blatant attempt to bring him and Levi together, even though a tiny part of him resented them assuming they were meant to be that way. Then he reconsidered. If Grammy had known how well suited they were, surely the others had picked up on the same vibes.

It's what they do, right?

Levi leaned in again. "Let's give them what they're obviously hoping for." He snaked his arms around Noah's neck. "Get a little closer. That's what slow songs are for, right?"

Noah placed his hands on Levi's waist, tugging him closer, molding his body to Noah's as they moved sinuously to the music. He bent lower and brushed his lips against Levi's ear. "Like this?" A shiver rippled through Levi.

"Yeah, like that."

Noah forgot about their audience, the rest of their friends dancing around them, and focused on Levi's face. That full, pink lower lip mesmerized him, until all he wanted was to lick it, tease it with his teeth and tongue…

Then the music changed, and it was another slow number, only this time, Noah knew the words by heart. Since his latest chat with Mark, how many times had Noah listened to Sakima's 'Show Me', acutely aware of how perfect the lyrics were? All the things he'd longed to say to Levi. Because Noah dreamed of letting their bodies do the talking, to show Levi how greatly he affected Noah…

How much Levi turned him on.

Noah held onto Levi's hips, moving them in harmony, a sensual rocking motion that had to speak louder than words ever could. Levi's gaze stuttered to his face, and Noah couldn't resist. He closed the gap between their mouths and kissed Levi, a lingering kiss accompanied by gasps from their friends.

When the song ended, reverting to a pulsing dance beat, they broke apart, Levi a little breathless. Noah leaned in and whispered, "When we get home? We need to talk."

You need a lesson on what makes me tick. And it might just surprise you.

Levi swallowed. "Okay."

They glanced at the faces surrounding them. Aaron appeared gob smacked, but Seb and Dylan reacted with a high five, grinning like idiots.

Finn stared at them. "Damn, we're good."

Noah took one look at Levi, and both of them erupted into laughter.

Aaron's gaze went from Noah to Levi, and back to Noah. He sighed. "Guys? I think the joke is on us."

"I don't know about you," Noah said with a smile, "But I need some air." And with that, he grabbed Levi's hand and led him through the bar, heading for the stairs that led to the upper deck. The others followed, and once outside in the cool night air, Noah went to the far corner and came to a halt. Aaron was the first to reach them.

"Okay. Spill."

"Isn't it obvious?" Noah exclaimed. "Your scheme worked. We fell madly in love on the dance floor." He found it difficult to suppress his laughter. "Good choice of slow songs, by the way. That last one in particular."

Seb glared at them. "How long has this been going on?"

Levi shrugged. "About forty-eight hours, give or take." By then, the rest had gathered on the upper deck.

"Then why didn't you tell us?" Dylan demanded. Shaun, Finn, Ben, and Wade echoed his question.

Noah raised his eyes heavenward. "Duh. Because it's Finn's bachelor party? We *were* going to let you know—eventually—but when you presented us with such an opportunity, we couldn't resist."

Aaron beamed. "This is for real? You're not saying this just so we feel better about our little ploy?"

Noah gave him a hug. "For real, I promise." Finn blinked back tears, and Noah gazed at him in concern. "What's wrong?"

"Wrong?" Finn widened his eyes. "Are you *kidding*? Two of my closest friends just discovered they're perfect for each other. What could be wrong about that? It's like… it's like you've given me an early wedding present." He hugged them both. "So freakin' happy for you," he whispered.

Noah knew the feeling. "Ready to go back downstairs and dance the night away?"

Finn chuckled. "I'll even wear my octopus."

Noah glanced at the others. "Let's dance, guys.

The party isn't over yet."

"I don't *wanna* dance," Seb protested. "I wanna hear how you two finally saw the light."

"Well, you'll have to wait. Like I said, this is a party, so let's go help Finn celebrate giving up being a single guy."

"Ben?" Finn winked. "I'll even let you film me wearing my octopus."

"Okay, we're done." Ben removed his phone from his jeans pocket. "I'm on this."

Noah waited as everyone trooped past him, heading for the stairs, until only Levi remained. "Ready to dance some more?" Noah grinned. "At least now we get to dance together."

"What you said just now… about us talking… Is it anything I should worry about?"

Noah kissed Levi on the lips, holding him close, feeling the heat radiating from him. "Nope."

"So can you tell me now?"

He smiled. "Nope."

"But why not?"

He leaned closer, and Levi shivered again. "Because we're wearing too many clothes for the conversation *I* have in mind," Noah whispered. He pulled back to find Levi staring at him

"I don't understand."

"You will, I promise."

"But… I thought—"

Noah pressed his finger to Levi's lips. "Patience. I'll spell it out for you later." He smiled as an idea came to him. "I might not even need words."

This is going to be delicious—in more ways than one.

Chapter Twenty-One

The Uber drove away, and Levi went to open the front door. The house was in darkness, apart from the lamp in the window: Grammy always left it on. They crept into the house and he locked up.

Noah nudged him, inclining his head toward the hall table. The envelope sat there still. "I don't think she's even looked at it," he whispered.

Levi could understand that reaction. "All these years she thought Mom was dead. She did her grieving a long time ago. Now this." It had to have opened a wound she'd believed long since healed.

They removed their boots, and Levi followed Noah up the stairs, his heartbeat quickening. All the way home, he'd been turning one thought over and over in his mind.

What on earth is coming right at me?

Noah's cryptic remarks had confused the hell out of him. And as for their little performance on the dance floor… *What is going on?*

He hoped Noah was about to illuminate him.

Noah stopped at Levi's bedroom door. "Can we talk in here?" he whispered. "It's the farthest from Grammy's room, and I don't want to wake her."

"Sure."

"Just let me go to the bathroom, and I'll be right back."

Levi entered his room, and went over to the

nightstand to switch on the lamp. *He said I wasn't to worry. But that part about wearing too many clothes... what was that all about?* Then the light dawned, and he saw through Noah's subterfuge.

I can't let him do that, not if it makes him uncomfortable.

Noah came into the room and closed the door. Before he could open his mouth, Levi launched. "It's okay. You don't have to do this."

Noah frowned. "Do what? And is it okay if I sit while we talk? My feet are killing me." He sat at the foot of the bed, shoving a pillow between his back and the footboard.

Levi climbed onto the bed and sat facing him, hugging a cushion against his body. "It's just that... the way we danced tonight... I know that was for the guys' benefit. You don't have to pretend it was for me."

Noah blinked. "Okay, *now* I'm intrigued. Where are you going with this? And what makes you think it was a performance?" He cocked his head to one side. "Didn't you like it when we danced?"

Levi's face grew hot. "Of course I did." He'd loved every second of it. Feeling Noah's body against his, the leanness of him, the way he smelled, the light in his eyes... And as for that kiss... He swallowed. "But... I remember every word you said at Aaron's cookout."

"Ah." Noah bit his lip.

"You said you weren't gay, for one thing. I figured that was either a lie, or something you've only just realized."

Noah cleared his throat. "It wasn't *exactly* a lie. I guess it was more of a denial kinda thing. And yes, then things changed—circumstances changed—mostly because of you, but also because I know and understand more about myself than I did before." He locked gazes with Levi. "You do believe me when I say I love you, don't you?"

"God yes." The words were torn from him. "You pour your heart and soul into your kisses. Can't fake that. But what I'm *trying* to say is… you don't have to pretend." He didn't break eye contact. "I understand. And I'll take you any way I can get you. I know you said things change, but I don't expect you to change that way overnight, just for me." He hoped to God this was making sense to Noah, because to Levi's ears, his words were a jumbled mess.

Noah became still, studying Levi's face. "So you'd be happy if we had lots of snuggling, kissing… but no sex."

"I know you have a sex life," Levi remonstrated. "You said as much. But I did a lot of reading on asexuality, and… I came up with a few solutions that might work for us."

Another blink. "I'm all ears."

Levi's heartbeat raced. "You still jerk off, right?"

"On occasion." Noah bit back a smile. "More occasions than I'll admit to. Although I keep my door locked these days. Grammy has a habit of sneaking up on a person."

"Well… I could do that for you."

Noah stared at him. "You're offering to give me hand jobs?"

Levi nodded again. "And you said you have toys. I… I could help you get off with them. It'd be something we'd share."

Noah expelled a long breath. "You really have thought about this." He narrowed his gaze. "And where do *you* fit in this scheme?"

"Me?"

"Yes, you. You've talked about getting *me* off, satisfying *my* needs… what about yours?"

Levi's heart pounded. "I can take care of those. I wouldn't expect you to—"

"Why would you do that?" Noah interjected.

"Because like I said, I'll take you any way I can get you, okay?" The words came out far louder than he'd intended, and he listened for any sign he'd woken Grammy. In the ensuing silence, Levi lowered his voice. "I've waited for you this long, I'm not going to lose you now."

I can't lose you.

Noah had known *something* was brewing in Levi's mind, but he'd had no idea it would be this… complicated. He'd put Levi's reluctance to bring up the sexual side of their relationship down to the fact he was a virgin.

He is, isn't he? He'd hinted as much. Maybe it was time to find out for certain.

"Tell me why you haven't had sex yet."

"I'll tell you—if you'll answer a question first."

"Okay." Noah waited.

"Who was your first?"

Noah arched his eyebrows. "Seriously?"

"I mean it. Who did you first have sex with?"

He had no idea where Levi was going with this, but if it meant they brought more out into the open,

Noah would play along. "A guy I met at a party, my first year in college."

"And what do you remember about that night?"

Noah still wasn't sure where this line of questioning was taking them, but he wanted to see what lay at its end. *I wanted us to talk about sex, didn't I?* At least this got them on the right track... kind of. "I think he was experimenting, but when it came down to it, he was horny, I was horny... I didn't make a big deal out of it, mostly because I'd already figured out my sexuality. I didn't crush on people, I didn't fantasize about guys fucking me, or me fucking them..." He could just about recall the guy's name. *Paul, maybe?*

Levi sighed. "I'm not like you. I guess I'm a romantic kinda guy at heart. I wanted my first time... to mean something. I wanted it to be with someone I cared for... someone I loved. Old-fashioned concept, I know, especially nowadays when all you have to do is swipe, and there are any number of hot guys practically on tap. But that wasn't for me. I was waiting." Noah stared at him, and Levi nodded. "That's right. I was waiting for you."

Noah's throat seized and his chest tightened. *Oh. Levi...*

"And then this summer, I came to my senses. I had to face reality. You... you didn't want me like that."

The words felt like a slap, and Noah heard the pain Levi must have gone through to reach that conclusion. "You decided not to wait any longer."

He nodded. "I put aside my romantic notions, bought myself some new clothes... and went to Maine Street."

Noah's breathing caught. "Oh my God. That night... you went there to get laid, didn't you?"

Another nod. "I met Daniel—who would've been more than happy to do the deed, I might add."

"Oh really?" Noah narrowed his gaze. "I may have to keep an eye on our mailman."

Levi chuckled. "You've got no worries on that score. Besides, it was then that I saw you walk from the dance floor with some guy, and... Well, Daniel got me out of there, and we talked. Mostly about you. Then when I got home, there was the whole conversation with Grammy... and I came to another decision." Levi looked him in the eye. "I'd show you how much you meant to me... and I'd take whatever you were willing to give, if it meant I could keep you in my life. I'd be whatever you needed."

Warmth swept through Noah. "You are probably the most selfless man I've ever known. You'd do all that—and miss out on a meaningful sex life—just to make me happy." He wanted to crush Levi to his chest, to kiss him to within an inch of his life, but he had a plan that required a little distance between them.

Kissing would come later.

Levi heaved a sigh of relief. "Yes. So you don't have to pretend. I do get it. More importantly, I'm okay with it."

It was Noah's turn to sigh. "No, you really *don't* get it at all. Remember I said I know and understand more about myself than I did before?" Levi nodded. "Well, one of the things I discovered was..." He smiled. "You turn me on."

Levi stared at him, his lips parted.

Noah couldn't stop now. "I also learned... a label is not for life. Like I said, circumstances change. But the most important thing I've learned is that I'm sexually attracted to guys I share a deep, emotional bond with. Except that's not quite right. There's only *one* guy." He met Levi's stare. "And that would be you."

Levi's Adam's apple bobbed sharply. "I see."

Noah smiled. "No, you still don't. Okay… I had an idea while we were dancing tonight—which, by the way, took a great deal of effort on my part. I knew the guys were watching—I knew *Seb* was watching, and those eyes don't miss a trick—so I was doing my best not to… get hard."

Levi coughed. "Never mind the guys—I think if I'd felt that, I wouldn't have known how to react."

"And then it came to me. You see, I'd expected us to have a conversation about sex, once we'd confessed how we felt about each other. And when you didn't bring it up, that got me thinking. So… I'm going to *prove* to you that you turn me on."

"You can't prove something like that," Levi replied.

Noah grinned. "Oh really?" He got off the bed, pulled his tee over his head and tossed it aside, unfastened his jeans, then shoved them down to his ankles before removing them completely. He sat facing Levi once more, his legs spread wide, his dick soft.

Levi's breathing became harsher. "What… what are you doing?"

Noah rubbed his nipples with his thumbs. "I want you to do something for me. I want you to listen to my voice, but keep your eyes on my cock."

Levi blinked. "Why? Is it going to do a magic trick?"

Noah smiled. "Kinda." What he had in mind was a somewhat extreme method of proving just how much Levi aroused him—but that was what would make it all the more effective.

He hoped.

And if it worked, he knew *exactly* how he wanted it to end.

Levi forced a chuckle. "Gotta say, it feels a little weird, staring at your dick." Noah's shaft lay to one side, pointing toward the mattress. It wasn't overly long, and the head was a lighter shade of pink than the rest of it. He raised his chin. "We don't—"

"Hey, keep your eyes down. And just keep looking," Noah told him. "And while you're doing that, let me tell you some of the things I've been thinking about recently. Thoughts about you."

"Do... do you think about me a lot?" Levi did as instructed, even though it still felt weird.

"Mm-hm. Especially when we're in the same bed, and I get to touch your warm skin."

His dick moved, only half an inch, but there was definitely upward motion.

"That night in the hotel in Philadelphia... You lay on your side facing away from me, and all I could think about was slowly pulling your briefs over your hips so I got to see your ass."

Another half inch, and damn, it thickened slightly. Levi breathed a little faster.

"I longed to stroke my fingers down your spine, right into that little furry cleft I only get to see when you've showered, and you turn away to step into your briefs."

Fuck, it was moving, lengthening a little, thickening some more…

"I think about kissing your shoulders, down your back, to that downy hollow just above your crease, then lower, tracing a path over that firm ass cheek with my tongue…"

Maybe thirty or forty seconds had elapsed—no longer than that—and yet now Noah's cock was pointing at Levi, twitching as it rose even higher.

Levi couldn't remain silent, his heartbeat quickening, his own dick hardening behind the zipper of his jeans. "Where else would you trace a path?"

Oh good *Lord*, Noah's cock pulsed, bobbing up and down.

"Where do you *want* me to go?"

Levi swallowed, thankful not to be looking Noah in the eye. Heat surged through him. "Over my hole. Can't tell you how many times I've watched a guy getting his ass licked, and it always sounds so freakin' hot. Like he can't believe how good it feels."

Noah's shaft passed forty-five degrees, more solid, more of it, and still rising.

"I want to hear the sounds *you'll* make when I push my tongue inside you."

Higher. Higher.

"I think hearing you moan will only make me more eager to slide my cock into you, feel your tight heat surrounding it…"

Levi almost choked. "Never mind that book you gave me to read from—you could write 'em yourself." He couldn't tear his gaze away from Noah's dick rising into the air, pointing upward, so much thicker than before, a bead of pre-cum glistening at the slit. "Oh God, look at you."

"And it's all for you." Noah groaned, and it was the sweetest sound. "Fuck, I want to be so deep inside you. I want to feel your heartbeat while we make love. Want to hear you call my name… Feel your fingers digging into my arms, my back, feel you clinging to me…"

Noah's cock stood at attention, pre-cum sliding in a thin trickle down his shaft, and Levi knew exactly what he wanted.

"Can I touch it?"

Noah rolled his eyes. "Thank God. Yes, get over here."

Levi launched himself along the bed, until he knelt between Noah's thighs, Noah's dick bobbing, pulsing, the veins on its side visible. Levi reached out to dip his fingertip into the sticky pre-cum, spreading it over the taut head. He ran his finger up and down the shaft, smearing it with the clear liquid.

"Want to know what it tastes like?" Noah's voice was husky.

Levi didn't trust himself to speak. He nodded, then lowered his head, until the flushed cock was barely an inch from his lips. He swiped his tongue over the slit, then jerked up to stare at Noah. "It's almost… sweet." Then without asking, he took the head in his mouth, his heart hammering, his blood pounding, and Noah's moans filled his ears. Levi hurriedly covered Noah's mouth with his hand. He reared back, staring at him. "Sh. You'll wake Grammy." Then he sucked on the flared head, loving Noah's stifled cries. Pride swelled in his chest, and he went a little deeper.

Noah gave a gentle push of his hips, and Levi moaned, his mouth full of hard cock. Levi curled his fingers around the solid shaft, sliding them up and down as he sucked and licked, tracing the veins with his tongue.

Suddenly Noah pulled free of his mouth, and warmth spattered Levi's cheeks and lips. Noah gripped his dick as it continued to pulse, shivers coursing through him. Levi licked his lower lip, tasting the slightly salty spunk. Then Noah tugged him higher, until Levi was in his arms, their lips locked in a fervent kiss.

Levi grinned. "You taste like me."

"Never come that fast in my life." Noah cupped his chin. "Well? Did I prove it?"

Levi was about to tell him he'd most definitely proved it, when he caught the sound of a toilet flushing. They froze. "She's awake," he whispered.

"Then we wait till she's gone back to bed, go to the bathroom, and clean up."

Levi reached into the nightstand drawer. "Better yet, I have some wet wipes. Use those. Then we should go to bed—after I've brushed my teeth." He gave Noah a hopeful smile. "You *are* staying in here tonight?"

Noah sagged against the pillows. "You think I have the energy to move, after *that*? You just blew my mind."

Levi chuckled. "I might have no experience, but I *thought* I blew your dick."

Noah kissed him again, a more leisurely kiss this time. "But now you've got some experience." His eyes sparkled. "You finally got your V card punched."

Levi stroked Noah's cheek. "What mattered most was who punched it."

Another night in Noah's arms, only, this night was different. Their journey had taken a new turn, and the thought of where it might lead him sent shivers of anticipation trickling through him.

He wants me.

He really *wants me.*

Life was perfect.

Chapter Twenty-Two

Sunday, July 18

Noah leaned out of the attic window. "Okay, Mark, send it up," he hollered. He watched as the last piece of the layout rose into the air, strapped to the top of the scissor lift. Feet thudded on the stairs, and a moment later, Shaun and Nathan bounded up the attic steps. They hurried over to him, and Dylan and Levi joined them. "Almost here."

The top of the lift came level with the windowsill, and he and Levi unfastened the straps. "Okay, guys, easy does it. Last time." The five men edged the layout through the open window, and when they'd cleared it, they carried their precious cargo to the space Noah had prepared for it on the framework.

Noah yelled down to Mark. "Okay, you can bring it back down now." The lift whirred into life and began its descent. Noah beamed at the sight in front of him. The layout would require wiring and slotting together, but it was finally *there*.

"Now *there's* a happy man," Levi said with a smile as he put his arm around Noah. "Everything is where it belongs. And now we can get on with designing the Ogunquit layout."

"Wait—there's more?" Dylan exclaimed.

Noah laughed. "Not yet, there isn't. We have models to make first." He gazed at the men. "Thanks, guys. I couldn't have done this without you."

"And as a thank you for stepping in at the last minute to replace Seb and Marcus, there's Grammy's lemonade and cookies in the kitchen." Seb had called that morning to say something had come up.

Noah had a good idea what that something was.

Shaun grinned. "*Now* you're talking." He and Nathan headed for the stairs.

"Got your speech ready?" Dylan asked Levi, a glint in his eye.

Levi coughed, and Noah patted him on the back. "He'll be ready. He just needs a little more practice." That made Levi cough even louder.

"I think I'd better go downstairs and give Grammy a hand." Levi leaned in and kissed Noah's cheek. "I'll pour you a glass." Then he and Dylan followed Shaun and Nathan.

"Never mind the lemonade—save me a cookie," Noah called out to him. He caught Levi's chuckle. He walked into the center of the attic, surveying the scene. There was a lot of work to be done, but the prospect wasn't a daunting one.

This time, Levi will be working on it with me.

Noah didn't think he'd ever been this happy.

The previous night's—well, early morning—discussion couldn't have gone better. Everything was out in the open, and things could only get better from then on. They'd both slept later than intended, and he'd awoken with a jump when Grammy knocked on the door to tell Levi breakfast was ready. A moment later, she'd knocked again, to tell them *both* to get their asses downstairs.

He'd wondered how she would react to them sharing a bed, but she didn't mention it. She did, however, seem a little out of sorts, and he hoped that wasn't down to them. Then he reconsidered. Grammy wasn't a prude, and if she had a problem, she usually spoke her mind.

And then some.

"Earth calling Noah, come in, Noah."

He blinked. Mark stood at the top of the stairs. Noah smiled. "Sorry. I zoned out there."

"You seem happier than the last time we spoke. Not that I'm surprised." Mark grinned. "I hear you had a good time last night."

"I had an even better time once we got back here."

Mark arched his eyebrows. "Should you be telling me this?"

He laughed. "Get your mind out of the gutter. Levi and I talked." Mark didn't need to know about what had followed the conversation. Unlike Seb, Noah liked to keep his sex life private. *Except I wouldn't change a thing about Seb.*

Mark beamed. "At last. So everything is hunky dory?"

"Not *exactly* hunky dory, but definitely better." Noah bit back a smile. "*Hunky dory*? Showing your age there, Mark."

That earned him a mock glare. "I was *about* to say, happy is a good look on you, but now I don't think I'll bother." Mark's eyes sparkled with humor, however. He inclined his head toward the stairs. "We'd better get down there fast, or there'll be no cookies left."

Noah tapped the side of his nose. "Don't you worry about that. I now have insider knowledge." He grinned. "I know where the cookies are kept."

"I take it back. You're awesome." Mark patted

his tummy. "But only one cookie. Gotta watch my figure."

"I think that's Dylan's job."

As they headed down the narrow staircase, Noah smiled to himself.

Life wasn't just better—it was as perfect as it could be.

Grammy got up from the table. "Think I'm gonna take out shares in Tums," she muttered as she left the dining room.

Levi piled the dishes up, and Noah gathered the silverware. "She's got indigestion again?" Noah inquired.

"Yeah." It seemed to be happening a lot lately, and each time, Levi had to wonder whether it *was* simple indigestion, or something more serious. They followed her into the kitchen. "You okay, Grammy?"

She scowled. "You're doin' it again. Quit fussin'."

"So I worry about you. Bite me." He walked over to her and kissed her forehead. "It's only because I love you."

Grammy chuckled. "Yeah, I know." She went back to loading the dishwasher. "I've been meanin' to ask. What did you end up gettin' Finn and Joel for a wedding present?" Her eyes gleamed. "That's assumin' it's not the kinda gift that would offend my delicate ears."

Noah laughed, but Levi stared at her, his heart

racing. "Aw hell." He'd been so preoccupied with the speech, Eli and Amy, Noah, that he'd forgotten.

"Uh-oh. I know that look." Grammy bit her lip. "You'd better get weavin', boys. At least you've still got two weeks before the wedding." She shooed them toward the door. "Get your brains into gear while I make coffee."

Levi left the kitchen, his mind in a whirl. They returned to the dining room, and Noah opened the French doors. They stepped out onto the patio, and Levi inhaled the scent of honeysuckle and jasmine.

"I'm just as bad," Noah said gloomily. "I guess we both had a lot on our minds."

"My only thought so far was that I didn't want to give them a gift card. I know that's what they asked for, having a new house and all, but... I wanted to give them something special."

"But do you have something in mind?"

"Maybe?" Levi got his phone out. He scrolled through his photos until he found what he was looking for. "I took these at Grammy's birthday party. I think this one of Finn..." He held up the phone. "And this one of Joel... would look really good together in a pencil drawing. It would be from us both."

Noah smiled. "Aha. You're thinking of Dean. But does he have enough time? And would he be able to fit us in? Aaron says he's painting up a storm right now."

"Let's find out." Levi went into Contacts and clicked on Dean's number.

After four rings, Dean answered. "Well, hello there. I hear congratulations are in order." He sounded a little breathless.

Levi smiled. "Thanks. I'm calling because we need your help."

"Oh? What can I do for you?"

Levi related the situation, and his idea. "If you can't do it in that time, please, say so, and we'll come up with something else."

"You've got Aaron's email address, right? Email me the photos now, and I'll be able to tell you. Drawing takes less time than painting, so I might be able to manage it."

"Hang on." Levi went into Email and attached the two photos. "On their way."

"One sec. Babe? Can you check your phone, please?"

"Now?" Aaron sounded incredulous.

"Yes, now, please." There was a pause, during which Levi could hear Dean and Aaron talking quietly. Then Dean was back. "That's fine. Once I've started, I'll text you with the dimensions of the frame you'll need. Pretty standard, so you shouldn't have any difficulty finding one. Then as soon as it's finished, I'll mail it—carefully packaged, of course."

"Don't forget to let me know what I owe you."

Dean chuckled. "No charge. That's my Congratulations gift to you. Sounds as if you two finally found your Happily Ever After. And now, I've gotta go. I'm in the middle of… something."

In the background, Levi heard Aaron say, "Well, *I* said it could wait, but *noooo, you* decided to take the call. Are you done now? Can we continue?"

Levi chuckled.

Dean cleared his throat. "Say hi to Noah for me."

"I will." He finished the call, then turned to Noah with a smile. "We're okay."

"Great." Noah gave him a quizzical glance. "Why the chuckle?"

"I think I interrupted them."

Noah frowned, and then his eyes widened. "Oops." He tut-tutted. "That's why I prefer to wait until nighttime. Less chance of being interrupted." He leaned in and kissed Levi's neck, making him shiver. "Tonight, for instance."

Levi coughed. "I thought you were going to work on the layout tonight."

"I'm not in any hurry. Not when there's something much better that I could be doing—that *we* could be doing." Another brush of his lips over Levi's neck. "I'll give you a hint. It involves you… me… and your bed. I'll bring supplies." He straightened. "And now I'll go help Grammy with the coffee."

Levi watched him saunter from the room.

Did he just wiggle his ass? Then he glanced at the clock on the sideboard.

There were *way* too many hours left until bedtime.

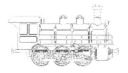

By the time Noah knocked gently on his door, Levi thought his heart was about to explode. He'd showered—twice—and then he'd trimmed his fingernails and given himself a quick tidy up down there with his shaver, wincing when a hair or two got caught. He hurried over, opened the door, and yanked Noah into the room, closing it behind him.

"Where have you been?"

"I had to wait until Grammy went to bed." Noah

paused. "By the way, did you see? The letter's gone from the hall table."

Levi nodded. "I noticed that when the guys left this afternoon." He had no idea if she'd read it. She hadn't said a word about it since he'd given it to her.

Noah held up a bottle of lube and a box of condoms. "Supplies."

Levi stared at the box. "When did you get those?"

"This morning after breakfast. Thank God for CVS. And before you say anything, yes, we're using condoms. And the first chance we get, we're driving to Portland to get tested."

"Oh." Heat surged to his cheeks.

Noah took his hand and led him to the bed. "Don't be nervous."

Levi snorted. "That obvious, huh?"

He deposited the supplies on the quilt, then pulled Levi to him. "We'll take things nice and slow, okay?" Noah cupped Levi's chin, tilted his head up, and kissed him, a light, chaste kiss that was just right—

Until it wasn't, and Levi wanted *more*.

He brought his hands to Noah's head and held him there, deepening the kiss, moaning a little when Noah explored his mouth with his tongue.

"Someone's hungry," Noah murmured against his lips.

"Are you surprised? I've been waiting a long time for this."

Noah groaned. "I've thought of nothing else all day. That box sat there in my nightstand drawer, and I *swear* I heard every single condom calling to me." He slid his hand over Levi's chest, moving slowly, until he reached his jeans. Noah molded his hand around Levi's stiffening cock, stroking, teasing it with his fingertips.

"Can't wait to have this inside me."

Levi stilled. "I think there's something else we need to discuss."

Noah smiled. "As in, who does what to whom? I'm easy. How about you?"

Relief flooded through him. "I guess I'm easy too."

"Good to know." Noah tugged him onto the bed, Levi tumbling onto his back. Noah lay on top of him, their lips meeting in another lingering kiss, only now, Noah rocked against him, a slow, sensual undulation that made Levi gasp when Noah's hardness met his own. He couldn't lie still, pushing up with his hips to meet Noah's sexy, leisurely thrusts, his breathing more rapid, his heartbeat climbing—

A dull heavy *thud* froze them both.

Noah was up and off him in an instant. "What was that?"

Levi clambered off the bed and ran out into the hallway. "Grammy? You okay?" He paused at her door, knocking. "Grammy?" Noah was behind him.

Muffled sounds came from behind the door, and he pushed it open. The bedside lamp had fallen onto the rug, and next to it was the opened letter. Grammy lay sprawled on the floor beside the bed, clutching her chest, struggling for breath.

Oh God.

He hurried to her and knelt on the rug. "Grammy? Describe whatever you're feeling right now."

She wheezed, "Can't seem… to catch my breath. Feels like… there's a vise… on my chest…" Her hands went to her jaw and neck. "Hurts."

Levi jerked his head in Noah's direction. "Call 9-

1-1. I think she's having a heart attack." Noah nodded and ran from the room.

Levi took Grammy's cool, clammy hands in his. "Hold on, Grammy, okay? You just hang in there."

He couldn't lose her.

He wasn't ready.

Chapter Twenty-Three

"Levi. *Levi.*"

He blinked. Noah stood beside the bed, holding two cups of steaming… something. He held one out to Levi, then sat in the chair next to his.

"Thanks," Levi murmured.

"You look exhausted."

Levi glanced at him. "Hate to break it to you, but you look just as bad." Noah's face was drawn, his eyes dull. Levi gazed at the bed where Grammy lay, surrounded by whirring machines, tubes, monitors… She seemed so *small.*

"They said she's stable, right?" Levi couldn't miss the anxious edge to Noah's voice.

"For now, yeah." Levi took a sip of what turned out to be hot chocolate. "While you were gone, I did some research on cardiac atherosclerosis." He'd done his best to take in all the information the doctor had shared with them, but a lot of it had gone over his head. All he could think about was Grammy. He'd registered the fact that whatever had happened had affected the right coronary artery.

He'd also registered the doctor's diagnosis of coronary heart disease—and that Grammy had known about it for a while, according to her medical records.

She kept it from me.

"So this balloon pump they were talking

about… it's helping her heart to function?"

Levi nodded. "The nurse said she'll spend twenty-four hours in the CCU, and then they'll move her to telemetry for monitoring." He swallowed. "Noah… I think she dodged a bullet."

"What do you mean?"

"The nurse was just here. She said it could've been a lot worse, given her age. She might have needed bypass surgery." The doctors had been able to successfully clear the artery and place a drug-eluting stent in there to keep the artery open.

"Thank God you knew where Grammy kept all her paperwork."

"She made sure of that. She told me last year when she set up her living will." Levi's chest tightened. "She knew this was coming. She *had* to know. And she didn't tell me." They'd waited while all the tests had been completed, the EKG, the blood tests, and the whole time he'd been praying.

Don't take her yet, Lord. I know you love her, but she can do far more good down here.

He took another sip. "I should call Eli and Amy."

"Levi… it's the middle of the night. They'll worry enough when they hear the news, and then they'll probably want to get in the car and drive here. Let them sleep a while longer."

Levi's throat tightened. "But what if she doesn't *stay* stable?" God, they'd only just learned they had another grandmother.

"If they thought she was likely to deteriorate, they'd have told us." Noah squeezed his shoulder. "You need to rest."

"I'm fine," he lied.

Noah sighed. "You're far from fine. You're worn

thin. And she's in good hands. The cardiac team here at York Hospital is second to none, my mom said. If there's any change, they'll call. We can be back here in twenty minutes. Please, Levi." He glanced at Grammy. "She wouldn't want you to wreck your health by tiring yourself out, not when there's nothing you can do here anyway."

Someone cleared their throat. Levi jerked his head to find the nurse standing close by them. She gave him a kind smile. "He's right. Some rest would be the best thing for you right now."

He peered at her badge. "Thanks, Lisa. Maybe a little sleep *is* a good idea." Maybe.

"And try not to worry about your grandmother. Her balloon pump is linked to the cardiac monitor, so we can see what's happening all the time from the central monitoring station."

"See?" Noah smiled. "She's in the best place. And if you're still not sure…" He gave Levi a hard stare. "What would Grammy tell you?"

Levi knew when he was beaten. He got up from his chair, walked to Grammy's bed, leaned over, and kissed her forehead as lightly as he could. "Goodnight, lady. Love you."

Then Noah took her hand and gave it a gentle squeeze. "See you soon, Grammy." He put his arm around Levi's shoulders. "Now let's get you home."

It felt as though fatigue had settled into his bones. "Yeah. Let's go home."

Sleeping might be another matter, however. He had to get his mind to stop turning before that could happen.

Noah got Levi through the front door and locked it. Levi had been quiet all the way home, not that Noah was surprised. He was still reeling from the shock. Grammy was in the best place, though.

Now he had to take care of Levi.

"Do you want some tea, or anything to eat?"

Levi shook his head.

"Then upstairs. A shower will feel really good before bed."

It took Levi a second or two to head in the directions of the stairs, but at last he got moving. Noah followed him up, and into Levi's room.

Levi sat on the edge of the bed. "She *is* going to be all right, isn't she?"

Noah wanted to tell him there was nothing to worry about, but he knew the words would taste bad if he uttered them and then Grammy took a turn for the worse, despite the doctor's optimism. "They're doing all they can, okay? Right now, *you're* the one who needs taking care of." He grasped the hem of Levi's tee.

Levi didn't move.

"Hey… arms, please?"

Levi blinked, then raised his arms into the air. Noah removed the tee before popping the button on his jeans. Levi watched him, his brow furrowed. Noah sighed. "You need to help me a little, okay? Unless you intend wearing your jeans in the shower?"

Levi stood, pushing his jeans to his ankles. Noah tugged them from his legs, then removed his briefs. He grabbed Levi's towel from where it hung on its stand, and gave him a gentle push. "Bathroom."

Levi moved as if in a daze, and Noah waited to hear the water running. When nothing happened, he went into the bathroom. Levi sat on the toilet, his cheeks streaked with tears.

Oh Levi…

Noah knelt in front of him and cupped Levi's face in his hands. "I know, I know. You can't think of anything else. But you have to be strong for her." He stood, and hurriedly stripped off, leaving his clothes in a pile.

Levi frowned. "What are you doing?"

Noah reached behind the curtain and flipped the shower on. "Washing you." He waited until the water ran warm, then took Levi's hand and pulled him to his feet. Noah held the curtain while Levi stepped into the tub before joining him, the flow of water cascading over them.

"This is new."

Noah smiled. "For me too." He poured the liquid soap into his palm, and commenced washing Levi's chest and shoulders, moving his hands in slow circles, noting how Levi relaxed into his touch. "That's it. Let me take care of you."

Levi leaned against him, and Noah wrapped his arms around Levi's slick body. "This wasn't how I envisaged the night ending," Levi murmured.

Noah chuckled. "Me neither, but there'll be other nights. I'm not going anywhere." He stroked Levi's back.

"Thank God."

Noah lifted Levi's chin with his fingertips. "I mean it. I've never given my heart to anyone—until now. You said you've been waiting years for me. Well, maybe I was waiting too." He kissed Levi on the lips, and Levi looped his arms around Noah's neck.

"Love you," Levi whispered.

"Love you too." The warm water tumbled over them as Noah held the man who owned his heart, lock, stock and barrel.

He needs me.

God knew, Noah needed Levi.

The shower done, they dried off, and Noah propelled Levi toward his bed. Levi closed his eyes the second his head hit the pillow. Noah climbed in beside him, switched off the lamp, curved his body around Levi's, and kissed his shoulder. He noted Levi's phone on the nightstand.

Just in case.

Noah closed his eyes. *I don't know if You're there, Lord, but Grammy believes you are. She's the best example of a Christian I've ever known. So please… watch over her tonight. Because if You decide to take her, so many hearts will be broken, and the world will have lost some of its light.*

Then he placed his hand against Levi's chest, feeling the reassuring beat of his heart, its regular rhythm lulling him into sleep.

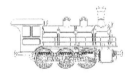

Monday, July 19

Levi glanced at his phone. "We should go."

Noah cleared his throat. "And we will—after you eat more than a mouthful of eggs. I don't cook eggs for just anyone, you know."

Levi had to smile. "They're good. I'm just not that hungry." From the moment he'd opened his eyes, his thoughts had defaulted to Grammy.

Noah narrowed his gaze. "What would Grammy say?"

He rolled his eyes. "Fine. I'll eat some more."

Noah grinned. "Hey, that really works. I'm thinking of having it put on a T-shirt. Or maybe a wristband." He pointed to the raisin toast. "Eat some of that, please. I even put out Grammy's lemon and ginger marmalade. You like that. And breakfast *is* the most important meal of the day."

Levi gave him a hard stare. "This is scary. It's like you're channeling her." He spread butter over a slice of toast. "I should call Eli and Amy before we leave for the hospital." Despite Noah's plea to let them sleep, he'd felt guilty about leaving them in the dark.

"I agree. Why don't you do that while I pour us another coffee?"

Levi caught Noah's arm as he stood. "Thank you."

"For what?"

"Last night for one thing. I was such a mess."

Noah leaned over and kissed him on the mouth. "You're welcome. Now make your call. Then we'll go see how Grammy is doing." He straightened and walked away from the table.

Levi sagged into his chair. So many turbulent emotions within him, all striving for dominance…Fear made his stomach clench, his chest tighten. *She's not out of the woods yet.* And if she did make it through this— *Please, God*—their lives would have to change. He'd look at what her diet should be, how much exercise she'd need to take…He was no fool. One heart attack could be the precursor to more of them, and he meant to lessen the chances of that happening, if he could.

And yet, beneath the layers of fear and anxiety, there was joy.

Noah loves me.

After all those years of longing, hoping, dreaming, something was *finally* coming right.

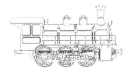

Tuesday, July 20

Levi sat beside her bed, holding her hand in his. The nurse—Sharon this time—said Grammy was taking a nap. Then her eyes had lit up as she'd commented, "Feisty, isn't she?"

Levi had chuckled. "You have *no* idea." They'd removed the intra-aortic balloon Monday afternoon, and she'd gone to Telemetry the same evening. The change in her had been amazing. She was still a little groggy from the sedative, but awake enough to complain about the six hours they'd made her wait before she could get out of bed and sit in her chair.

The doctor had been to see them, and the prognosis seemed positive. If she continued to make steady progress, the likelihood was she'd be home by the weekend.

The trickle of relief that had begun the previous day had swelled into a steady stream. *She's going to be okay.* Levi had lost count of how many times he'd thanked God. Noah's tight expression had finally relaxed. *He loves her too.* As if that had ever been in doubt. There'd been numerous calls from the others, and those living closest promised to visit in a day or two, once Grammy was fully on the road to recovery.

"Levi?"

He jumped. Grammy's eyes were open and looking right at him. "Hey," he said with a smile.

Grammy frowned. "Can I g' home now?" She wasn't totally awake.

Levi sighed. "No, not yet. You had a heart attack, remember?"

She let out a sigh. "Yeah." She glanced at the beeping monitor next to the bed, and the IV tube that went to the crook of her arm. Then she scanned her room. "Where's Noah?"

"He's gone to make some calls."

"Lettin' the gang know, huh?"

It was more a case of working out who would be visiting and when. "Something like that. I told Eli and Amy what happened. They'll be here this weekend. And barring any unforeseen incidents, you should be home by then." Levi met her gaze. "Why didn't you tell me?"

She blinked. "Tell you what?" Before he could respond, she sighed. "I'm sorry. There I go again, treatin' you like a child, and you're not. I should've said something, I know that, but…" She swallowed. "Can I have some water?"

Levi stood to find the nurse, but Sharon was already on her way. She did her observations, then poured water into a cup with a long bendy straw. "Don't gulp it this time."

Grammy gazed at her with narrowed eyes. "I was thirsty, all right?" She drank, then nodded. "That's better."

Sharon did a final check, then left them.

"You were saying?"

Grammy held out her hand, and Levi took it. "I don't have an excuse. Ignorin' it was a stupid thing to do. But all the advice that fool doctor was givin' me… 'Eat more whole grains.' 'Cut down your salt intake.' 'Don't eat processed meat.' 'Get more exercise.'"

Levi could almost hear the unspoken 'blah blah blah.'

"None of that sounds like bad advice to me," he remarked. He stroked her hand. "In fact, it sounds pretty sensible." And from what he'd read, she was about to receive the same advice once she got home.

She stared at him. "He told me to cut out sugar-sweetened beverages. Can you imagine me *not* havin' sweet, iced tea? The world would stop turnin'." Her eyes twinkled for a moment. "I talked with the doctor here, though. He said seein' as I'm not diabetic, I can keep drinkin' my tea. Ha." Then her face fell. "Oh my Lord, the stuff they've been feedin' me. I swear, they sucked all the taste right out of it. And *then* the doctor said I'll have to follow a special diet. If *that's* the sort of food I have to eat, they might as well order my coffin now, 'cause life won't be worth livin'."

Levi had heard enough. "You're seventy-one. Have you *really* had your fill of living so much that you'd ignore sound medical advice? *I'm* hoping you'll still be around to see your eighties and nineties."

She swallowed. "Sound kinda selfish, don't I?" Grammy let out a sigh. "Don't you be worryin' 'bout me. I ain't ready to meet my Maker just yet."

Levi bent over her and whispered. "Good. Because I'm not ready to lose you yet." When she closed her eyes, he stood. "You're still tired. I'll let you rest."

Grammy tightened her grip on his hand, her eyes popping open. "Want... want you to do something for me."

"What?"

"When you get home... go to the living room. You know that little drawer in my writing desk?" He nodded. "There's a key for it in my jewelry box. Open it, and you'll find something. Only one thing in there. Bring it to me, please?" Levi nodded once more, and she smiled. "Okay. Now let an old lady sleep some more."

He kissed her cheek. "And when you wake up, I'll be here."

Chapter Twenty-Four

Levi glanced at the pizza box. "Better get rid of the evidence before she comes home this weekend." They'd stopped at Seacoast Pizza on the way home from the hospital, after it became obvious neither of them felt much like cooking.

Levi was still buzzing. *She's going to be all right.* The weight of the last few days had slipped from his shoulders, and he felt lighter than air. All it had taken was the look in Grammy's eyes when she'd groused a little at her nurse. *That's my Grammy.* She wasn't going to be doing handsprings anytime soon, but the difference in her after forty-eight hours was enough to give him hope.

"Yeah, Grammy's not a fan of takeout." Noah chuckled. "Just how often do you go there?"

"Not that often." The words came out more defensively than he'd intended.

"Mm-hm." Noah's eyes sparkled. "Is that why they greeted you by name when you walked in?"

Levi stared at him. "Okay, so I *might* be a regular."

"And does Grammy know that?"

"No, and after our conversation today, she's never *going* to know." Her diet was going to have to change, and knowing Grammy, she'd complain about it. Then he recalled the rest of their talk. "She asked me to bring her something from her writing desk."

Noah widened his eyes. "Ooh. You have permission to open it?"

Levi chuckled. When they'd been growing up, Grammy's writing desk had been forbidden territory. He wasn't even allowed to *breathe* on it. He'd glimpsed inside it a couple of times, and had concluded its interior was definitely *not* a reflection of Grammy's usual ordered universe: there had been papers stuffed into crevices, receipts, letters… *Why wouldn't she let me anywhere near it?*

The worst thing Levi might have done was to tidy it.

"I'll go find the key." He went upstairs and into her room. Noah had righted the fallen lamp, and as Levi gazed at the rug beside the bed, his stomach clenched, recalling how frail she'd seemed, lying there…

No… She's going to be all right, remember?

Grammy's plain oak jewelry box sat on her chest of drawers. He smiled as he raised the lid to the sound of tinkling music. Levi could remember countless occasions as a little boy when he'd ask Grammy to let him hear its melody.

There was only one key sitting in the top tray, ornate and made of brass. He hurried downstairs, aware of Noah humming to himself in the kitchen. Levi had to smile. He stood in the doorway, watching as Noah filled the dishwasher and unashamedly staring at his ass, his jeans tight over it as he bent down.

For the first time in two days, Levi's dick showed a flicker of interest, and he resisted the urge to stroke his burgeoning erection.

"What *is* that tune you're so fond of?"

Noah closed the dishwasher, then straightened,

his face flushed. "Oh... that. It's from a show my grandpa used to watch all the time when I was a kid. *Casey Jones*. It was about a railway engineer who drove a train, the Cannonball Express. Grandpa said it only ran for one season. He loved to watch the reruns."

"You know every word of the theme song, don't you?" Levi grinned.

"And what if I do?" Noah's eyes gleamed, and he wiped them quickly. He gave Levi a sad smile. "Memories." He lowered his gaze to Levi's hand. "You found the key? Do we get to see what's in there?"

Levi had a good idea that was where Grammy had stored her letters from Granddad. "It's not locked. It never was. I just had to promise not to go in there." And because he feared the touch of Grammy's broom on his backside, he'd kept that promise.

They went into the living room, over to the varnished writing desk sitting in the corner. On top of it was a framed photo of Grammy and Granddad on their wedding day. Levi smiled at the image. Granddad wore a pale blue suit with black satin-edged lapels and matching bow tie, and Grammy had tiny white flowers in her hair, an abundant veil, and a white dress with a high lace collar.

He opened the desk and slotted the key into the lock of the tiny middle drawer. Inside was a small black velvet box.

"That looks like a ring box," Noah observed.

Levi opened it. Nestled in black was a plain gold band. He eased it from its slot and peered at the inside. "It's engraved." He smiled. "This was my granddad's wedding ring. I wonder why she wants it?" Levi put the ring back in its velvet bed and closed the box. He shook his head as he gazed at the chaos inside the desk.

"How does she ever find anything?" He placed the box on top of the desk.

"Knowing Grammy, I'd bet she knows exactly where to find something if she needs it." Noah leaned in to peer closer. "Although I don't know…" He picked up a receipt and chuckled. "This one is dated 1997."

Levi scanned the contents, and caught sight of a battered envelope on which was written *Report cards*. He plucked it from the stack of similar items and looked inside. "Aw. I think she's got all of them in here." He replaced the envelope. "What else has she kept?"

Noah pulled out a stiff card. "Oh wow. Your award for Awesome Attitude."

Levi flushed. "She was so proud of that one."

Noah nudged him with his arm. "That's because you won one every year." Then he stilled.

"What have you seen now?"

Noah reached into the bundle of papers and spiral-bound notebooks that filled one section of the desk. He carefully removed a notebook. "Isn't this your English notebook from high school? I recognized the cover."

Levi stared at it. A pale blue Happy Bunny wore a set of headphones, and the wording read *It's cute how you think I'm listening to you.* "You're right. What on earth is it doing in here?" Noah handed it to him, and Levi flicked through the pages to the front. "Oh wow. My notes on *The Importance of Being Earnest.* This was my last notebook before graduation." Why Grammy should have kept it, he had no idea. He leafed through it, smiling at the doodles he'd made, obviously when the class had gotten boring. But when he reached the back, his heartbeat quickened as he spied one word.

Noah…

Levi's heartbeat raced. *Oh Lord.* That *notebook.* He closed it, but Noah grabbed it.

"Was that my name I saw?"

"It's nothing," Levi said quickly, heat blooming in his cheeks. "Please, give it to me."

Noah arched his eyebrows. "Oh, now I *have* to see it." He thumbed through until he reached the final pages. "It's a letter. Why did you write me a letter and never give it to—" His lips parted, and a soft sigh fell from them.

Levi's heart pounded.

Noah raised his head and stared at him, his eyes glistening. "Oh, Levi…" He swallowed. "This is beautiful."

Levi couldn't recall what he'd written word for word, but he knew well enough the emotions that had given rise to its creation. "Ten, almost eleven years since I wrote that." He took a deep breath. "I couldn't quote from it, but… my feelings haven't changed."

Noah's Adam's apple gave a sharp bob. "This part… 'I guess it's easier to put everything in a letter than say it out loud. And there's so much I want to say to you." His gaze rose briefly to meet Levi's, then he went back to reading. "'When I was fourteen, something happened that made me realize I was gay. I met *you.* Can a person fall in love at fourteen? Stupid question, because I knew I was in love with you.'" Noah gazed at Levi with shining eyes, then went on reading. "'The way I feel about you has changed a little during the past four years. If I had to sit here and write exactly why I love you, I think I'd run out of paper. I love your sense of humor. It's uniquely *you*—dry, intelligent, observational…. I love your generosity.

These are all good things. So yes, I love you like a brother. You're my best friend. What you don't know is… I want to be more than that.'" His breathing hitched. "'I dream of holding you, kissing you…Okay, I dream of doing more than that, but I have a feeling that if I committed <u>those</u> thoughts to paper, they'd scorch the page." Noah's chest rose and fell. "'But college is right around the corner, and I have no idea where our different paths will lead us. I have to face reality. All those wonderful things I've dreamed of doing with you will probably stay in my head. But if just *one* of them could come true…which would I choose? Well… I think I know.'"

Oh God. Levi suddenly remembered the next part.

"'I sat in the cafeteria this morning, listening to Ry Cyr bragging to his buddies about how he'd hit a home run with Teresa Young last weekend. Not that I was surprised to hear that—those two have been dating since forever. No, what shocked me was, I listened to him sharing intimate details of what they'd done while his parents were away, and all I could think about was doing all those things—those deliciously dirty things— with you. Except I'd never tell a living soul. I'd want to keep the memory of my first time with you all to myself. Some things aren't made to be shared.'"

Heat barreled through Levi, his pulse racing, his breathing shallow and erratic.

Noah closed the notebook. "I don't think I need to read any more, do you? So let's put this back where it belongs." He inserted it into its original place, then turned to Levi. "You could've told me all this back then, you know."

Levi shook his head. "I was too scared. I didn't know if you were gay, straight, bi… I just knew I wanted you. But I couldn't make a move on you." He bit his lip. "Although… there *was* one time I tried to… to see if I could make something happen between us."

Noah frowned. "When?"

"That camping trip we all took… the one Aaron set up?"

"Yeah." Then Noah's eyes widened. "You sneaky little fucker. You said you'd forgotten to bring your sleeping bag, then asked if you could share mine."

Levi chuckled. "Too subtle?"

He laughed. "It's the kind of stunt Seb would pull."

"Where do you think I got the idea from? Seb did the same thing when we stayed over at Finn's one time." This time they both laughed.

"You didn't try anything, though," Noah commented. "At least, I don't think you did."

"Too chicken. Plus, all the guys were sleeping a few feet away from us. Not one of my better ideas."

Noah closed the desk, took Levi by the hand, and drew him toward the door.

"Are we going somewhere?" The effort it took to keep his voice even…

Noah smiled, his eyes glinting. "Yes, we are. We're going upstairs to your room…to do *deliciously dirty things*—together." He cocked his head to one side. "I think you've waited long enough, don't you?"

"That's a rhetorical question, right?" Levi managed to get out as they climbed the stairs, his heart thumping. *Oh dear Lord.* His whole body was vibrating with excitement, his stomach churning. When they reached his room, he chuckled. "I'm having déjà vu. I swear we've been here before." The levity didn't ease his pounding heartbeat, or the shivers that multiplied with each step.

Noah opened the door and led him inside. "Only this time, there's no one here but us. No interruptions...and all the time in the world." He sat at the foot of Levi's bed. "Supplies in the nightstand drawer?" Levi nodded, and Noah smiled. "Good, but we don't need those just yet." He cupped Levi's face and drew him down into a lingering kiss. Noah's lips were soft and warm, his tongue on a mission to explore Levi's mouth. Levi opened for him, his hands on Noah's neck, his fingertips registering the beat of Noah's heart.

"I think," Levi murmured between kisses, "that this could soon become... my favorite thing to do."

"I'm glad." Noah edged up toward the headboard, tugging Levi with him until Noah lay on his back and Levi was on top of him, one thigh inserted between Noah's. He cradled the back of Levi's head in his hands, looking into his eyes. "I have to tell you... this feels as if it's my first time too."

"What do you mean?"

"This is different. You know I'm no virgin, but... sex has always been a means to an end—and the end was an orgasm. I guess you could say I liked the outcome, but tolerated the guys who got me there. But now?" Noah pulled him closer, their lips meeting in a sweet kiss. "I want to savor this. I want to feel every shiver, hear every sigh and moan... I want to watch you lose it, watch you unravel..."

"So you're going to unravel me?" Levi's voice came out husky.

Noah nodded. "Starting with your clothes. Kneel up."

They knelt on Levi's quilt, facing each other, as

Noah removed first Levi's shirt, then his own tee. He ran his hands over Levi's chest. "Sexy man. Love this hair." He lowered his head and kissed Levi's nipple before teasing it with his tongue.

Levi shuddered, his breathing staccato, unable to hold in the low moans of pleasure that tumbled from his lips with every flick of Noah's tongue. Then he gasped when Noah pushed him onto his back, their mouths meeting once more in kiss after kiss, while Noah rocked against him.

"*Definitely* having déjà vu," Levi groaned as Noah's hard shaft met his.

Noah nuzzled his neck. "Feels good, doesn't it? Your dick pressing against mine."

"Oh yeah," he groaned. "You like that too?"

Noah gave a raw chuckle. "I think it could become *my* favorite thing." He snaked one hand between them, attempting to unfasten Levi's belt.

"Want some help with that?" Levi's fingers felt like thumbs as he pried the metal prong free of the hole it sat in. Between them, they got the task done, and Noah slid the belt from its loops and tossed it aside.

"Pants off." Noah tugged them, dragging them from his legs and throwing the garment to the floor. "And the briefs." There was less haste this time as he eased the black cotton over Levi's hips, freeing his erect cock that rose into the air, bobbing stiffly. Noah leaned in, kissing his dick, Levi's briefs around his knees. Then he removed his own jeans and the briefs, insinuating his legs between Levi's and kneeling there.

Noah crooked his finger. "Come here." Levi sat up, and Noah kissed him, his cock poking Levi in the chest.

Levi had to chuckle. "Well, that's a new

sensation." There was some weight to it, and he shivered at the thought of it penetrating him, filling him, stretching him…

There was no shadow of a doubt he wanted that.

Noah cupped the back of his head. "Tease my nipples?"

He didn't have to ask twice. Levi leaned in, his hands on Noah's belly and chest as he lapped the nipple with his tongue, loving the shudders that coursed through Noah. His heart soared to give Noah such pleasure, and in that moment the act they were about to unite in took on a whole new dimension.

They were *connected*.

He and Noah already shared years of friendship, of brotherhood, but this would create a different bond, one based on something Levi had longed for—love.

He tilted his head up to gaze at Noah. "Love you," he whispered.

Noah caught his breath. "Love you too, so much." He wrapped his hand around both their shafts, rubbing them against each other. The sensation was exquisite. Then Noah grasped his hand and guided it to their cocks, already slick with pre-cum. "Now *you* do it."

Levi nodded, moving his hand gently up and down, his breathing ragged.

Noah closed his eyes. "Oh, that's it." Levi thought his heart would burst. Noah cupped his chin, gazing into his eyes. "Want to taste your dick."

"Oh God, yes." He could still recall the noises that had poured from Noah when Levi had given his first blow job, and he couldn't wait to discover how good it could be.

Noah gave him a push, and Levi was once again on his back, his cock standing proud. Noah lay on his front, his hand curled around Levi's shaft, his lips tantalizingly close to the wide head of his dick. That initial lap of Noah's tongue over the knot of nerve endings under the flared ridge sent a violent shiver through him, and he arched up off the bed.

Noah grinned. "Oh, you like that."

Levi craned his neck to glare at him. "And yet you stopped." Noah laughed and resumed his flicking and licking, pausing to drag his tongue over Levi's balls before sucking them into his warm, wet mouth, one at a time. Levi shuddered. "Yes. Fuck, yes. Don't stop."

Noah's head bobbed as he took Levi deep, working the shaft with slick fingers. He pulled free, his lips glistening. "I think you're hard enough." He gave Levi's cock a squeeze. "I want to feel every inch of this." He gave the head a hard suck, and Levi groaned.

He gaped at Noah. "And now I want to feel that too." The prospect of sliding into Noah's body sent a trickle of hot anticipation through him, and his shaft swelled even more in Noah's mouth.

Noah moaned around his cock, pulled free, and flipped onto his back. "Get the supplies." He drew his knees toward his chest, and Levi had his first glimpse of tight puckered flesh set in a downy cleft. Noah cleared his throat. "Lube?"

Levi forced himself to tear his gaze away, and fumbled in the drawer. He dropped the bottle of lube and the box of condoms onto the bed, within reach of Noah.

"Get some lube on your fingers," Noah instructed. When Levi did so, Noah spread his ass cheeks, stretching the skin around his hole. "Now… slowly… push one inside."

Levi took a couple of deep breaths and eased a

single finger into Noah's body, catching his breath at the warmth that surrounded it. Noah nodded, his eyes focused on Levi's face, and encouraged, Levi pushed it all the way in, up to the knuckle.

"Aw fuck, yes." Noah's breathing quickened. "That's it, get me ready for your dick." Levi moved it in and out, keeping the movement gentle, until Noah was pushing down hard, fucking himself on it. "Add another." Levi stretched him a little more, loving the way Noah's channel clung to his fingers, sucking him in, so tight around them.

Noah grabbed him by the wrist. "Now, Levi. Please." His knees were at his chest, his feet in the air, his toes curling.

Levi opened the box, took out a condom, and tore the wrapper, his fingers trembling. Noah lent a hand to unroll the latex down his rigid cock, then squeezed lube over the head, smearing it along its length. He tossed the bottle onto the bed. "Kneel as close as you can."

Levi shuffled forward, and Noah stroked his gloved dick. He brought the head to his hole, his stomach quivering. "Now, put it in me, but slowly, okay?"

He nodded, his heart hammering, his chest slick with sweat. A gentle push, a little resistance, and *holy fuck*, he was inside Noah. He couldn't move, his dick sheathed in Noah's body.

Noah's chest was equally damp. "Kiss me?"

Levi shifted forward, and Noah rested his calves on Levi's shoulders, Noah's arms around him, holding him close as they kissed. Levi gave an experimental roll of his hips, and Noah rewarded him with a low moan. "You feel so good," he murmured.

Joy surged through Levi. "So do you." They kissed again, and then Levi picked up the pace a little, his breathing quickening as Noah clung to him, meeting his thrusts, moving in harmony with him.

And there it was again, that feeling of being connected, of it being so much more than a physical act joining them. Noah's groans punctuated his thrusts, and soon they were rocking together, both of them covered in a sheen of perspiration, his nostrils filled with Noah's scent, aware of him in a way he'd never been before.

Noah gasped. "Oh, holy fuck, the way you feel…" He rolled his hips up off the bed, locking them both into a rhythm. "Never… never felt this amazing. Don't want it to end." Levi sped up, and Noah locked gazes with him. "Can't last," he croaked.

Levi curved his hand around Noah's cock and gave it a few good tugs. "Then come," he demanded. "I won't be far behind." It didn't matter. *Nothing* could detract from the exhilaration that filled every part of him, the elation, the sheer fucking *joy* of making love to Noah.

Then Noah shot, and *oh God*, his body clamped down on Levi's cock, imprisoning him as Noah's warmth creamed Levi's hand. The sensation pushed Levi to the edge, and he came with a low cry, his dick throbbing inside Noah. Levi buried his face in Noah's neck, inhaling his smell, his cock still wedged in Noah's ass.

"Fuck." Noah grabbed Levi's nape, and then they were kissing, breathless, eager kisses that in Levi's mind only served to deepen their connection—joined in both body and soul.

Noah broke the kiss, panting. "Wow." He locked gazes with Levi. "That was off the scale." He gave Levi a fierce kiss. "Love you," he murmured against Levi's lips.

Levi couldn't speak. His throat was tight, his chest too. He held Noah's face in his hands, pouring his heart into every kiss.

Noah pressed his lips to Levi's damp forehead, then pulled back to look at him, his eyes shining. "Was that deliciously dirty enough?"

That joy he'd experienced was still bubbling close to the surface, threatening to spill out of him in a torrent of bright laughter. Levi stroked his cheek. "No. I think we need to try harder."

Noah laughed, and Levi felt it all the way through his dick still inside him. "Don't worry. I'll do better next time." Noah smiled. "And maybe next time, we should change things up a little."

Levi's pulse raced. "I like the sound of that." He'd imagined it often enough, and feeling Noah's body writhe beneath him only increased his desire to experience *everything*.

Well, maybe not everything. Some things he'd leave to Seb and Marcus.

Thirteen years of longing and hoping had culminated in him lying in the arms of the man he loved. "We got there in the end," he whispered.

Noah chuckled. "Sooner or later, you're going to have to come out of me."

"If I do that, then it's really over." He wanted to hold onto this moment for as long as he could.

Noah kissed the tip of his nose. "But if you don't, it'll make round two a little difficult."

Levi eased out of him in a heartbeat. "That was all the incentive I needed." He tied up the condom, and Noah handed him a tissue. After a quick clean up, they curled up together beneath the sheets, the sound of Noah's breathing lulling him to sleep.

Chapter Twenty-Five

Wednesday, July 21

Noah's phone buzzed, and he peered at the screen. "Aw damn."

"Problems?" Levi inquired. It was almost four o'clock, and it wouldn't be long before Sharon would be shooing them from Grammy's bedside. Then he smiled to himself. Grammy was quite capable of doing her own shooing.

"It's from a client. I'm working on his accounts at the moment."

Nestled in a pile of pillows, Grammy cackled. "He prob'ly thinks he needs a bigger rebate."

Noah pocketed the phone. "I'll go outside and call him."

"I won't be far behind you," Levi told him. "You might as well wait in the car."

"In that case…" Noah stood, went to Grammy's side, and leaned in to kiss her cheek. "Goodnight, Grammy. "I'll see you tomorrow."

She caught hold of his hand and squeezed it. "Go take care of business." She peered at his hand clasped in hers. "You got hands like my Robert. Always said he had elegant hands, long, slim fingers… You can tell a lot about a man by his hands." Then she released it. "Now get outta here. You got work to do."

Noah glanced at Levi. "See you at the car."

Once he'd left, Grammy beamed. "It's official.

I'm definitely comin' home Friday. Doctor said so this afternoon."

"Great." Levi grinned as he moved his chair closer to her. "I suppose I'd better clean up then. You know, get rid of all the beer bottles, the pizza and Chinese takeout boxes…" Not that there was anything to clean up. Neither he nor Noah was a slob.

Grammy cackled again. "It's been party, party, party while I've been in here, hasn't it? And don't think I haven't spotted the odd pizza box on the back seat of your car." She bit her lip. "Or was it supposed to be a secret?" Then she laughed. "You have your pizza. Just don't go buyin' me none. Never did understand what folks saw in it." She stared at him. "But the house had better be shinin' like a new pin when I get home."

He chuckled. "It will be. You're still way too handy with that broom." That earned him another cackle.

She pointed to a folder sitting on the table beside her bed. "That makes for depressin' readin'."

"What is it?" Levi picked it up and opened it. "Ah. Diet sheets. Well, you knew it was coming. You can't go through something like this and not expect to have to make changes to your life afterward."

Her brows knitted. "Fine, but why'd they have to make the food so boring?" She nodded at the folder in his hand. "That don't give a body anything to look forward to." Then her eyes twinkled. "The only bright spot on the horizon? That doctor I spoke with… He says I'll have more energy than I've had for a while. And that's because my heart is workin' properly now." Another scowl. "I guess I'll need that energy for all the exercise he wants me to get."

"And if all this means we have you with us for

longer, then it'll be worth it." He took her hand in his. "Not ready to lose you yet, lady."

She smiled. "Well, that works out just fine, 'cause I'm not ready to leave. Got too many things I wanna see happen before that." She peered at him. "I asked you to bring me something. Didn't you find it?"

Levi gave an apologetic sigh. "I'm sorry. I forgot it yesterday." He reached into his pocket and removed the ring box. He handed it to her. "This was Granddad's, wasn't it?"

She nodded, opening it and gazing at the gold band. "We almost made it to our silver weddin' anniversary, but he died the month before." She stared at her own ring. "Sharon says they took mine off before surgery—not that I remember—and then put it back after. My mom said hers never left her finger from the day my dad put it there." She took Levi's hand in hers, turned it to face palm upward, and placed the small box there. "I want you to have this."

His throat tightened. "Why?"

"You'd get it anyway, when I'm gone. But I wanted you to have it before then. You never know, you might want to wear it… one day." She stroked his cheek. "I wish you'd known him."

"Yeah, so do I." He plucked the ring from its black velvet bed. "Not sure this would fit on my fingers, except maybe on my pinky."

Grammy snorted. "Y'know, there's these wonderful places called jewelers, where they can alter a ring size. Because I'm told—believe it or not—that not everyone has the same size fingers."

Levi put the ring back in the box and returned it to his pocket. "You'd better make yourself look pretty—except you always look pretty—because a little bird tells me you're having visitors this evening."

She grinned. "I guess the gang's comin'."

"Not all of them. Ben and Aaron couldn't make it, but they send their love. Finn and Joel should be here though, as well as Shaun and Nathan, Dylan and Mark, and Seb and Marcus."

Grammy laughed. "Sharon will have conniptions if they all turn up at the same time."

"I'll tell them to stagger their visits, okay? Only two at a time."

She preened. "Makes me feel like royalty."

"Eli called. He and Amy are coming on Friday. I'll make sure the guest room is ready for them."

Grammy let out a sigh. "You're a good boy". She swallowed. "And I know I'm repeatin' myself, but I'm so damn happy about you an' Noah." The nurse arrived and Grammy squinted at her. "Now what? You checkin' I'm goin' to the bathroom regularly? Jeannie Crummel, I can't wait to be outta here."

The nurse aimed a hard stare at her. "We've already had this conversation, haven't we?"

Grammy bit her lip. "Sorry, Sharon. I know you're only doin' your job, but I haven't been this inactive since… forever."

Sharon smiled. "I know, but you'll be home soon." She glanced at Levi. "Your grandmother is a formidable lady."

Levi chuckled. "That's one word to describe her." He waited until Sharon had walked away before leaning in. "Grammy… Something I've always wondered about. Why do you say Jeannie Crummel?"

Grammy coughed. "I got into the habit when I was a teenager, I guess. Jeannie Cromwell was a woman who lived a few doors from us. Truth be told, she was just plain weird. Anyhow, I wasn't allowed to swear—you know, to take the Lord's name in vain, or even say Jeezum crow."

He chuckled. "Wow. That didn't last long, did it?" He could recall hearing the latter all the while he'd been growing up.

She grinned. "Yeah, that one slips out now 'n' then." Levi couldn't hold in his snort. "So instead, I said Jeannie Crummel."

Levi smiled. "I can't believe it's taken me this long to ask you." Then he remembered what else he'd discovered along with the ring box. There was still a mystery to be solved. "I have another question for you. When I went into your writing desk to find the ring, I found a lot of other stuff. Report cards, awards… And then I found something else—my English notebook." He stared at her. "You didn't keep any of the others—I know, because I checked—so I guess I'm curious as to why you kept that particular one."

She settled back against the pillows. "When you went to college, I tidied your room. There was so much stuff. I put all your textbooks on the shelf, but that left all your notebooks. I think I stored most of them in boxes, and shoved them out into the garage. But one caught my eye. That blue bunny on the cover…" Her eyes twinkled. "It made me smile. I looked through it mostly out of curiosity, to see if English studies had changed since I was in high school." She chuckled. "Not much, I can tell you. And then I got to the back…" She cleared her throat.

Oh God. Kill me now.

"You read my letter." His cheeks were on fire. Thank the Lord he hadn't written anything too graphic.

"Ayuh." Her face pinked.

"You never mentioned it."

She coughed. "It wasn't the kinda thing I thought you'd want to discuss."

"But that still doesn't explain why you chose to keep it."

She sighed heavily, then fell silent.

"Grammy?"

Her gaze met his. "Because I hoped that one day... you'd send it."

His mouth fell open.

Grammy took his hand in hers. "You held a torch for that boy for so many years, waitin' for him to see what was right under his nose. Well, after I read that letter, *I* was waitin' too." She smiled. "*Now* you know why I was so happy when you told me you were together. I knew how long you'd waited for this." Her smile widened. "You deserve a happy ending."

Levi did his best not to choke.

Grammy cocked her head to one side. "Has he read it now?"

He nodded. Then her confession hit home. "So all that stuff you said about noticing how I looked at Noah..." He widened his eyes. "You lied. You knew *exactly* how I felt about him, because you'd read the letter."

She blinked. "Oops?" Then she laughed. "Okay, I lied. Like Seb keeps sayin', bite me." She bit her lip. "I guess things are gonna be a little different when I get home. And I'm not talkin' 'bout the diets or the exercise. I'm gonna be sharin' the house with a couple. That might make life kinda... interesting."

This was definitely *not* a conversation Levi wanted to be having.

Then she grinned. "But I *have* come up with a

solution."

"A solution?" *To what?*

She nodded. "Something to spare *all* our blushes." Another grin. "I was chattin' 'bout you two with one of the nurses—don't you worry, I didn't go into specifics—but she came up with somethin' that I'll definitely have to invest in."

He did an exaggerated swallow. "I'm afraid to ask."

Grammy's eyes glittered. "Seems there are these amazin' things called noise cancelin' headphones."

Yeah, Grammy could still make him blush.

"And now we've got *that* out of the way…" She fixed him with a firm gaze. "Finn's wedding is soon, isn't it?"

He nodded. "Ten days from now. And they're moving into their new home on the twenty-eighth."

"Good for them. But what I wanted to say was… I'm goin' to the wedding."

Aw hell. "Fine. But you'll be going there in a wheelchair." He'd rent one for the day if he had to.

Grammy arched her eyebrows. "Good luck with that."

"Grammy," he protested. "I know you get around *way* better than a lot of people your age, but can I just state the obvious? You just had a *heart attack.* You need to take it easy for a while."

She narrowed her gaze. "Are you sayin' the only way I get to see Finn 'n' Joel married is from a wheelchair?"

"No. I'm saying you use a chair to get you to the venue. I don't expect you to stay in it for long. I know you too well. But at least, let me have the *illusion* of getting my own way."

That glint was still in her eyes. "I can do that. Jeezum crow, it's not like I'm about to get down an' boogie on the dance floor, all right?"

"'Boogie'?" He chuckled. "Showing your age there, Grammy. *And* you let it slip out again."

"You're not gonna let me forget that, are you?"

Levi grinned. "Not a chance."

He slipped his hand into his pocket, his fingertips brushing against the velvet ring box.

Maybe I won't need to resize it after all.

Chapter Twenty-Six

Thursday, July 22

Noah opened his eyes to find Levi sleeping on his side, facing him, his hand resting in the gap between them, as if he'd been reaching for Noah in his sleep.

Noah loved that idea.

Then Levi opened his eyes and blinked. "Why're you watching me sleep?" The drowsy edge to his voice was adorable.

"I wasn't watching you sleep. I opened my eyes and there you were."

Levi grinned. "Lies. You just want to stare at me."

Noah smiled. "And why would I do that?"

He shrugged one shoulder. "'Cause I'm gorgeous?"

Noah chuckled. "Okay, you got me there. You're gorgeous. You're also pretty cocky."

Levi laughed.

Noah shifted his leg across the gap and nudged Levi's morning wood with his knee. "Yup. That feels like cocky to me." He didn't miss the hitch in Levi's breathing.

"You got any strong feelings about morning breath?"

Noah raised his eyebrows. "You brushed your teeth last night, didn't you?" He grinned again.

"Because I know when we kissed goodnight, I couldn't taste my cum on your lips."

Apparently, that was the response Levi had been waiting for. "Then what are you doing over there? Come and kiss me."

Noah closed the gap between them and rolled onto him, kissing, Levi's arms around him. It wasn't long before Noah was writhing against him, both of them hard as nails.

Levi's breathing quickened, and his kisses grew more impassioned. "Have I mentioned... how much I like it... that you sleep naked too?"

Noah slid his shaft over Levi's, eliciting a groan of pleasure. "That feels just as good without the jeans." Then frotting gave way to sucking and licking, and Noah's heart pounded when Levi grabbed his head and held it steady while he fucked Noah's mouth.

That's it, Levi. Show me how you like it.

Noah pulled free, and gave Levi's solid cock a squeeze. "Seems a shame to let this go to waste." Minutes later they were both on their sides, Levi curled around Noah's back as he guided his gloved, slick shaft into him. Noah shuddered to feel Levi's cock fill him to the hilt.

"This is the only way to start the day," Noah said with a moan as Levi slowly withdrew, only to enter him at the same leisurely pace.

Levi leaned in and kissed his neck. "Maybe not the *only* way."

Noah twisted his upper body and they kissed, Levi's arm around him. "And now you've given me something to look forward to."

"Can't wait," Levi murmured. He groaned as he slid into Noah's body. "That feels amazing."

"Feels pretty amazing from where I am too." He put his arm around Levi's shoulders and kissed him, a deep, exploratory kiss that sent a wave of pleasure through him. "Love you."

"Love you too."

The combination of unhurried strokes, languid kisses, and whispered words of joy was just as mind-blowing as their first time, and the thought of more sensual discoveries to come sent a shiver of anticipation up and down Noah's spine.

Mark was right. I've found my person.

And now they were together, Noah couldn't let anything part them.

Levi glanced at the clock on the fireplace. "We should be at the hospital by now."

Noah smirked. "And whose fault is it we're still here? Hmm? I don't recall asking you to get into the shower with me."

Levi gave him a mock glare. "Didn't hear you protesting either." His phone buzzed, and he grinned. "That'll be Grammy, wanting to know what's keeping us." He glanced at the screen, and stilled. "It's Eli." He clicked on answer. "Hey. Is everything okay? You're still coming tomorrow, right?"

"Yeah, everything's fine. It's just… Do you think we might find a quiet moment for a chat? Not now—I can't talk about this over the phone. And besides, Dad's here."

"This doesn't sound as if everything's okay."

"Nothing wrong, I promise. Just… something I need to share, and I know you'll understand." A pause. "Oops. Dad's got that look in his eye. I've gotta go. See you tomorrow. We should be there by dinner time."

"See you then." Levi ended the call.

"What's up?" Noah inquired.

"Eli wants to talk." Then his phone buzzed again, and he smiled. "Okay, this time it really *is* Grammy. She wants me to bring some clothes for tomorrow."

"Then let's go check out her closet."

Levi followed Noah up the stairs. "I'm glad she's coming home, but—"

"But it's been awesome having the place to ourselves," Noah finished. "Once she's back, we need to decide if we're going to share a room permanently. And if so, which one."

Levi grinned. "That's an easy choice. The one farthest from Grammy's." Then he sighed. "Things will have to be very different for a while, at least until she's fully recovered."

"Is that what you're going to tell her?"

Levi shrugged. "It's a conversation that has to happen."

Noah snorted. "Good luck with that."

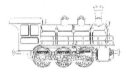

The first things Levi noticed as he approached Grammy's bed were the flowers. They were *everywhere,* their colors so bright against the white walls. There was even a teddy bear sitting on the cabinet, clutching a bunch of rainbow-colored balloons.

Levi placed the bag at the foot of the bed. "You have a few more cards than yesterday. Among other things."

She cackled. "That's 'cause I had a stream of visitors. Three guesses who, not that you need that many." Grammy regarded them with gleaming eyes. "I *was* gonna ask why you weren't here first thing, like you've been all week. Then I realized I knew better than to open my mouth." She pointed to the bag. "What did you bring?" Levi opened the overnight bag to show her, and she smiled. "Good choice."

"Have they given you any indication when they'll discharge you?" Noah asked.

Grammy shook her head. "All I know is I have to wait till the doctor gives the all-clear. As soon as that happens, either they'll call you, or *I* will." Her eyes still held a gleam. "I guess it'll depend on who gets to the phone first." She gave a wistful smile. "Can't wait to get back in my kitchen."

Noah cleared his throat, but Levi got in first. "It looks as if your visitors did you a power of good. I hope they didn't disturb any of the other patients."

"They were angels," Grammy insisted. Levi blinked, and she burst into laughter. "Okay, they weren't *that* good." She inclined her head toward the drawer in the cabinet. "Take a peek in there," she whispered, giving a furtive glance toward the nurses' station.

Levi was intrigued. He pulled the drawer open, and found three boxes of chocolates. He frowned. "Why have you hidden them?"

She widened her eyes. "Because I don't want

some fool doctor seein' 'em and tellin' me I can't have chocolate."

"But you *can*," Levi insisted. "In moderation, of course. It's not as if you're diabetic."

Grammy blinked. "Really?"

He sighed. "It's time we had The Talk."

She snorted. "As long as it isn't like the one I gave you. I think that kind of… activity has passed me by." Then she squinted at him. "And before you start layin' down the law, you need to keep something in mind. I may be seventy-one—and I love you more than my luggage—but push me too far an' I'll tell you where to go, how to get there, *and* I'll give you cab fare." She grinned. "I've been wantin' to use that luggage line ever since I heard it in *Steel Magnolias*."

"But you *are* going to listen to what I have to say, aren't you?"

"What *we* have to say," Noah corrected him. "Because I'm with Levi on this."

Grammy locked gazes with Levi. "You're gonna be regular pains in the backside, aren't you?"

He folded his arms. "If it keeps you healthy, then yes." He grinned. "Bite me." Levi perched on her bed, and took hold of her hand. "I've been looking at the hospital's Cardiovascular Health page."

"Hmm. They told me to check it out too," she muttered.

"Good. Then we're on the same page—literally." He cocked his head. "Have you looked at it yet?"

"No. Figured I'd wait till I was outta here. But I can guess the kind of thing I'll see on it. Diet, exercise…" She cackled. "I'm not about to take up swimmin' in the ocean."

"You don't have to. Quest Fitness isn't that far

from us, and they have a great indoor pool." Levi folded his arms. "And I'll bet the Cardiology department will have a list of other places where you can go."

Grammy huffed. "Yeah, you'd win that bet." She peered at him. "You've really done your homework on this one. But then, you always did, so I shouldn't be surprised."

Levi smiled, leaned over, and kissed her cheek. "And you wouldn't have me any other way."

She sighed. "Ain't that the truth?" She squared her shoulders. "What else did you read?"

"Well, one of the first things they talk about is cardiac rehab. It's a program designed to help you recover."

"Program?" She frowned. "How long does it last?"

"About three months. And it's only a couple of times a week. They'll just supervise, and offer you support and coaching." Levi could have left the talk until she was home, but he wanted to be straight with her—well, as straight as it was possible for a gay man to be. "It sounds as if it's worth doing, especially if it helps you prevent another heart attack."

"You know all those naps you've been taking recently?" Noah smiled. "Well, you keep right on taking them, at least until you get your strength back." He held up his hand. "Yeah, I know you *feel* fighting fit, but you're not. You need to take it easy for a while. That's all we're saying. Because if you do that now, you could be back in that kitchen in a few weeks."

She stared at him. "Back in the—who's gonna be doin' the cookin', may I ask?"

"We are." Levi squared his jaw. "You got

something to say about that?"

She bit her lip. "Not where I can be overheard in polite comp'ny, that's for sure. I think I'd better increase my life insurance premiums. I wonder if my policy covers poisoning?" Her eyes twinkled.

"But one thing *is* going to change." Levi locked gazes with her. "If you have *any* of the symptoms you had before—pain in your jaw or chest, shortness of breath, tiredness—then you *tell* us, you hear? You don't try to hide it."

Grammy sagged against her pillows. "You don't have to tell me twice. I should've said something, I know that. And I promise I'll tell you if I'm feelin' ill." She stilled. "But you're gonna be stickin' to those diet sheets, right?"

He nodded. "More fruit and vegetables. Fish, chicken, or tofu instead of red meat. I'll keep an eye on saturated fats too. Less salt—and less fried food."

She rolled her eyes. "Jeannie Crummel, you're gonna suck all the joy out of eatin', aren't you?" But before he could respond, she took his hand in hers. "Don't you mind me. I'm still adjustin'. I'll come around." She smiled. "It's hard to be annoyed with someone who's only lookin' out for ya 'cause they love ya."

"We do," Noah confirmed. He walked around her bed and sat on the other side.

Grammy held their hands. "Love you too, boys. I'm sorry I gave you such a scare. I don't ever wanna do that again."

"So you'll be good?" Levi asked.

She grinned. "Well, I wouldn't go *that* far."

Chapter Twenty-Seven

Friday, July 23

Levi walked into the bedroom, rubbing his hair with a towel. Noah sat on the bed, naked, leaning back on his hands, his dick pointing to the ceiling.

Levi chuckled. "Are you trying to get my attention? Because it worked."

"I was just thinking…"

He let out another wry chuckle. "Yeah, and I can see where it took you."

Noah gave him a mock glare. "Can you stop thinking about my cock for a second? It just occurred to me, this is our last chance for a while to be alone."

Levi sighed. "I had the same thought while I was in the shower. I mean, I'm happy she's coming home, but at the same time…"

Noah bit his lip. "Didn't we have this conversation yesterday?"

"Yes, but…" Levi's gaze drifted lower to Noah's erection. "There's something I'd like to do *before* she comes home. Something I'd like a little… privacy for."

Noah's eyes widened. "Oh."

Levi nodded. He unfastened the towel from around his hips, letting it fall to the floor, his dick springing up. He walked slowly toward the bed, and Noah sat upright.

"You sure about this?"

Levi gestured to his hard cock. "What does that tell you?"

Noah laughed. "That I'd better get the supplies ready."

"About that... Do you think we could maybe drive to Portland soon?"

"Tired of latex already?"

Levi cleared his throat. "I don't want anything between us. Not even latex. Is that wrong?"

Noah's pupils enlarged a little. "No, not at all." He reached into the nightstand drawer and removed the lube and condoms. Then he crooked his finger. "Come here."

Levi joined him on the bed, and they kissed, their hands all over each other, stroking, caressing, teasing... Noah pushed him onto his back, kissing his way up Levi's body until he reached his lips. He rolled his hips, sliding his shaft over Levi's, and Levi moaned. "My favorite thing. You remembered."

Noah bent down to kiss his neck, eliciting a shiver. "You owe me some sounds."

"Huh?"

He propped himself up on his hands, looking Levi in the eye. "Remember the night I proved to you how much you turn me on?" Levi nodded, his heart lurching into a higher gear. "You told me where you wanted my tongue, about watching guys getting their asses licked, and how hot it sounded. You said something about how they couldn't believe how good it feels."

Oh God. Levi's heart was hammering. "And you... you said you wanted to hear the sounds I'd make—"

"When I pushed my tongue inside you. Well...

don't you think it's time we *both* get what we want?"

He swallowed. "Yes." Then Noah kissed him on the lips, a sweet, tender kiss as soft and comforting as his quilt. Levi wrapped his arms around him and deepened the kiss, heat flooding through him at the thought of what was to come. Noah nuzzled his neck, then moved lower, planting a trail of kisses down his torso, dipping his tongue briefly into his navel before burying his nose in Levi's pubes.

"Love how you smell," Noah murmured. He raised his chin and grinned. "Except you smelled better *before* the shower."

Before Levi could respond, Noah grabbed his thighs and pushed Levi's knees to his chest, rolling his ass up off the bed. "And there it is. Such a pretty little hole."

Levi stared at him, his breathing erratic. "Holes aren't pretty."

Noah's eyes gleamed. "Yours is. All tight, pink, and puckered, just waiting for me." He licked over it, and Levi gasped. Noah grinned again. "Hey, what do you know about that? It's delicious too." The next moment, Levi's breathing hitched when Noah pressed the tip of his tongue against his entrance, exerting a little pressure. Levi's shivers multiplied, and he couldn't lie still. He rocked, and Noah pushed his face into Levi's crease, licking over his hole again and again.

"I've changed my mind," Levi blurted. When Noah blinked, he shuddered. "*This* is my favorite thing."

Noah's eyes sparkled. "Mine too." And then he went back to teasing and licking, until Levi couldn't take much more.

"You're gonna make me come."

Noah shifted in a heartbeat. "Not yet." He knelt up, grasped Levi's ankle, and brought his foot to his lips. Noah kissed his toes before sucking on them, sliding his tongue between them.

"Oh my God." Levi's body tingled, and something fluttered deep in his belly. Noah didn't stop, and Levi couldn't take his eyes off him. "That is so… *hot.*"

Noah pulled free. "Another new favorite?"

Levi shook his head. "It's good, but your tongue on my hole has it beat."

Noah grabbed a pillow and stuffed it under Levi's ass. "That'll help. It changes the angle. Or we could do this doggy style, or you could ride me. That might be easier."

Levi bit his lip. "And if I wanted to do it in this position?"

Noah smiled. "You're in charge, seeing as it's your ass." Then he reached for the bottle of lube, and squeezed some onto his fingers. "I think the best is yet to come." He nodded to Levi's knees. "Hold them." Levi did as he was told, holding his breath as Noah pushed a single finger into his body, taking his time.

Noah stilled. "Breathe, Levi. You'll find the more you relax, the easier it is to take a dick."

Levi struggled to draw air into his lungs. Noah's finger in his ass felt *huge,* so he could only imagine what his cock would feel like. But Noah remained motionless, and little by little, Levi willed himself to relax.

"That's it." Noah's voice was warm. Then he leaned over to kiss Levi's mouth while he slowly moved his finger in and out. Levi moaned into the kiss, and as the minutes passed, his discomfort ebbed, until he was eager for more. Noah added another finger, and for a moment that burning sensation returned, only to fade when Noah applied more lube.

"Tell me when you're ready," Noah whispered.

Levi locked gazes with him. "Now?"

Noah smiled. He sat up, knelt at Levi's ass, and unrolled the condom over his rigid cock. He swiped slick fingers over it, then brought the head to Levi's pucker. Levi did his best to breathe through it as Noah penetrated him at the same leisurely pace. When he was fully seated, Noah bent to kiss him, and Levi flung his arms around Noah's neck. Noah gave a gentle roll of his hips, withdrawing a little, and Levi's breath stuttered.

"You okay?"

Levi nodded. "It feels good, but it hurts too." He looked Noah in the eye. "Don't stop though."

"I won't. And it feels incredible." Another slow thrust, and Noah was all the way in again. They kissed as Noah moved in and out with a rocking motion. Levi's discomfort faded, as the first waves of pleasure surged over him. Levi held him in his arms, his heartbeat racing, electric tingles zapping through him with every measured thrust.

Noah picked up the pace a little, then slowed once more, drawing a long sigh from Levi. "*Oh*, that's good." He gazed at Noah's flushed face. "This is heaven. Holding you, feeling your body against mine, you inside me... the way you smell..."

Noah smiled. "You were right, of course." When Levi managed an inquiring glance, Noah kissed him, then whispered into his ear, "You *are* gorgeous." He arched his back, moving a little faster. "Still can't believe this is real."

"Come here," Levi pleaded. Noah covered him with his body, and Levi clung to him, his hands on Noah's back. "Now kiss me."

Noah's lips met his, and Levi rocked with him, losing himself in the sensations that threatened to overwhelm him: the slick sound of Noah's cock as he drove it in and out; the musky, warm smell of Noah's body against his; the glisten of sweat on Noah's brow and chest; and the glorious feeling of being filled, again and again.

It was too much.

He groaned against Noah's lips. "Coming."

Noah's scorching kiss only hurried his approaching orgasm. "Then come. I'm close too." He curled his hand around Levi's dick and gave it a couple of tugs, and that was all it took. Levi shot, his body jolted by the tide of euphoria that crashed over him, lifted him, and left him trembling in its wake.

Noah's moan reverberated around the room. "Oh, fuck." He slammed into Levi then froze, and Levi shivered when Noah's cock pulsed inside him, aware of every throb. Noah kissed him, shaking. They lay together, their chests slick with sweat.

Levi shuddered out a breath. "And now... I need another shower."

Noah kissed his neck. "Want me to wash your back?"

He smiled. "You can wash whichever parts of me you want."

Noah eased out of him and flopped onto his back, one hand holding onto the condom. "New favorite thing?"

Levi laughed. "I think I'll need to try it one more time. Just to be sure."

"Mm-hmm." Noah removed the condom, tied it, and placed it on the torn wrapper. "Well, can I suggest you wait a while before round two? I speak from experience."

Levi shifted onto his side, and laid his head on Noah's damp chest. "Whatever you say." He craned his neck to gaze at Noah. "And in case I forget to mention it… that was… amazing."

Noah cupped his chin. "That's because *you* are amazing." He glanced at the alarm clock.

Levi sighed. "I know. We need to get ready. The hospital could call at any minute."

"There's always tonight," Noah murmured.

Levi gaped at him. "But… she'll be across the hall. Plus, Eli and Amy will be in the next room."

"Then we'll be quiet."

He frowned. "I'm not sure I can be *that* quiet."

Noah shrugged. "Well, it's either that, or… we don't have sex again while she's in the house."

There was a pause before Levi found his voice. "I'll be quiet."

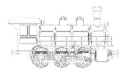

Grammy glared at the wheelchair. "It's goin' back to the hospital, right?"

Levi sighed. "We've talked about this. It's staying for a while. Now, is there anything you'd like?"

"I s'pose coffee 'n' cookies are off the menu," she groused.

Levi bent down and kissed her forehead. "If

you'd read the diet sheets like you were told to, you'd know coffee is fine. Maybe limit it to four or five cups a day, though." He paused. "Cookies, on the other hand…"

Her face fell. "Yeah, I thought as much."

"It's the sugar."

"And you're already sweet enough," Noah quipped from the couch by the front window.

Grammy arched her eyebrows. "Lord, but he's got a smooth tongue."

It was all Levi could do not to choke.

"They're here," Noah called out.

Levi hurried into the hallway to open the door. Eli led the way, carrying an overnight bag. Amy tugged a carry-on after her.

"Moving in?" Levi teased as they stepped inside. Amy deposited her case by the stairs before giving him a hug. Then she headed into the living room. Grammy's exclamation of delight made him smile.

"I'm here till Sunday afternoon," Eli told him. "Amy wants to stay longer, so I'll go home and help Dad. Then I'll come back for her a week today." He cocked his head. "You have a wedding to go to soon, right?"

"Yeah, the thirty-first."

Eli glanced toward the living room door. "And we can talk at some point?"

"Sure. How about after dinner?"

He smiled. "Sounds great. Now I've got to see Grammy." He hurried into the living room, just as Noah emerged.

"I'll get started on dinner, now they're here." He smirked. "You got out of there awful fast."

"I had to, just in case Grammy wanted to say

something else about your smooth tongue."

Noah leaned in and whispered, "But you *know* it's true." Then he made a dash for the kitchen when Levi tried to smack his butt.

Where did the quiet, contemplative Noah go to?

Not that Levi was complaining. Noah 2.0 promised to be a lot of fun.

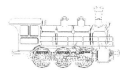

Levi went into the kitchen where Noah and Eli were chatting while Noah loaded the dishwasher. From the dining room came the strains of piano music.

Noah inclined his head toward the sound. "What's she playing? That's beautiful."

"Satie," Eli informed him. "One of his 'Gnossiennes', number one, I think. Amy's been working on it to play for Grammy. It's all she's played since our last visit." He smirked. "You *can* have too much of a good thing, y'know."

Levi pushed the door to. "Okay, Grammy's having her own personal concert. Suppose we talk in here? Unless it's something you'd rather not discuss in front of Noah?"

Eli shook his head. "No, that's fine. He might be able to help too." He pulled out a chair and sat at the table.

"This is all very mysterious." Levi sat in the chair facing him.

Eli rested his chin on his steepled fingers. "The thing is… You know you asked me if there was anyone? And I said no."

"Let me guess. You were lying—or there is now."

Eli's face flushed. "Okay, I was lying… kinda. You see, there's this guy who's a regular customer at the store. Comes in maybe once a week. But…"

"But what?" Levi asked in a low voice.

"It's sort of… complicated."

Noah chuckled. "*Life* is complicated."

"Clearly, something is stopping you from saying anything to this customer," Levi surmised. "The most obvious thing being… he's not gay."

Eli's brow furrowed. "I think he might be. I mean, sometimes I catch him looking at me. But no, that's not it. What stops me from making a move on him is… his age."

"Older guy, huh?" Levi leaned back in his chair. "How old are we talking?"

"Really old. Maybe in his thirties."

Noah smothered a snort, and Levi tried not to laugh. "Okay. Let me point something out here that might make you feel better about approaching this guy. You've heard us talk about our group of friends, right?" Eli nodded. "Well, out of six of them, one has a partner in his thirties—and four have partners in their forties."

Eli widened his eyes. "Seriously?"

"But what's *more* important is that the age difference hasn't mattered once to any of them," Noah remarked. He gave Eli a kind smile. "It's only a problem if you let it be. There's nothing wrong with someone your age dating a guy in his thirties. Although, if I can just say something here… When we take you and Amy to Aaron's cookout in August, *please*, don't voice the opinion that someone in their thirties is really old."

Levi chuckled. "What he said."

Eli heaved a sigh. "Then you think I should say something to him?"

"Only if you're sure he's not going to give you a smack upside the head," Noah advised him. "That's always a worry when it's not obvious whether a guy is into men or not. Just… play it by ear."

"Thank you." Eli sagged into his chair.

"What's he like, this mystery customer?" Levi inquired.

Eli's face glowed. "He's a good-looking dude. Taller than me, looks like he can take care of himself. And he rides a Harley."

Levi arched his eyebrows. "A biker?" He peered at Eli. "Have you ever ridden a motorcycle?"

"Nope." Eli's eyes sparkled. "But there's a first time for everything, right?"

In the dining room, the beautiful, haunting music came to a stop.

Levi stood. "We'd better get in there, before Her Majesty starts hollering for us."

Eli rose, and hugged him tightly. "Thanks."

Noah frowned. "That's the front door opening. Did Amy forget something?"

They left the kitchen and went into the living room. Grammy pointed to the front of the house. "Did either of you check the mailbox today?"

Levi shook his head. "We were in too much of a hurry, coming to collect you." Amy came into the room, carrying a familiar brown package. She handed it to Grammy, who grinned.

"I hoped it might get here today. I ordered it a couple days ago." She didn't make a move to open it, however.

"Well? Don't we get to see whatever it is?" Noah asked, his eyes twinkling. "Or is it a surprise?"

Levi swallowed. Suddenly he had a very good idea what lay concealed in the package. He grabbed Noah's arm. "Let's go make the coffee," he suggested, tugging Noah from the room.

Once they were in the hallway, Noah gave him a perplexed glance. "What's going on with you?"

Levi opened his mouth to reply, only to be interrupted when Amy asked in her clear voice, "But why do you need noise-canceling headphones?"

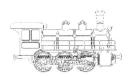

Wednesday, July 28

"Is that it?" Noah demanded, flopping onto a plastic-covered couch next to Levi. "Because I don't think I could carry another box if you paid me." It had taken them most of the day—and one U-Haul and several cars—to move every last bit of Finn and Joel's belongings to their new home on Water's Edge Drive, Lincolnville. With more than two hours' driving time between the house and Goose Rocks Beach, there was only ever going to be one trip.

Finn walked into the living room, carrying a bucket filled with cans of soda nestled in ice. "I think we can all use one of these." He set it down on the hearth.

Ben grabbed a couple of cans, and handed one to Wade. "Well, if the house you build for us is anything like this one…" He beamed. "I'll be a very happy man.

This is amazing." He gazed at the fireplace. "I love this. And as for that dining room…" His eyes shone. "There's a view of the ocean."

"You'll have a similar view," Finn told him. "And once the wedding is out of the way, I can get started on your place."

"You have a lovely home," Nathan said with a smile. Finn thanked him.

"The U-Haul is empty," Mark declared as he and Dylan entered the room. "And I hope there are snacks, because I'm starving."

Joel chuckled. "I think we can do better than that. We've booked tables at Franny's Bistro in Camden. Great food, great atmosphere… It was the least we could do after everything you all did today." A chorus of *whoops* greeted his words.

Finn scanned the room. "I thought it was quiet in here. Where's Seb?"

"He and Marcus went for a walk," Levi told him. "Just to the water's edge and back, they said."

Aaron joined them, depositing a box on the floor. "Finn… Something I've been meaning to ask. Does your dad know you're getting married?"

The others fell silent. All the friends knew why Finn's parents had divorced. He'd never made a secret of it.

Joel walked over to him and put his arm around Finn's waist. "We don't think so."

"It's not as if I could send him an invite, right?" Finn said brusquely. "There hasn't been word of him since the divorce. For all I know, he's drunk himself to death by now." He squared his shoulders. "Fuck him. Let's talk about something else."

Joel kissed him on the cheek. "Good idea."

Despite Finn's set jaw and steely gaze, Noah figured it still had to hurt.

He has us now. And as families went, they were an awesome group of guys.

"Hey, Levi?" Dean piped up. "I've got that book you lent me. It's in my truck. Remind me to give it back before we go to dinner." He gave Levi a meaningful stare.

Levi frowned, and then Noah nudged him with his elbow. Levi coughed. "Oh. Yeah. I'd forgotten. How about we do that now? That way, neither of us will forget."

"Sure." Dean headed for the door.

Levi got up from the couch and followed him, Noah quickly joining him. When they were outside on the gravel driveway, Levi chuckled. "I'm sorry. I guess I must be tired."

"Are you pleased with it?" Noah asked as they went to the back of Dean's truck.

"It doesn't matter if I am or not—*you're* the clients." He removed a large brown paper bag, and handed it to Levi, who peered inside. "I *was* going to mail it, until I remembered about today."

"Oh, Dean." Levi pulled the bag open so Noah could get a better look. "It's beautiful. You've really captured them."

Noah studied the delicate pencil sketch. "They'll love it. What do we owe you?"

"You don't, remember? This is my gift to you two." His expression grew serious. "How is Grammy?"

Noah smiled. "She's doing well." He nudged Levi. "*Someone* didn't want to leave her today, until I reminded him Amy's there, and Grammy would've killed him if he'd said he was going to stay on her account."

"I can believe that," Dean murmured. He glanced toward the house. "I didn't know about Finn's dad."

"His mom will be there, that's all that matters," Levi told him. Then he clammed up as the front door opened, and everyone came outside. "Looks as if it's time to eat. I'd better put this book someplace safe," he said in a stage whisper.

Noah chuckled. "Good idea."

K.C. WELLS

Chapter Twenty-Eight

Saturday, July 31

Levi peered through the open barn door toward the shady ceremony grove where most of the guests had already gathered, seated on long wooden benches. The treetops met over the seating and the flower-covered arbor, and the dappled sunlight created a romantic atmosphere. Hidden speakers poured out piano music, low and unobtrusive.

Noah appeared at his side. "Can you see her?"

Levi scanned the assembled guests and smiled. "Found her." Grammy had ditched the wheelchair—no surprise there—and was sitting with Finn's mother, Carrie, and Eric. Then he spotted a couple of women with them, who had to be Joel's sister Megan and her wife Lynne. Joel's daughter Laura wore a long dress of pale green satin and one of her customary wide-brimmed hats, decorated with matching satin ribbon. The handsome young man standing beside her had to be Nate's boyfriend, Carter.

Levi smiled to himself. *Nate has good taste.*

"I'll go see if we're nearly ready." Noah left the barn and headed along the gravel path toward the grove.

"Is it time?" Finn hadn't been able to stand still ever since Levi had brought him to the barn.

He chuckled. "Almost. We're still missing one very important part, however."

Finn's eyes widened. "You have the ring, right? Don't tell me you left it at our place."

Levi patted the tiny pocket in his waistcoat. "Relax. It's here. And I was talking about Joel."

"He's with Nate... somewhere." Finn smiled. "Nate looks so cool in his suit. Carter does too." He stilled.

"Something wrong?"

Finn bit his lip. "I wanted to thank you for sharing with me... about your mom. I guess you've really been through it the last couple of weeks."

"I think Grammy's heart attack was brought on by all the stress." Levi sighed. "But I can't wait for you to meet Eli and Amy."

Finn smiled. "That's the one good thing to come out of this. You got yourself a brother and sister."

"It's not the *only* good thing," Levi corrected him. "I learned the truth. My mom never stopped thinking about me and Grammy, not once." He paused. "Just like somewhere, your dad might be thinking about you."

Finn's breathing hitched. "That's why you told me about your mom. You think I should try to find my dad? After what he did?"

Levi held up his hands. "It was a long time ago, you've said as much. And maybe he got help, like my mom did. Maybe somewhere, he's waiting for a phone to ring, because he's too scared to do it himself." He took a deep breath. "What if he's an older, sober man, who just wants to make amends?"

Finn swallowed. "I always said you were the peacemaker of our little band."

"Then you'll think about it?" It had been on Levi's mind since the moving day, hearing the bitterness in Finn's voice.

Finn said nothing for a moment, and Levi wondered if it was simply a step too far. Then he nodded. "After the wedding, okay? I'll talk to Mom. Maybe we can get a lead on where he is." Levi crushed him in a tight hug, and Finn gasped. "Hey, you'll wrinkle my suit." He gestured to his body. "Do *I* look okay?"

Levi placed his hands on Finn's shoulders. "You look great. Now please, breathe? Everything is going to be perfect."

"That's what I've been telling him for the last week," Joel said, joining them. "Anyone would think he was nervous." His eyes twinkled. He wore an elegant dark grey suit, and there was a red rosebud in his lapel.

"That's because I am!" Finn retorted. "Not about marrying *you*—I just want this whole day to go without a hitch."

"And it will," Joel assured him in a low voice. He leaned in and kissed Finn on the lips. "You're about to make me the happiest man on the planet."

Finn shuddered out a breath. "Love you."

"Love you too." Joel pointed to the tables behind them, covered in snowy white cloths, with sparkling glasses and gleaming silverware, each with a centerpiece of red roses. Chandeliers spilled warm light around the barn's interior. "And this looks pretty perfect to me."

Finn followed his gaze. "It does, doesn't it? Plus, I like the idea of leaving the barn door open while we eat. Kinda brings that peaceful, leafy backdrop into the room with us." His eyes twinkled. "Did we tell you about this place? They've got this deal going. It's called Love/Give. A percentage of the proceeds goes to a charity of our choice." He clasped Joel's hand. "We chose the Trevor Project."

Levi's chest swelled. "I think that's awesome."

Noah appeared at the door. "Guys? We're ready for you. Nate's waiting by the arbor."

"Then I'd better join him." Levi gave the two men a hug, then he and Noah walked briskly along the path. By the time they reached the green arbor, its posts covered with climbing roses, the piano music came to a stop, and instead, a guitar played. It was a recording of Eva Cassidy's soulful rendition of 'Songbird'. The guests rose, and everyone turned to watch Finn and Joel walk slowly toward them, holding hands.

The front rows on the left were taken up with their friends, and Levi didn't miss Ben wiping his eyes as Finn and Joel drew closer. Not that he was the only one displaying such emotion—Seb's eyes glistened too. Noah took his place next to Aaron, and gave Levi a nod.

Love you, he mouthed.

Levi mouthed back at him, *Love you too*. Then he gave all his attention to the approaching couple.

Finn and Joel stood in front of the celebrant, and the ceremony began.

Levi was half-listening, his mind someplace else. His speech was in his inside pocket, but he wasn't worried about it. He'd done enough practice runs with Noah to feel more confident about speaking in front of the guests. Besides, what he'd written was tame compared to the books Noah had made him read aloud from.

What occupied his mind was something else entirely.

It came as a shock when Finn coughed, giving him a meaningful stare. Levi hurriedly removed the ring and handed it over. Finn bit back a smile, then proceeded to look into Joel's eyes as he slipped the ring onto Joel's finger. Joel repeated the process, not breaking eye contact as he intoned his vows.

When the legalities were over, the celebrant turned them to face their guests. "I have the honor to present, Joel and Finn Hall."

Nate let out a *whoop*, then threw handfuls of rose petals over them. "Congratulations!" Laura joined in, and the two men were caught up in a blizzard of petals.

"I think you've thrown enough," Carrie said in a warning tone.

Joel brushed the petals from his shoulders, and Finn chuckled. "It looks as if you have dandruff."

Joel arched his eyebrows. "I think we're missing something." And before Finn could respond, Joel took him in his arms, dipped him toward the floor, and kissed him on the lips to rapturous applause. Finn threw his arms around Joel's neck and returned the kiss, the two of them locked in a lingering embrace.

Seb coughed. "Get a room."

"Could say the same to you two," Megan commented dryly. Her wife snorted.

The guests laughed.

Finn righted himself, grinning. Joel took him by the hand. "This way, *Mr. Hall.*" They walked down the aisle toward the barn, Mendelssohn's Wedding March playing loudly, amid cheers and hollers from the guests following them.

Noah held Levi's hand as they strolled toward the barn. "Ready for the next part?"

Levi squared his shoulders. "As ready as I'll ever be."

"Want me to be prompter?"

He narrowed his gaze. "No, I do *not*. I can do this, okay?"

Noah raised Levi's hand to his lips and kissed it. "You can do *anything*."

Levi breathed more easily. "Yes, I can—because I have you."

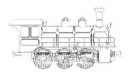

Levi clinked his glass with his fork. "If I might have your attention? And yes, Seb, that includes you too." That got him a few chuckles from the nearest tables where their friends were seated. He gazed at the expectant faces of the guests, then caught sight of Noah's smirk. That was all it took to remind Levi of his practice sessions with Noah's 'scripts', and he picked up his glass to hastily gulp down some water to cool his burning cheeks.

Noah was chuckling, the little fiend.

He searched the tables for Grammy, who was sitting with Carrie and Eric. She beamed at him. He made a mental note to keep a watch for any signs she was getting tired, but so far she seemed to be coping well.

Time to do this.

Levi took a deep breath. "A friend gave me some well-worn advice for those giving a speech. You've all heard it before, I'm sure. The one about picturing your audience naked?" He smiled. "Well, I just tried it, and it doesn't work." He paused. "Okay—it did, but it was so distracting I mentally dressed you all again." That raised a few laughs. "I'm here to embarrass—I mean, talk about—Finn." More laughter. "There is so much I could tell you, but I don't think he'd thank me."

"Spoilsport," Seb yelled. The rest of his table cackled.

"I've known Finn for a long time, and the one thing anyone who knows him will tell you is, he has a great sense of humor. However, this has, on occasion, led him to try out a few pranks." Levi grinned. "Like the time after gym class, when he put chicken bouillon cubes in the locker room showerheads. The coach kept asking who'd brought fried chicken in their lunch box. Or the time he saran-wrapped Seb's car."

Seb's eyes bulged as he gaped at Finn. "That was you?" Finn gave a half bow, and some of the friends applauded.

"Then there was the fake snake he left in Dylan's sleeping bag when we all went camping," Levi continued.

Dylan gasped. "I thought that thing was real!"

Joel said to Finn in a stage whisper. "I can tell I'm going to have to keep an eye on you."

Noah's eyes lit up, and Levi wagged his finger at him. "Do *not* go getting any ideas."

"Spoilsport," Noah said with a grin.

Levi cleared his throat. "Finn has been one of my closest friends since we were teenagers, and that is why I am so, *so* happy to be standing here, helping him celebrate finding the man of his dreams." He turned to Finn and Joel, and raised his glass. "To the grooms. May they love each other more with each passing day."

"To the grooms." The toast echoed around the barn as everyone lifted their glasses.

Levi took his seat, with a glance at Noah, who

gave him the thumbs-up.

One less thing to occupy him.

Only one thing left to accomplish.

Finn stood. "Levi is a hard act to follow, but there's something I wanted to say." He gestured to the group of friends who sat together. "I need to mention these guys right here. I've known them since high school, and they're the finest kind of friends a guy could ever wish for." He glanced at Joel. "And what's really amazing is, Joel and I might have been the first to find each other, but every last one of us found love. Ben and Wade... Seb and Marcus... Dylan and Mark... Shaun and Nathan... Aaron and Dean... and now Levi and Noah. The story of how I met Joel? Well, find me later and I'll tell you all about a man walking his dog along a beach, and the guy who dreamed of finding enough courage to speak to him." His eyes glistened, and Joel handed him a tissue. Finn chuckled. "See? This man came prepared. He *knows* me." He gazed at the group of friends. "And all these guys have a story to tell too. They might not have been looking for love, but it sure found 'em." He picked up his champagne. "So... I'm asking you to raise your glasses, and join me in a toast." Finn looked at Levi as he held his glass aloft. "To friendship."

All the guests rose to their feet, their raised glasses sparkling in the light from the chandeliers. "To friends." Everyone drank.

"And before you sit," Joel added, rising to stand beside Finn. "I'd like to publicly thank Linda Brown for being the best surrogate mom—to all of us." He lifted his glass. "To Grammy, who loves Levi's friends as if they were her own. Lady, you are awesome."

Levi glanced at Grammy, just as Carrie passed her

a tissue. "I think we just witnessed a miracle," he murmured to Noah.

"What do you mean?"

He smiled. "She's at a loss for words."

Levi sighed as he and Noah danced to a slow song, his cheek pressed to Noah's. "In case I forget to tell you… you're a wonderful dancer." Noah's scent filled his nostrils, and his arms felt so good around him.

"You're pretty awesome yourself." Noah brought his lips to Levi's ear. "I did it, by the way. I called my mom and told her she could stop trying to fix me up. I said I was well and truly spoken for."

Levi pulled back to stare at him. "What did she say?"

Noah snorted. "That she wasn't in the least bit surprised. Then I heard her telling my dad. He laughed, but in a good way." He glanced at the guests dancing around them. "I always thought I wasn't a romantic, but…"

"Changing your mind?"

He smiled. "All of this… the chandeliers, the music, that ceremony… having you in my arms… The whole day has been filled with romance—and I love it." He paused. "Is Grammy okay? I saw you talking to her a while ago."

"She's getting tired, but you know what she's like."

"Stubborn as a mule?" Noah said with a smile.

Levi laughed. "Mules have nothing on Grammy." He didn't want to leave just yet, but he knew it wouldn't be long. Grammy was chatting with Finn's mom.

Noah let out a sigh, and Levi peered at him. "What was that for?"

"Believe it or not, I was thinking about my trains."

Levi chuckled. "Oh, I'd believe it."

"I was just looking forward to creating that layout with you, that's all."

"How long did it take your granddad to amass all his trains, and make his layouts?"

"I guess he got interested in model railroads when he was in his twenties, so maybe… fifty years or more?"

Levi smiled. "Think of what *we* can achieve in the next fifty years." Then he realized he'd skated too close to what lay in his heart.

Noah stilled. "Don't look now, but we're wanted. Seb is gesticulating like crazy."

Thank God for Seb's timing.

"As long as we get to dance some more before we leave." Thank goodness they didn't have an hour's drive home to think about. The hotel wasn't that far away. "Let's go see what Seb wants." They left the dance floor and strolled over to one of the long tables, their friends and their partners seated on both sides. Finn and Joel were there too, looking relaxed and happy.

Seb grinned at them. "I thought you two would never stop dancing. We managed to get the grooms to stop mingling and sit with us a while."

"This takes me back to Ry and Teresa's wedding.

Remind me to thank them next time we see them," Finn remarked as Levi and Noah sat facing each other at the end of the table.

"What for?" Shaun asked, leaning against Nathan's shoulder.

"It was being at their wedding that made me realize I wasn't meant to be alone."

Joel kissed his cheek. "I think the thanks should go to Bramble for running off that day."

"And he's being rewarded." Finn's eyes sparkled. "We're getting a puppy. We're gonna be a two-dog household."

"Great!" Ben grinned. "The baby can play with both of them."

"'Baby'?" Joel and Finn said.

Ben shrugged. "You two would be great dads— well, Joel already is. Just sayin'."

Joel coughed. "I think we'll stick with a new puppy for now." He glanced at the long table toward the rear of the barn. "All those presents… I can't wait to see what people have brought us, but at the same time—"

"You're thinking about where we're going to put them all." Finn chuckled. "I was thinking the same thing. That house was empty four days ago—now look at it."

Levi caught Dean looking at him, and they smiled. *They'll love it*, Levi mouthed.

Ben peered at Aaron, who sat next to Dean, the two of them holding hands. "We still going away on a trip together?"

"As soon as I can find somewhere that can accommodate all of us."

Joel leaned back in his chair. "I guess the really

important question is… who's next to tie the knot?"

Ben laughed. "We've only just finished celebrating your wedding. Besides, not all of us want that."

Wade nodded. "We're happy as we are. We don't need a piece of paper, but hey, not everyone feels that way. Whatever floats your boat."

Dylan glanced at Mark. "I don't know… maybe?"

Mark blinked. "Was that a proposal?"

Dylan grinned. "Maybe?" Then he chuckled. "No, not just yet."

Seb gestured to their surroundings. "Can't see me doing all this."

Marcus nodded. "I agree. If we ever decide to make things legal, it would be a very different kind of affair."

"Yeah." Ben's eyes gleamed. "It'll probably be held in one of those New York clubs, you know, with lots of leather, paddles, slings…"

Both Seb and Marcus blushed.

"Oh really?" Aaron said with a grin.

"Leave them alone," Shaun said in a low voice. "But I think Ben's right. Marriage isn't for everyone."

Aaron nodded. "I think we should just let things happen. No rush."

Levi cleared his throat. "But when you *know* there'll never be anyone for you but the guy who holds your heart, why wait?" And speaking of hearts, his was hammering.

Aaron gazed at him. "Does Noah hold *your* heart?"

He took a deep breath. "Yes. He has done since we were teenagers. It just took us a while to realize we were meant to be." He reached into his suit pocket and removed the small box he'd been aware of the whole day. Levi got off his chair and knelt at the end of the table where Noah sat.

A hush fell over the nearest tables, and Levi's heart quaked.

Noah stared at him, shaking. "Levi?"

Levi raised his chin and looked Noah in the eye. "So I guess this is me, a boy, kneeling in front of another boy, asking him to marry me." He swallowed. "There has only ever been you. There will only *ever* be you." He opened the box. "And on your finger is where this belongs—if you want it to."

Noah made a choking sound and hauled Levi to his feet. "If I *want* it to? Why would I not want that?" He threw his arms around Levi and kissed him with a passion that robbed Levi of breath and made his heart soar. "Yes, yes, yes," Noah murmured against his lips.

Levi managed to take the ring from its velvet bed, and held it to Noah's left hand. "Let's see if you really do have hands like my granddad." His own hand trembled.

"Jeannie Crummel!" They turned their head to find Grammy standing behind them, her eyes wide. "And you say *I'm* sneaky?"

Levi laughed. "Can you just let me do this first before you bawl me out?" He slid the ring onto the third finger. "It could've been made for you." Levi kissed Noah on the mouth, then turned to Grammy, beaming. "Okay—*now* you can finish."

Tears trickled down her cheeks. "What's there to say, except you've made me happier than a body has a right to be."

Levi glanced at their friends, and his throat tightened to see their tears and smiles.

Then the barn erupted into a riot of whoops, hollers, and applause, and Levi and Noah were surrounded by friends and family, congratulating them and heaping good wishes on them.

Levi curved his hand around Noah's cheek. "Love you."

Noah seized him in a hug. "Love you too."

He smiled. "We have a lifetime together to look forward to."

Noah beamed. "And an attic to fill."

The End

THANK YOU

As always, a huge thank you to my beta team. Where would I be without you?

Kazy Reed, you are awesome. Thank you for being there.

Jack Parton, thank you for our trip through Maine that made me change a few details, and add even more, and for all our conversations about this book. I look forward to researching for the new series.

Miski Harris, for your time and expertise – and for making sure Grammy was in good hands.

Jason Mitchell, who had SO MUCH going on in his own live, and still found time to chat about books…You ROCK.

And a special thank you to George Parton. I couldn't have written about Noah's trains, layout, or grandfather without you. Thanks for patiently answering my emails. So much of the help you gave ended up in this book.

ALSO BY K.C. WELLS

Learning to Love
Michael & Sean
Evan & Daniel
Josh & Chris
Final Exam

Sensual Bonds
A Bond of Three
A Bond of Truth

Merrychurch Mysteries
Truth Will Out
Roots of Evil
A Novel Murder

Love, Unexpected
Debt
Burden

Dreamspun Desires
The Senator's Secret
Out of the Shadows
My Fair Brady
Under the Covers

Lions & Tigers & Bears
A Growl, a Roar, and a Purr
A Snarl, a Splash, and a Shock

Love Lessons Learned

First
Waiting for You
Step by Step
Bromantically Yours
BFF

Collars & Cuffs
An Unlocked Heart
Trusting Thomas
Someone to Keep Me (K.C. Wells & Parker Williams)
A Dance with Domination
Damian's Discipline (K.C. Wells & Parker Williams)
Make Me Soar
Dom of Ages (K.C. Wells & Parker Williams)
Endings and Beginnings (K.C. Wells & Parker Williams)

Secrets – with Parker Williams
Before You Break
An Unlocked Mind
Threepeat
On the Same Page

Personal
Making it Personal
Personal Changes
More than Personal
Personal Secrets
Strictly Personal
Personal Challenges
Personal – The complete series

Confetti, Cake & Confessions
(FREE)

Connections
Saving Jason
A Christmas Promise
The Law of Miracles
My Christmas Spirit
A Guy for Christmas
Dear Santa

Island Tales
Waiting for a Prince
September's Tide
Submitting to the Darkness
Island Tales Vol 1 (Books #1 & #2)

Lightning Tales
Teach Me
Trust Me
See Me
Love Me

A Material World
Lace
Satin
Silk
Denim

Southern Boys
Truth & Betrayal
Pride & Protection

Desire & Denial

Maine Men
Finn's Fantasy
Ben's Boss
Seb's Summer
Dylan's Dilemma
Shaun's Salvation
Aaron's Awakening

Kel's Keeper
Here For You
Sexting The Boss
Gay on a Train
Sunshine & Shadows
Double or Nothing
Back from the Edge
Switching it up
Out for You (FREE)
State of Mind (FREE)
No More Waiting (FREE)
Watch and Learn
My Best Friend's Brother
Princely Submission
Bears in the Woods

Anthologies

Fifty Gays of Shade
Winning Will's Heart

Come, Play
Watch and Learn

K.C. WELLS

<u>Writing as Tantalus</u>
Damon & Pete: Playing with Fire

ABOUT THE AUTHOR

K.C. Wells lives on an island off the south coast of the UK, surrounded by natural beauty. She writes about men who love men, and can't even contemplate a life that doesn't include writing.

The rainbow rose tattoo on her back with the words 'Love is Love' and 'Love Wins' is her way of hoisting a flag. She plans to be writing about men in love - be it sweet or slow, hot or kinky - for a long while to come.

Printed in Great Britain
by Amazon